P9-ELX-629

*The woman had strength, the raw animal
strength that comes from fear.*

She tried to break the man's Adam's apple with the side of
her palm. He parried the blow with the hand that held the
gun. Though the man was vastly stronger, he could not control the woman with one hand. When she started to scream
in an effort to attract attention, the man laid the pistol down
on the bench and clamped his hand over the woman's
mouth.

That was the first mistake I'd seen him make.

I came through the curtain. He still had his back to me as
he bent the woman's arm behind her. With measured force,
he hit her just below the breasts, knocking the wind out of
her. Then he twisted his fingers into her long black hair and
forced her face toward the glowing furnace.

I grabbed him around the neck with one arm. Then I
raked the front sight of my gun across the thin skin just
above his eyebrow, drawing blood. He twisted his head suddenly and gave me an elbow shot, stuck his chin in the
crook of my arm, and slipped out of my grip. Then he ran. I
could have killed him before he got to the door, but I saw no
real advantage in it.

The woman watched me with haunting amber eyes.
"Who are you?" she asked.

"I'm the guy who just saved you from a third-degree facial. My name is Fiddler."

**JUST ANOTHER DAY
IN PARADISE**

Bantam Books offers the finest in American mysteries
Ask your bookseller for the books you have missed

Rex Stout
AND FOUR TO GO
BAD FOR BUSINESS
THE BROKEN VASE
DEATH OF A DUDE
DEATH TIMES THREE
DOUBLE FOR DEATH
A FAMILY AFFAIR
THE FATHER HUNT
FER-DE-LANCE
THE FINAL DEDUCTION
GAMBIT
THE LEAGUE OF
   FRIGHTENED MEN
MURDER BY THE BOOK
PLOT IT YOURSELF
PRISONER'S BASE
THE RED BOX
THE RUBBER BAND
SOME BURIED CAESAR
THREE DOORS TO DEATH
THREE FOR THE CHAIR
TOO MANY CLIENTS

R. D. Brown
HAZZARD

Robert Goldsborough
MURDER IN E MINOR

Rob Kantner
THE BACK-DOOR MAN

William Kienzle
MIND OVER MURDER

Ross Macdonald
BLUE CITY
THE BLUE HAMMER
THE GOODBYE LOOK
THE MOVING TARGET

Ted Wood
MURDER ON ICE
DEAD IN THE WATER
LIVE BAIT

Just Another Day in Paradise

A. E. MAXWELL

BANTAM BOOKS
TORONTO · NEW YORK · LONDON · SYDNEY · AUCKLAND

This low-priced Bantam Book
has been completely reset in a type face
designed for easy reading, and was printed
from new plates. It contains the complete
text of the original hard-cover edition.
NOT ONE WORD HAS BEEN OMITTED.

JUST ANOTHER DAY IN PARADISE
A Bantam Book / published by arrangement with
Doubleday & Company

PRINTING HISTORY
Doubleday edition published February 1985
Bantam edition / September 1986

All rights reserved.
Copyright © 1985 by A. E. Maxwell.
Cover art copyright © 1986 by Bantam Books, Inc.
This book may not be reproduced in whole or in part, by
mimeograph or any other means, without permission.
For information address: Bantam Books, Inc.

ISBN 0-553-25789-7

Published simultaneously in the United States and Canada

Bantam Books are published by Bantam Books, Inc. Its trademark, consisting of the words "Bantam Books" and the por-
trayal of a rooster, is Registered in U.S. Patent and Trademark
Office and in other countries. Marca Registrada. Bantam
Books, Inc., 666 Fifth Avenue, New York, New York 10103.

PRINTED IN THE UNITED STATES OF AMERICA

KR   0 9 8 7 6 5 4 3 2 1

For

Liz and Jim Trupin:
friends, agents,
Keepers of the Faith.

1

Like the rich, California is different. But not that different. One of the new cities up the coast from me has a motto that says it all: "Just another perfect day in Paradise." Honest to Christ. People will believe anything, but anyone over the age of twelve should be smart enough not to say it out loud.

Still, that motto runs through my mind every time I look out the big window of my house on the bluff. When the cottage was built, picture windows were the technological equivalent of silicon chips. The glass is so old that it has ripples and tiny bubbles. The flaws add texture to the streamers of gold and red, purple and cobalt that make up the standard southern California sunset. Yes indeed. Another day in Paradise.

But I didn't say it out loud.

If the ocean at the western edge of California has a failing, it's a certain lack of texture. Fine color, outstanding light, but not too much character. Out beyond the smog that hugs the water on some summer days, Catalina is the color of unfiltered wine. The island's blunt stone cliffs are all that save the Gold Coast from being just another pretty face.

What I call the Gold Coast stretches along the California shoreline about fifty miles, from Malibu halfway to San Diego. Even though I invented the name, I'm sure other people must use it, too. It's the only name that fits. Los Angeles doesn't really touch the Gold Coast. Sure, LA has a couple of windows to the sea in the Palisades and the Marina, and a kind of Polish Corridor to the Port of San Pedro. But the Gold Coast is the rest of Southern California, the outer city to LA's inner sprawl. The Gold Coast's capital is Newport

1

Beach. Its other major cities include Laguna Beach and the People's Republic of Santa Monica. Seven million dreams and disillusionments with nothing in common but the Pacific Ocean.

Besides having the most beguiling climate on the North American continent, this stretch of the Pacific rim is characterized by a lack of tradition that's either alluring or appalling, depending on whose column you're reading. Houses older than twenty-five years qualify for attention from the local historical society. Basically, everybody is inventing the place as they go and spending a great deal of money in the process. It's a place where the pecking order changes with the interest rates, which means there is a continuous shoving match for seats above the salt shaker. The competition gets a bit fierce at times. Along the Gold Coast, cocktail parties are a form of blood sport.

I like the place, because I like to invent life as I go along. The Coast, as natives call it, is the magnet that has drawn the best, brightest, meanest, and most aggressive folks in the hemisphere. In the world, if you include the Vietnamese and Iranian contingent. I'm not talking about Boat People or fanatic Muslim students; I'm talking about the people who got out flying their own planeloads of gold while their countries blew up around them.

There is, of course, a social hierarchy on the Gold Coast, but it's almost an inverted pyramid. The more important the individual, the less likely he is to be recognized as such. Even oil princes keep a low profile. On this scale any elected politician is, by definition, unimportant. No man of real significance would expose himself to such humiliation. The less visible and more wealthy, the more important.

That makes it convenient for me. A low profile has survival value.

Where do I fit in this scheme? I've asked myself that question a few times, especially after I got enough money to sit on my butt until it went numb. How much money? Like I said, enough. Enough money is when you never have to think about it. Yeah, I hear you. If you don't think about it, how do you get it, much less keep it? Simple. You have an uncle three years older than you who dies penniless and leaves you with a steamer trunk full of greasy $20s, $50s, and $100s. Then you happen to be married at the time to a honey-blond tiger shark of an investment banker whose middle name is Midas.

In no time at all you have more money that you can count, an ex-wife, a numb butt, and a desire to kill something. Anything. You've discovered that the only thing worse than not liking your work is not having any work to *dis*like. After you've bought everything you thought you ever wanted, drunk ancient and unpronounceable wines, eaten ancient and unpronounceable cuisines, chased and caught the best ass on this or any other coast—what then?

Numb butt, that's what. And rage. The Chinese knew what they were doing when they cursed their enemies with a single phrase: *May your fondest wish come true.*

Not that I'm mad at Fiora. She was only doing what she does best—make money. I don't ask those suicidal questions anymore: Who was wrong and who was right, who was innocent and who was screwed. I just sign the contracts she puts in front of me. We get along a lot better now than we did when we were married. I don't even get mad at her when she spends my money. After all, she earned it, with some help from Uncle Jake, and he's in no position to object to how his ill-gotten gains were laundered.

There is, of course, still some problem with having that much money, particularly when you weren't raised with it. Being proud of doing nothing was not one of the things they taught me in northern Montana. You may not have to be born into wealth to enjoy it, but indolence is something else. It wasn't the guilt that got to me. It was the boredom.

For a time I even considered going back to fiddling. Serious fiddling that is. The kind you do with an orchestra. I had been a nine-day wonder with the violin when I was younger. They told me I was good. The best. I might have been, but not to my own goddamned ear. Perfect pitch. Human hands. The twain only meet in my dreams. Long ago I threw that ravishing, bastard violin under the wheels of a southbound Corvette. But with more time, enough money to buy the best . . . ? So I picked up a violin, felt the strings vibrate through my soul as I drew the bow down, and was haunted by a perfection I couldn't touch.

Maybe when I'm sixty, and perfect pitch is only a memory. Maybe then I'll play again.

Finally I struck on an idea that comforts me in about the same way libraries comforted Andrew Carnegie. It's called giving people a hand. I figure that I got lucky and other people didn't. So I'll spread my luck around as long as I have it.

That's how I got the extra crack in my skull, my nose rearranged, and a few odd scars over my body. As the government would put it: Interfering in other people's business can be hazardous to your health. I keep sawing away, though, fiddling with the world's distribution of bad and good luck.

I never fool myself into believing I do it for anybody but me, to make *me* feel better. Well, almost never. Every time I forget, I get myself into trouble. Take my wife. Or my ex-wife, to be precise. And that is both halves of the problem—ex and wife. I am still absolutely mad about the woman that I was once married to. Fiora feels the same way about me, which is why we end up chasing and catching one another every few months. She has the smallest waist and the most beautifully formed breasts of any woman I have ever seen, and, in some ways, she's the smartest person I know.

Every couple of months, for one night or even two, we have an absolutely wonderful time with one another. Then the old troubles set in. We are cursed. Same appetites, different metabolism. No matter what time or how thoroughly Fiora was bedded the night before, she bounces up from our sheets full of the sharp desire to slay dragons, always not much more than five minutes before or after 6 A.M. She varies about as much as your average vernal equinox.

On the other hand, I'm likely to need a jump start from a twelve-volt system. If I'm out of bed before 9 A.M. it's only because the day is going to be too hot to run after then. The pounding of three miles on pavement, a modest round of

weights and mantras, Mencken or whoever, and I'm ready
to face the world. But just barely.

Fiora never understood that about me. And I never understood what it's like to face dawn with a predatory smile.
Midnight, now—yeah, that's different. Like I said; same appetites, different metabolisms. A fact of life that we both
curse with regularity. In another era we probably would
have remained married and made one another miserable for
forty or fifty years before we reached our angle of mutual
repose. But in our modern and supposedly enlightened
age, we split the blanket after a few years of trying. I wish to
hell I knew whether that was the smart thing to do. So does
Fiora. We probably won't know for another thirty or forty
years. All I know is that sometimes she can crush my heart
with a single look. She says I can do the same to her. Sometimes. When the times mesh, it's extraordinary. When they
don't—well, there's always next time. Isn't there?

The hope of a next time was why I was sitting in her office
on the nineteenth floor of one of the smoked-glass commercial cathedrals along Century Park East in Century City. I
was there even though I knew that, at the moment, Fiora
was keeping company with a slick European named Volker.
Fiora and I were together long enough that we're pos-
sessive, but we owe one another enough that we don't keep
track. So when Fiora called me this morning, at least half an
hour before I'm normally human, and asked me to drop by
about 11 A.M., I replied with one word:

"Sure."

I should have stayed in bed.

Fiora schedules her time to the half minute. She's one of
the highest paid investment counselors on the West Coast.
For her the time-is-money cliché is a flat statement of truth.
Even if it weren't, her Scots efficiency would prevail. Such
a structured life would—and did—drive me crazy.

I turned up at her office at eleven-thirteen. Later I realized that if I had to show up at all, I should have been on
time. The lost thirteen minutes cost two lives that I know of.
Those minutes were the ones Fiora had allotted to brief me
on one of my least favorite subjects: Danny, her twin

brother. But I didn't know I was there to hear about him, so I had less information than I needed to deal with the government team that was camped on Fiora's lovely tail.

I knew how worried Fiora was when she didn't complain about my tardy arrival. Instead, she came around from behind that Louis XIV desk—the one that does a hell of a good job of letting her male clients catch a polite but provocative glimpse of her slender, beautifully formed calves and ankles—and met me halfway. She was wearing my favorite kind and color of blouse, a sea-green silk that outlined her perfect breasts and hinted at the nipples beneath. She dresses for power in her own way.

"Thanks, Fiddler," she said, looking at me out of her big hazel-green eyes before she gave me an extra-long hug, extra fierce.

For a slender woman she has real strength. She smelled like lavender and warm nights. I knew that she had used green silk and lavender scent this morning for their impact on me. I hugged her back, felt her softness and her strength, and let her go. The last was the hard part. She fit too well. I was faintly aware of a weakness that had settled in back of my knees.

"Trouble?" I asked.

"I don't know," she said, lowering long lashes. She turned a cheek to accept the kiss we used to show how cool we could be about our present, between-times relationship. "Some government men are coming in a few minutes. They want to talk to me about Danny."

Ah yes. Danny. She and her brother shared the intimacy of fraternal twinship. I didn't care much for him. I suppose I was always a bit jealous of their closeness. For Danny, Fiora was never scheduled to the half minute.

"Why don't they just talk to Danny?"

"He's disappeared," she said.

With a studied nonchalance that was devastating, she ran a handful of fingers through her dark blond hair. She focused inward for a moment, caught between distraction and anxiety. Then she looked directly at me, letting me see the green and gold flecks in her lovely eyes. Her full lower lip almost trembled.

"I'm scared, and when I get scared, I turn to you, don't I?" Fiora smiled quickly, apologetically. "I'm sorry that I'm so much trouble for you, Fiddler."

I doubt if my smile was very pleasant. Watching her expression change, I was sure of it. "You don't have to do that, Fiora."

"Do what?"

"Run me through the sexual wringer. You want something? Just ask. That's all you have to do. Ask." I showed her my open hands, palms up. No threat.

Fiora's eyes narrowed as she studied me. "Was I really coming on that strong or are you just jealous of Volker?"

"Yes. Twice."

"And you're completely innocent," she retorted.

"What the hell does that mean?"

"Damn you, Fiddler? Did you have to wear that fitted gray chamois shirt? You know I love the feel of it." Her voice was mocking but her eyes weren't as she looked me over. "Six feet two in your naked feet, all of it hard and warm, brown hair made for a woman's fingers, a mustache that tickles in all the right places and gray eyes that should be cold but are hot enough to melt Scots granite." She gave me that heart-crushing smile. "In short, you don't have exclusive use of that sexual wringer."

Fiora's smile turned down at the corners. "I know you're angry about me and Volker. I'm sorry, but I need your mind right now, not your body."

"You've got it," I said, watching her. "Pretty thing like you can write her own ticket with men. Isn't that what your daddy always told you?" We do this kind of clawing thing when we aren't sleeping well, either one of us.

"Fiddler," she said, "don't—"

The intercom buzzed on Fiora's desk before she could finish telling me what I shouldn't do. She hesitated, then spun around and lifted the French phone from its ivory cradle, listened for a moment, and snapped:

"Three minutes, then bring them in."

Fiora hung up and turned to me. Or on me. Her voice was very much that of a financial counselor. "These guys are your kind of people, Fiddler. Night prowlers. Trouble-makers. Government gumshoes. I don't know what they want with me."

"What *do* you know?" I asked abruptly.

"They called this morning and demanded an interview. The subject is Danny. I told them I hadn't seen him in about two weeks. They think I know more than that."

"Do you?"

"No."

"How about his business partner? Does the noble Volker know anything more?"

"Fiddler, please."

"Does he?"

"No, damn it!" said Fiora. "Quite being a jealous ex-hus-band."

"I'm an ex-husband whose ex-wife just gave him the best feel he's had in a week." That wasn't entirely true but I wasn't in the mood for pure truths.

There was a knock, then the outer door opened, and her secretary entered. Jason was a slim-hipped type who wore thin pastel shirts. He's one of the few genuine fags I've ever liked.

"Ms. Flynn, these men are impossible!"

We weren't left to wonder which men Jason was talking about. They pushed the door against Jason's heels and walked into the room. Jason looked both irritated and un-easy.

"Mr. Sharp, U.S. Customs," said Jason, pointing to the first man through the doorway. "The other gentleman didn't bother to introduce himself."

"Good morning, ma'am," said Sharp.

Sharp was a type I recognized from my days with Uncle Jake on the border. Sharp had the look of a junkyard dog. No barker, this one. Quiet and dark-eyed and mean. He wore a pair of blue jeans—definitely not designer—that were rolled once in late 1950s style. Below the jeans was a beautiful pair of custom-made boots. Above the white shirt, the man's skin was weathered and red-brown, desert style. The skin was still pliable, like the soft leather coat he wore, but it would someday turn brittle and split. His belt buckle was a chunk of antique turquoise that would have done credit to a Navajo chief.

Family G-man. Genus Customs. Species *Border* Cop. I knew the type from some experience, usually unpleasant, over the years. The line between two countries is always a wild place, wilder than usual when the two countries are the United States and Mexico. Sharp had the tempered look that comes from the desert sun and the constant friction of two cultures. My guess was that he spoke fluent Spanish, Texas English, and Spanglish, and he could kick ass in any language known to man or gila monster.

It was easy to overlook Sharp's partner. Perhaps partner is the wrong word. The man who walked into the room after Sharp is a better description. Those two would be partners the day they held the Winter Olympics in Jamaica. The second man was around forty, medium height, gray-brown hair, gray-brown eyes, gray-brown suit, gray-brown—you get the idea. If you looked away from him you had to remind yourself that he was there. He was a three-dimensional definition of bland, which made the orchestra in the back of my head start tuning up.

Cacophony, of course. It's always that way before the overture begins, what with all the stringed instruments picking and pulling toward the same note. My own fiddle was a part of it, sawing away as inharmoniously as the rest. The only pure note was one simple truth: Being gray-brown inconspicuous takes a lot of talent, intelligence, and hard work. This man reminded me of all the bleached, fiercely bright blonds who have made a fortune playing dumb for drooling males.

Neither man smiled at Fiora. The man in the expensive boots looked at her carefully, top to bottom, appraising her hair and her face and her breasts and her waist and the rest of her. There was nothing sexual about his inspection. I got the impression that he had sex the same way he took a

dump—with his boots on. The gray-brown man cataloged
Fiora with a single innocuous glance.

Both men passed over Fiora quickly and moved on to me,
trying to figure out where I fit into whatever tune they were
playing. My boots were as good as Sharp's, which was saying something. I wasn't as invisible as the gray-brown type,
but I was just as silent.

"Identification, boys," said Fiora crisply, looking at her
watch. One minute of their allotted fifteen was gone.

Sharp and the man who wasn't there had just made the
most common mistake committed in a woman's office. They
had oriented themselves toward the man in the room. Fiora
was the wrong woman to slight like that. She was used to
dealing with bankers, stockbrokers, multimillionaires,
and—worse, from her point of view—motion picture pro-
ducers. She could reduce the most reflexive chauvinist to
sliced bacon with a few words.

The ghost recovered before Sharp did. But instead of
showing any ID, the invisible man shook his head very
slightly, so slightly that I wouldn't have noticed it if I hadn't
been staring impolitely. Sharp reached into his jacket
pocket, pulled out a folding wallet, and flipped it open to
reveal a hard brass badge. He showed how thoroughly he
had recovered by giving the wallet to Fiora rather than just
waving it under her nose. Without looking, she handed the
wallet to me.

"Special Agent Aaron Sharp, U.S. Customs," he said for-
mally, giving the nod that was the Southwestern equivalent
of a bow.

Considering the situation, Sharp's nod was as off-key as a
wet violin. He didn't introduce the ghost. He didn't even
look at him. Maybe he wasn't really there at all. I checked
Sharp's credentials quickly, knowing that they were as real
as the turquoise in his belt buckle. I looked at the ghost. He
looked back at me.

"He's just along for the ride," said Sharp. "We're going
out to lunch later."

I wanted to ask who was eating whom, but decided it
wouldn't be polite. Just like pointing out the obvious lie

JUST ANOTHER DAY IN PARADISE 11

wouldn't be polite; Government agents don't bring along anyone for the ride.

"What can I do for you, Special Agent Aaron Sharp?" asked Fiora, her voice making it clear that the inquiry was of the polite, empty variety.

"Introduce me to your friend."

Fiora looked at me.

"Fiddler," I said.

Fiora smiled at Sharp. The gesture revealed the edges of her pretty white teeth. "He's just along for the ride. We're going out to lunch later."

In our case, it was the truth, but Sharp didn't like the excuse any better for that. His lips thinned down to nothing. His pale eyes squinted at me, showing the tiny fine lines that came from staring into the white hot light of a desert sun by day and the elusive green light of a star scope by night.

"Just Fiddler, huh?" he grunted. "Dressed like that, you could be a producer, a lawyer, a pimp, or a coke dealer."

I smiled, showing that I have nice white teeth, too.

Fiora went and sat behind her desk. The man who wasn't there took a chair off to one side, leaving Sharp and me to the dainty blue velvet loveseat. We divided it evenly between us. I was more at ease with the loveseat than Sharp, but I'd had more practice looking at home on the damned thing.

Fiora looked at her watch, then at Sharp. He got the message.

"Miss Flynn, I have a few questions to ask you about your brother."

"Is this a civil or criminal investigation?" I asked casually, stretching out my legs and crossing my boots. I sensed the ghost's increased interest in me like a cool wind on my neck. I didn't like turning my back on him, but the furniture arrangements left me no choice.

Sharp gave me a sideways look. "Criminal."

He left it open whether the word referred to me or the investigation.

I turned to Fiora. "Since Agent Sharp hasn't read the

Litany of St. Miranda to you from his little plastic-coated card, you aren't the target of the investigation. You still, however, have the right to tell him to go shit in his hat."

Sharp's look told me that he'd like me to exercise my right to silence, immediately. With barely concealed impatience, he turned back to Fiora. "Will you tell me where to get in touch with your brother?"

Fiora looked at her perfectly manicured nails. Peach, like her lips and tongue. "No, I can't." She looked up swiftly, trying to catch Sharp off guard. "And that's can't, not won't."

Sharp shrugged. Can't or won't gave him the same result. Nothing.

"Why is Danny being investigated?" she asked.

"I'm not at liberty to say." Sharp didn't look away from Fiora's beautiful mouth.

"What are you at liberty to say?" snapped Fiora.

"Nice office you have, ma'am."

I stood up and walked to Fiora's side. Having my back turned to that ghost was more than my sixth sense would put up with. I leaned over Fiora and spoke so softly that Sharp could only hear if he strained and the ghost couldn't hear at all.

"Mr. Sharp is trying to say that he gets to ask all the questions, and we get to answer them," I murmured.

Fiora grimaced, flicked a quick glance at her Piaget, and said, "I haven't seen my brother for more than a month. I believe he was going to San Jose and then to Europe. Business, not pleasure. I don't know when he'll be back."

At the mention of the word "Europe," the ghost's eyes became a good deal less vague. Sharp grunted and tapped his finger against the turquoise at his waist.

"By business do you mean Omnitronix, his electronics exporting firm?" asked Sharp.

"Yes."

"What can you tell me about that business? Are you involved in it in any way?"

Sharp had a lot of questions lined up. You could see them crowding against his tongue, one after another without pause. It's a technique that reporters, cops, and investigators use—just keep 'em coming and sooner or later people will tell you something they don't want to.

"Back up, Sharp," I said, my voice soft enough that the ghost had to strain to hear. I wanted to bug him as much as the sour notes in my head bugged me. "If you thought Fiora was a principal in Omnitronix, you'd have read her the same rights you're going to read Danny when you find him. Now cut the bullshit, or she'll start charging you the same hourly rate she charges her clients."

"The government couldn't afford that, ma'am," Sharp said, almost smiling at Fiora and ignoring me entirely. Then he shrugged again and looked at me with eyes as opaque as old lava. "Okay, Fiddler, or whatever your name is," he said. "We're conducting a criminal investigation. The matter is before the grand jury. It would be a misdemeanor for me to tell you anything about the case. We want to talk to Daniel Flynn. If one of you can't tell us where to find him, we have nothing to talk about."

"Then good-bye, Agent Sharp," said Fiora.

I was watching the gray-brown man the way a bird watches a snake. If I hadn't been, I'd have missed the instant of anger that made his face memorable instead of anonymous. That was one tough hombre. But he said nothing, only stood and prepared to leave.

I turned so that I was plainly speaking to both Sharp and the other man. "Maybe we can keep this from being a total bust, gentlemen," I said. "If all you want is to talk to Danny, we'll try to get in touch with him and have him call you."

The ghost's eyes said *no* before Sharp opened his mouth. "This can't be handled by phone," said Sharp. "We need to speak to Mr. Flynn in person."

"Go to Europe, then," said Fiora crisply. "If you don't have his German address, I can give it to you."

Bingo. Depend on Fiora to get to the bottom line. It was an offer I'd been dying to make, but coming from me it would have gotten nothing but a horse laugh. Sharp gave Fiora a reluctant nod of admiration. Turning down her offer of Danny's German address would be more revealing than anything Sharp had said so far today.

"Thank you, ma'am, we have the address." There was a faint Oklahoma twang to Sharp's voice. I suspected it had something to do with the anger that had flattened his lips into a mean line. "What we don't have is the authority to talk to him in Germany, as I'm sure your, er, friend will tell you."

Fiora lifted one slender eyebrow. No one mentioned the word "extradition" but it was on everyone's mind. "Then perhaps you can answer my question, Customs Agent Aaron Sharp. I thought customs agents were worried about items coming into the country. Danny is in the exporting business. Naturally, I'm confused as to why you want him."

I could have enlightened Fiora, but I didn't. Neither did the ghost. Sharp looked at her for a long moment, then shrugged again. "The U.S. has laws about exports as well as imports. Particularly high tech exports."

"Like the equipment Omnitronix ships?" said Fiora.

Sharp stood up and straightened his coat. Only someone who was looking for it would have noticed the slight bulge at the small of his back. His coat had been cut to fit seamlessly over the gun and holster. I'll bet that he had at least a small gun in his boot, too. It's a good place to carry a gun, once your ankle gets calloused in the right place.

"Good-day, ma'am. Thank you for your help."

Fiora accepted Sharp's irony with a brilliant smile. "You know how welcome you are, Agent Sharp." She turned away, then said over her shoulder, "Does all this mean that Omnitronix is suspected of having violated some export control laws?"

"No," said Sharp. "All it means is that smugglers live on both sides of the border."

He nodded to Fiora and to me but didn't offer to shake hands with either of us. I looked for the ghost but he had already left the room. Through the wall, no doubt.

I stood there watching the door closing behind Sharp and wondering idly whether now wasn't a pretty good time to go into the dope smuggling business. I'd had a taste of it, years ago, with my mother's much younger brother, Jake. The sight of Uncle Jake lying face down in the cactus just outside a no-name Mexican village had convinced me there was no future in dope. But if the Customs Service had pulled the likes of Sharp off the border in pursuit of high tech rather than highs, it might be time to consider going back into the business.

"Don't even think about it," said Fiora. "I need you here."

She always did know me too well.

2

I gnawed on the morning's business as we approached Beverly Hills. The interview had left a nasty flavor, like diet drinks sometimes do. I was driving the Cobra, a primordial eight-cylinder beast, because Fiora had asked me to. I should have been tipped off by that. She normally prefers a more sedate, disciplined form of transportation than she gets with the Cobra's English Bristol body and huge Ford engine. Mercedes is her favorite.

We didn't talk much. That's one of the things I love about Fiora. Aimless conversation irritates her, too. And until I had a chance to think, whatever I had to say about Danny and the morning would be aimless if not destructive.

The problem at one level was simple: Fiora and Danny shared that twins' unbreakable bond of love and trust. Over the years, she and I had argued about her wild young brother, who was nearly as beautiful in his way as Fiora was. Danny had Fiora's intelligence but none of her discipline, sensitivity, or drive. He always seemed to fail, although not spectacularly, at whatever he attempted. He was the only wealthy young man I knew who hadn't been able to negotiate the MBA program at the University of Southern California, the new version of Imperial India, the eternal sinecure of Anglo-Saxon remittance men.

Fiora, on the other hand, had negotiated Harvard's MBA, had graduated third from the top, and had never looked back. But this intelligent, perceptive woman had never been able to regard her own brother with anything like the bottom-line insight she brought to a stock prospectus.

"I can hear 'I told you so' doing push-ups on your tongue," Fiora said finally, moving restlessly in the Cobra's passenger seat.

I sighed. "Fiora, in my own cynical way I worry about Danny almost as much as you do. He can be a charming child." *He can also be a pain in the butt*, I added silently.

"He's not a child," she said reflexively, old response to an even older argument. Then, in a tight voice, "I thought it would be different this time. Volker has told me more than once that Danny was doing a 'masterful' job of running his end of Omnitronix."

If I thought a line of bullshit would get Fiora into my bed, I'd sing paeans to Danny, too. But I managed to hold my tongue. If you don't learn from past mistakes, the pain of them is pointless. "Why don't you fill me in on the thirteen minutes we didn't have this morning. Starting with Omnitronix."

Fiora looked at me for a long moment, saying nothing, as though she were having second thoughts about trusting me. That really reached me. I downshifted hard, letting the Cobra snarl for me.

"Look, pretty lady," I said. "You called me, remember? This is one hell of a time to start doubting me—unless you already know something about Danny that you don't want me to know."

Fiora touched me quickly, fingertips warm on the back of my hand, sliding down to my wrist. "It's not doubt, Fiddler. Never that. I trust you more than I trust myself. That's why I called you." She took a deep breath. "I'm just not sure that I want to know what's going on with Danny and Omnitronix," she admitted.

For a woman of Fiora's intelligence and pride, that wasn't an easy admission to make. When she continued, her voice was so low I had to strain to hear her.

"If Danny is doing something illegal, common sense says Volker is probably involved, since they are partners. But I don't really want to know because I don't trust myself to deal with it. So I called you, knowing that even if it hurts you, you'll protect me from myself—if it comes to that. God, I hope it doesn't come to that."

The more I heard, the more it sounded like Volker had his hooks into more than Fiora's twin. The Cobra snarled again.

"I'm sorry," she said. "I know this isn't fair to you."

I downshifted again, double-clutching, then nailed the accelerator. The Cobra went into full cry, second gear on the freeway, dark blue hell on wheels.

Fiora knew me well enough not to protest. In fact, she closed her eyes and almost smiled, for once enjoying the Cobra's unleashed power. That, too, told me that beneath her manicured exterior, Fiora was seething. Usually she only showed her capacity for emotion in bed. There was no experience quite like having her come apart in my hands.

That line of thought didn't do me a damn bit of good. I swore and backed off the Cobra. When the decibel level dropped, I said, "Omnitronix." I didn't look at Fiora, but I could see her out of the corner of my eyes as I turned off the freeway.

"It boils down to a brokerage operation, really," said Fiora. Absently she ran her fingers through her loose, honey-blond hair. With some women that's a come-on. With Fiora, it was a rare signal of nervousness. "Omnitronix works mostly for European clients, buying high tech items in Silicon Valley or down in Irvine and then shipping them overseas. From what Danny said once, a lot of their inventory is custom-made. Semiconductor manufacturing equipment, that sort of thing."

"Defense stuff?" I asked as I cut in front of a Mercedes and made a right onto Wilshire, heading for the Rodeo Drive Hotel. It wasn't my favorite place to lunch in Beverly Hills, but Fiora had insisted.

"I just read spread sheets and annual reports, not engineering specs," Fiora said. "Volker can tell you, though."

I looked at Fiora, hard and fast. My expression must have revealed more of my thoughts than it usually does. Or perhaps it's just that she knows me too well. She touched me again, tried to smile, and failed.

"Yeah," she said. "We're having lunch with him."

I looked at the Seville slowing on the street in front of me and thought what a satisfying crunch it would make if I rammed its clumsy ass. Then I told myself I was acting juvenile about being conned into having lunch with the man who was sleeping with the woman I had married and divorced and still loved. I mean, we're all adults, right?

Like hell we are.

"That's your free one for the year," I said, jabbing the brakes to save both the Cobra and the Seville. The tires gripped, and we snapped to a stop. "You pull this crap on me one more time before midnight, December 31, and I'll start keeping score."

I didn't say anymore. I didn't have to. When it came to score, I could count every bit as fast as Fiora could and one hell of a lot meaner. It was one of the problems we'd had.

"Fiddler, I'm sorry," she said in a husky, pleading voice. "I'm in over my head."

"Danny or Volker?" I asked bluntly.

She hesitated, started to speak, then stopped. That set off alarms. Fiora is not the sort who dithers. "Yes," she said finally.

"Yes which?"

"Just yes."

". . . shit."

I didn't know what else to say. Ever since we had been divorced, there was always the chance that one of us would meet someone else. That thought kept me awake at night from time to time—like every time Fiora kept the same man around for more than a week or a month. She had said some things that told me she spent some nights worrying about me, too. But that wasn't any guarantee she would never meet a man she loved and could live with, too.

The Cadillac in front of me finally got out of the way. I gunned the Cobra onto Rodeo Drive.

"Okay, Fiora," I said after a pause that was too long and too hard to be comfortable. "Maybe your great and good friend Volker can figure out why the government is sniffing after your twin. So we'll have lunch, but that doesn't mean

I'm going to take on a full-blown consultation. There are
certain people I've learned not to fiddle with. Your Danny is
one of them."

"Thanks," Fiora said, touching my mustache lightly, a
gesture from a lot of yesterdays. "I just want a little advice."

Bullshit. We both knew it, but neither of us said anything. We had learned some things the hard way. Silence at
the right time was one of them. We kept it that way until we
were walking into the patio restaurant she had chosen for
lunch.

The Beverly Rodeo Hotel is just about what you would
expect for the neighborhood—lots of wood and glass and
classy rattan, relentlessly cosmopolitan. The food is hotel,
the service okay if you look rich, and the ambience too self-
conscious to be impressive. I'd been prepared to dislike
Volker; when I found out he was staying at the Beverly
Rodeo Hotel, I shrugged at the confirmation of my in-
stincts.

But nothing is ever as simple as we would like it to be.
Volker was no exception.

First of all, he was so goddamn handsome.

He had the build of a gymnast, which I later found out he
was. He was shorter than he looked, perhaps five nine, narrow hips, broad shoulders, and cleanly muscled. He moved
with an elegance that was utterly masculine as he rose from
a table at the far edge of the garden. He was dressed in a
navy blue blazer, gray slacks, and a white silk shirt open at
the neck. Neither the clothes nor the shoes came off anyone's rack. His assurance went deeper than hand-made
clothes. His smile was welcoming but not ingratiating. You
didn't have to smile back if you didn't want to. He would
understand. His smile understood everything.

The orchestra in my head started sawing up cacophony
by the cord. Yeah, the sound was as bad as the pun, but the
pun made me feel better. When you've already lost the contest once, you'd just as soon your competition had arthritic
hands and concrete ears. No such luck with Volker. World
class all the way.

"Volker, this is Fiddler," said Fiora as Volker kissed her on the cheek she offered. "Fiddler, this is Danny's partner."

Fiora's lover too. But silence is golden—or at least silver. I shook Volker's hand. I expected a weak European handshake. I didn't get one. There was real strength in Volker's smooth, manicured hands.

"I have wanted to meet you for a long time, Fiddler," he said. "I admit to jealousy. Fiora often talks about you. You mean a great deal to her happiness."

What the hell can you say to that, even if she is sleeping with the guy? Especially if she is. On top of that, Volker's smile was genuine and warm. With his translucent skin and ash-blond hair he had the aspect of a mature Billy Budd, angelic without being insipid.

With the strong hand Volker had offered me, he drew me toward his table. There was no possibility of holding back. Volker's charm was like the Southern California sun—sublime, generous, unforced, falling on everyone equally. It warmed you to your bones.

And then I knew why Fiora was afraid. God in heaven, Volker's kind of charm was as rare as Caruso's voice, as rare as true goodness or flawless beauty. A genetic freak, like my own "gift" of perfect pitch. The gift that was my private curse, the thing that finally drove me to throw my violin beneath the wheels of a passing Corvette. Not that I wasn't good enough to play with the best. I was. But I wasn't good enough to equal the perfection I heard in my mind. So I fiddle in other ways now—but when I sleep, I dream of perfect sounds.

And in his sleep, Volker smiles.

As I felt Volker's charm enfolding me like a benediction, I wondered if he had found a satisfying way to live with the gift God or Lucifer had given him. I would have felt sorry for Volker—no intelligent person likes being captive to his genes—but how can you pity the sun?

"I was afraid I was going to have to finish the first bottle of Chardonnay myself," Volker said, laughter just beneath his voice. It was a good voice, of course, more supple than my own bass rumble.

Volker had us both seated at the table, wineglasses in hand, before I could say yes, no, or maybe. The smile on Fiora's face told me she had already said yes. I didn't blame her. Flowers were born to come unwrapped in the sun. I did wish I could hate Volker, though. I wasn't born to turn the other cheek. If I had been, I'd still play the violin.

"So. How was your meeting?" Volker asked, raising his glass to toast us.

The wine was wonderful, not too cold, as it usually is in a place like the Rodeo. I gave the pale, fragrant liquid the appreciation it deserved, then put the glass down and smiled at the most charming person I'd ever met.

"You should have been there," I said. "You would have enjoyed Sharp, and I'm damn sure he'd have been delighted to meet one of the principals of Omnitronix."

I glanced at Fiora. She didn't meet my eyes. I didn't point out that Sharp would be pissed when he found out that Volker had been within reach and Fiora hadn't mentioned it.

"Sharp didn't ask about Volker," murmured Fiora, sipping her wine with unusual interest.

I couldn't help wondering what would have happened if Sharp had asked. Would Fiora have lied to protect Volker? Had she already lied to protect Danny? Was she damn well lying to me right now?

After another sip of wine I turned my attention back to Volker. He was watching me with light blue eyes, his expression open, his body language telling me that he was fascinated by whatever I might want to say. The best reporters come across like that. The poor schmuck being interviewed is so delighted to have a good listener that he gives you chapter and verse and thanks you for the chance to do it.

But even though I understood the process, it was difficult to resist the pull. Conscious or unconscious, nurture or nature, Volker was good. So I told him about the meeting.

"We said hello. Sharp wanted to talk to Danny. We didn't know where Danny was." I shrugged. "We said good-bye."

"So concise," said Volker approvingly, pouring more wine

for me and then for himself. "I am a guest in your country. I do not understand how your system works. Do they plan to arrest Danny?"

"Why would they want to do that?" I asked, saluting Volker with my glass.

I didn't mention a grand jury, warrants, perjury, and other variants of bad luck that attend men like Special Agent Sharp, or the ghost whose face I could only remember with an effort. Fiora gave me a sidelong glance, then returned to her wine. She could always tell Volker later, I suppose, but I gave her points for letting me handle it now.

Volker shook his head in gentle bemusement. "Danny, Danny," he sighed. "I wonder what forms he forgot to fill out this time. So—impetuous, is that the word? I am sure it is nothing serious."

It wasn't really a question, though Volker's voice ascended slightly on the last word. Not asking, mind you. He wouldn't be that crass.

I relented slightly. "The export control laws were mentioned, although not in any detail."

Just then the waiter approached. He pressed for answers with a lot less class than Volker. I glanced quickly at a menu. The prices suggested that the fish was fresh, although I was skeptical. Volker and I ordered Petrale sole at the same instant. Fiora smiled as though she had just won a bet with herself. She chose the seafood salad.

Volker turned to Fiora as soon as the waiter left. "I am happy there was no need for you to worry." Again, not quite a question. Volker's English was a bit formal, very subtly accented. The result was like hearing every word for the first time. It was part of his charm.

Fiora simply shook her head and looked toward me.

"It's not that easy, Volker," I said. "The questions could get nasty, especially when they find out that you're floating around on this end of the Polar Route."

Volker's smile changed, more male and less sunshine. "If they found out, it would be both awkward and futile. I have little patience for red tape, as you say here. That is why I hired Danny Flynn." Volker's pale eyes measured the distance between us with intelligence and real interest. "Will you tell your government that I am here?"

I shrugged. "For the time being, I'm enlisted on the side of free enterprise and international trade," I said. "Provided, of course, *I* get some answers."

As Volker studied me, his eyes changed, clearer and deeper now. The effect was like looking into the center of a freshwater iceberg. Color concentrated around his slightly dilated pupils. He glanced once at Fiora. She looked at him, then at me. He shrugged in the European manner, as much with his hands as his shoulders. "Fiora trusts you. Then I must, too."

"Exactly what is Special Agent Sharp going to find when he catches up with Danny and looks inside Omnitronix?" I asked.

Volker studied his wineglass, then took a drink. "I enjoy California wines," he murmured. "What a pity we cannot get more of them at home." There was a flash, a moment when his eyes changed again, focusing inward. Then he blinked and returned to the present. "Your government will find a company with all its records intact. Danny is a very capable partner," he said, touching the back of Fiora's hand; her fingers moved, touching his. "Omnitronix has valid export licenses, shipping orders, all of the, ah, 'books' expected of a legitimate electronics brokerage firm."

"Are the books rare, medium, or well done?" I asked dryly.

Fiora tightened, a reflexive drawing in that told me I was getting close to her private fears. Cooked books, the second oldest game in the accountants' casino. The oldest is called double entry. Or triple. Whatever gets it done.

Volker's smile broadened. It was more trouble than it was worth for me not to smile back.

"I fall upon your marvelous Constitution," Volker said turning his hands palms up, giving himself into my safekeeping. "'Taking the Fifth.' Is that the correct idiom?"

For a moment I wondered if the handsome, charming German had any more sense than Danny. "Right idiom, wrong man," I said in a clipped voice. "I'm not a cop. But unless you're on the next flight out of here, get a lawyer. American law isn't as simple as counting to five."

"Fiddler, please," said Fiora, her voice strained.

"Not to frown," murmured Volker, leaning over the table and smoothing away the lines between her silky eyebrows with his fingertip. "I will trust your former husband's judgment about numbers and lawyers."

"Sharp could be very dangerous if you were involved in something. . . ." Fiora's voice trailed off. "You aren't, are you?"

"Of course not," Volker said.

"Good," she sighed, smiling up at him.

Fiora hadn't given me the up-from-under look since the third night of our honeymoon, when a plate of oysters and and a will of iron had given me the strength and resilience of three—or four, I forget which—in the span of an hour. Volker had the look of a man who didn't need oysters. I've seen the type before. Like a good whore, they can go all night long, probably because they never feel anything.

Or maybe it was just my jealousy showing. I was frowning but nobody was smoothing my brow.

Fiora looked at me. Her smile slipped. "Excuse me," she said quietly.

Volker and I watched silently as Fiora stood and crossed the patio. We weren't the only men watching. I looked away. I'd had a lot of practice at that. One day I might even get good at it. I took the last sip of my wine. It had turned as warm as piss in the sun.

"Okay, Volker, it's show-and-tell time," I said. "What kind of trouble is Danny in?"

Volker squinted at me through the pleasant California sunshine. His skin and hair were pale, almost translucent, giving him an aura of delicacy that was as misleading as hell. Just like me. At six feet two, with long bones and big hands, I'm always expected to be slow and clumsy. I'm not knocking it—it saved my hide more than once—but it also taught me about appearances. Volker was about as delicate as a falling mountain. His mind had the unemotional precision of an engineer or an assassin. Not a stupid man at all. That was the other half of his attraction for Fiora. She liked her men with equal parts of intelligence and meat.

Volker shrugged again, making his shirt pull across his muscular chest. He had the pectorals of a well-trained welterweight.

"Fiora has told me about your work as a journalist and as an, ah, free-lance investigator. She believes you are gifted as a synthesist."

"I've been a lot of things. Reporter is one of them. Licensed investigator is another."

"And unlicensed things, too," Volker said, smiling, displaying a cynicism to equal mine.

"She told you?"

"No. Meeting you is like looking in a recurved mirror, seeing myself. Different, of course, but still essentially me." Volker looked at himself reflected in my eyes, assessing me and himself without flinching. "What a pity that so much is between us," he said with soft finality.

It wasn't the kind of statement that required an answer. Which was just as well. There were too many ways to interpret what he had said. He was like a diamond. Every word, every gesture revealed another facet. But the light he threw off concealed rather than revealed his interior. I put away Volker's words to chew on sometime when my plate wasn't already full.

I didn't know then that "sometime" would be too late and Volker would be added to my long list of midnight regrets. As the saying goes, so soon old, so late smart.

Volker smiled crookedly and saluted me with the last of his sun-warmed wine. "How much do you know about the high technology business?"

"I have a few friends in the computer business, software geniuses, mostly. I use a personal computer. I'm not an expert. I can't write my own programs, and I don't have a gut understanding of electronics, like most fifteen-year-olds today."

"What do you know about the business end of electronics?"

"Not much," I said. Nice and ambiguous. The first rule of interviewing is that you don't learn by knowing it all.

"Omnitronix buys equipment in the United States and exports all over the world," said Volker. "It is a very profitable business, therefore very competitive. Time is vital. *When* we ship is as important as *what* we ship. If we are too slow, too fastidious, there are a thousand companies waiting to take our place. That is why the bureaucrats from the Customs Service can be so damned inconvenient."

I was beginning to get the picture. It was about what I'd expected. The gray market in electronics is as old as silicon chips. To you and me that's not very old. Ask the kids, though. They'll tell you it's a lifetime.

"I'm listening," I said to Volker.

"Yes, you are good at that."

"Like looking in a mirror."

Volker smiled ironically. When he spoke again, he was looking into the empty wineglass, watching light curve and flow as he rolled the crystal between his hard fingers.

"Almost every piece of electronics gear made in the U.S. is subject to export controls," he said. "If the equipment uses silicon chips, export licenses are required, no matter how old the chips might be. Red tape, as you Americans call it. In Europe we call it foolish. The Eastern Bloc may be ideological enemies but they are good customers to a great many businessmen. Much of Europe does not share the pathological fear your government has of the Soviet system."

Volker waited for my response. I nodded, letting him make of it whatever he wanted. Another trick out of the reporter's repertoire. You pass judgment in print, not in person.

"I myself do not wish to trade with the Eastern Bloc," continued Volker. "France is an excellent market, as are some of the Middle Eastern and South American nations." The crystal glass spun between his fingers with a speed that made light flash. "But even to trade with them, I must have licenses. It may take six months to get approval to export a handful of unsophisticated semiconductor chips. Are

French factories going to shut down for six months while Omnitronix goes from bureaucrat to bureaucrat trying to get export licenses for chips that are all but obsolete in the U.S?"

Volker looked up from the spinning glass. I waited.

"Your red tape simply creates a natural, very profitable gray market for chips that would have been shipped anyway after a few months and kilometers of red tape," said Volker simply. "It is so very easy to place those tiny chips in your clothes and board TWA's Flight One for Frankfurt, Zurich, or Paris."

"Did Danny's pockets bulge when he got on the plane?"

Volker's smile was as beautiful and hard as the crystal flashing between his fingers. "I did not say that. I was merely describing the way in which some people in our business operate. The gray market, I believe you Americans call it."

"What do you call it, Volker? Business as usual?"

He laughed in genuine pleasure. "You are darker and bigger than I, but every bit as quick. I would not burden you with any difficult truths. Think of the delicate position that would put you in with Fiora, who believes that the sun rises in Danny and sets in you."

"Not to mention Special Agent Sharp," I said, "who doesn't give a damn where the sun is so long as sunlight isn't on the restricted list."

"Then you understand why I can say no more. Not even to the man Fiora trusts more than she trusts herself."

That hit me like a fist in the gut. Volker saw. He stopped smiling.

"I knew you still loved her," said Volker. "I did not know how much." He leaned forward suddenly, focusing on me. "Listen to me, Fiddler. I am going to offer you something. Before you say yes or no, you should know more about me. I was a gymnast once. A very good one. I was being groomed for international competition at the highest level. It meant a great deal to me, because my parents were outcasts and thus so was I."

When I would have asked why, Volker made an abrupt

gesture with his hand, denying my question. I sat back, wondering where Volker was trying to lead me, wondering what he could offer me that I might possibly want. Yet he was very serious, the black centers of his eyes expanding as he spoke.

"In the final contest, I finished the parallel bars in first place. The second event was the horse. It was my weakest event. I was very determined. I executed a very difficult exercise. Almost perfectly. Almost. When I landed, I broke a small bone in my left foot. I heard it snap, felt bone grind against bone. I told no one. I bound the foot and went to the last event, my strongest event. The rings. I remember each movement, each twist and hold. . . ."

Volker's eyes closed for a moment, then opened again. Black centers and splinters of blue in every shade.

"I remember the dismount very well. A controlled fall from nearly four meters. Double somersault, land, then hold. The landing could not be done on one foot. I knew that before I began the event. I accepted it, just as I accepted the pain that would come."

My thoughts must have showed on my face, for Volker nodded. "I do not enjoy pain, but I do not fear it, either. I do what I must to win." He leaned forward even more. "Do you understand, Fiddler?"

I nodded. I'd taken my share of beatings for things I believed in. I was doing it right now, but there was no point in telling Volker that. He already knew how I felt about Fiora. "I understand, Volker. What's the punch line?"

"My offer?"

"Yes."

"Take Fiora away for a time, Fiddler. A week or a month. And then I will find you, and she will decide. It would be so much *cleaner* that way."

It was the most tempting, most gentle bribe I had ever received.

There are days I wish to God I had taken it.

3

Fiora and the sole arrived at the same moment. Her timing was superior to the Petrale. Not that the sole was bad. It was simply—fish. No matter how much money I might have, I resent paying extraordinary prices for ordinary food. The worst of it was that Volker and I took a bite, looked at each other, and started laughing. It would have been so much easier if I could have hated the son of a bitch.

We garnished the food with conversation about bear versus bull on Wall Street, good Spanish wines (all two of them), Washington power brokers, the price of gold and gasoline, and British politics as a modern incarnation of the nineteenth-century French bedroom farce. Volker was as witty as he was handsome. I tried not to like him. It was a losing battle. He had that rare ability to make the people around him feel special.

Finally Fiora smiled equally at both of us, stood gracefully, and murmured something about catching a cab back to the office. Before she left she bent over, ran her fingers through my hair and kissed my cheek. "Call me ASAP," she murmured, too low for Volker to hear. Then she turned, kissed Volker's cheek, and said something I couldn't hear. Yes, she ruffled his hair, too. And his nerve endings. Equal treatment all around.

The lady had her moments.

We watched Fiora leave, then turned and looked at each other. Neither of us needed to say anything. We both knew that Fiora would not be a topic of any conversation between us. It was common sense and a healthy dose of survival reflex. Neither of us wanted to probe beneath the other's layer of civility. You could lose fingers that way.

30

Volker looked at his watch. It was a slice of gold almost as thin as a silicon chip. Like everything else about him, the watch was elegant without being effeminate. It's an Old World trick that few Americans have learned to pull off.

"I have an appointment in San Jose at four," said Volker, pushing aside the last of his lunch. "As it took me almost an hour to get a cab the last time I was here, I had better begin bribing the bell captain immediately."

"Are you flying out of LAX?"

He nodded.

"I'll drop you off. It's on my way."

Volker didn't conceal his pleasure. "That is kind of you." He paused, then smiled widely. "Is it too much to hope that you have brought your Cobra?"

Bingo. Volker was the reason Fiora wanted me to bring the uncivilized roadster. That was also the reason she had faded out so conveniently. Three in a Cobra is a workable definition of "ménage à trois."

"I brought it. Hope you don't have much luggage."

Silently Volker pulled an airline ticket out of his breast pocket.

"That shouldn't tax the Cobra's trunk," I admitted.

Volker and I spotted the waiter and signaled for the check at the same moment, but Fiora had taken care of it on her way out. Like I said, the lady had her moments.

As we strolled across Rodeo Drive to the parking garage, Volker said, "I am in your debt, Fiddler. I have never even seen a Cobra, except in photographs. Will you understand if I admit that it was the possibility of seeing your Cobra that lured me down here today?"

"It's quite a car," I said, believing in understatement.

Volker laughed softly. "The Shelby Cobra is the quintessential Anglo-Saxon automobile," he said, his voice rich with the kind of excitement and enthusiasm that can't be forced, "the ideal union of American internal combustion power with British styling. Anyone in the world who cares about automobiles is fascinated by the Cobra."

He was absolutely right, of course. The Cobra has a 427-cubic-inch Ford engine mounted in a slightly modified and greatly reinforced automotive chassis that had been originally made by A.C. Bristol Motor Works in Coventry. An open roadster body as clean as a haiku and raw power on the straightaway: zero to one hundred to zero in fourteen seconds. Fewer than five hundred Cobras had been manufactured by Carroll Shelby, a crazy Texas chicken farmer with a bad heart and a wild appreciation of life.

As we approached the drive, a big Mercedes came roaring out of the parking garage, showing complete disdain for pedestrians. Volker leaped left and I leaped right. He was a hair faster than I was and a damn sight more graceful. I caught him assessing my reflexes. He nodded and said nothing. After all, who talks to his reflection in a mirror?

The Cobra was parked next to the booth where the attendant, a young Iranian with the black eyes and quick movements of a wild mallard, could keep an eye on it. He had done his job. Not even a drool mark on the wax. I gave him the larger half of the $20 bill I had torn in two when I parked.

Volker took one look at the dark blue Cobra and began making sounds of appreciation in several languages. He walked around the car, touching it from time to time as though to reassure himself that it was real. I couldn't help smiling. I'd done the same thing when I first saw the Cobra. It was one of the few things money could buy that was worth what it cost.

"Drive it?" I asked quietly, flipping Volker the key in its soft leather case, surprising myself almost as much as I surprised him.

Volker snatched the key out of the air and looked at me the way cavemen must have looked at Prometheus. Without a word he opened the door and lowered himself into the Recarro seat. I didn't bother with the door. For a man my size, it was easier just to step over the door and into the passenger seat. I strapped myself in with a lap belt.

"The belt helps to keep you right side up," I said.

Volker looked at me sideways, then strapped himself in. I showed him the right combination of toggles and key, cautioned him about the stiffness of the clutch, and then shut up. The sideoiler fired up with a snarl. Volker laughed, sheer exhilaration, contagious.

"In the mornings, it sometimes coughs flame back through the carburetors," I said.

"Like the dragon of myth," said Volker approvingly.

He rapped the accelerator once and listened to the tight, snapping exhaust. His pale blue glance roamed over the dials and gauges, missing nothing. Through his fingertips he drank the powerful vibrations of the leashed engine. He found the friction point on the clutch without killing the engine, a trick most people don't master the first time or even the second.

The tires squeaked on the smooth concrete floor as we slid up to street level and then out onto Rodeo Drive. He tapped the footfeed and felt the Cobra's full power for the first time. He swore softly, more prayer than curse, the sort of words a man might call out at the instant of hottest passion.

Volker slowed smoothly to keep from running up the exhaust of a Carrera Porsche, then settled down to drive. Any niggling worries I might have had about turning over the Cobra to Volker disappeared. He was a skilled driver, strong and decisive, with the reflexes of a gymnast.

Traffic and common sense restricted Volker to first gear and, rarely, second gear, most of the way to the San Diego Freeway. But when he made the cloverleaf turn onto the freeway, we were suddenly confronted by an unexpected Southern California treasure—clear road, four lanes wide. It was a siren call as sweet as any man has ever heard.

I looked for cops, saw none, and said, "The Cobra was made to drive."

Volker didn't need it gilt-edged and engraved.

He slipped down into first, double-clutching with the speed that only came from experience. He stabbed the accelerator, burned through first and into second with a speed that flattened us against the seats. The Cobra rose up on its shocks as the engine went from throaty to nasal roar. The front end dipped for an instant again when Volker executed his remarkably smooth power shift into third. The Cobra's weight snapped onto the back wheels again as we accelerated.

Cars appeared in front of us like still photos glued to a concrete page. The world divided, flowing by us on either side in a multicolored stream as we went past one hundred mph. At that moment there was nothing I wanted more than a second Cobra. Nevada was a mountain range away, roads straight and empty, country made by a God who loved raw power almost as much as Carroll Shelby had.

With another Cobra, Volker and I could have had God's own race.

I heard someone laughing and realized it was me. When I looked at Volker he was wearing a Comanche grin, wild and hard, the smile of a man who doesn't take prisoners. And he never even got to run the Cobra up into fourth gear.

With tangible reluctance Volker backed off the accelerator, letting the Cobra slip back into sync with the rest of the world. He downshifted into second for a few moments just for the undiluted joy of hearing the Cobra breathe. Then he shifted up into third and drove sedately all the way to the PSA terminal. He pulled alongside the curb, put the car in neutral, and stroked the accelerator lovingly, letting the Cobra's sweet music rip.

"I am fluent in five languages," Volker said finally, "but for some things there are no words." He got out and turned to me. His eyes were brilliant, compelling beyond such soft words as *charm* or *charisma*. He was a man, unique. "No matter what happens, Fiddler, no matter how it ends . . ."

Volker held out his hand. I shook it and he was gone, swallowed up by the massed anticipations and anxieties of an international airport, leaving behind the emptiness of fading adrenaline.

There was a lot for me to think about on the way back down the coast. I knew Fiora was in her office by now, waiting for my call. I didn't know what I was going to tell her.

My conscience flogged me off the freeway at the edge of a grubby little suburb called Fountain Valley. The place used to be known as Gospel Swamp, back before they drained it and planted houses. Another piece of Paradise, complete with legless reptiles and gas stations with public phones.

Fiora picked up her private line on the first ring.

"Thanks for lunch," I said.

"It was the least I could do," she murmured.

"Amen."

"What do you want me to say?" asked Fiora, her voice sharp, uneasy.

"That you renounce all the things that alienate me and that you will never look at another man until next Tuesday."

Her laugh was helpless, short. Then she gathered herself together and gave me the address of Omnitronix in Irvine. "Volker said he'd get the key to you by tomorrow."

Interesting. He must have already figured out that I was not going to disappear with Fiora.

I made a noncommittal sound and waited.

So did she.

"What do you want me to say?" I asked.

Fiora couldn't say it. Or wouldn't.

So I did.

"OK, OK. I'll look after your interests," I said. "But you'll have to pay my special consulting fee."

"You mean the one you made the Ice Princess from Norway pay?" she shot back, suddenly regaining the use of her sharp little tongue.

I had to chuckle. I didn't think Fiora had found out about Ingrid. Not that it really mattered. We don't keep that kind of score. It was just faintly unseemly. I had met the archetypal Scandinavian in Fiora's living room. I normally don't fish that close to home.

Such as home is.

"Actually, I had in mind the price that you paid last time I bailed you out—when the Internal Revenue Service wanted to punch your ticket."

"Yeah," said Fiora softly, "that was fun, wasn't it?"

There was a surprising depth to her voice. You forget about Fiora's intensity if you haven't slept with her for a while, or danced with her or fought with her.

"Fiddler, what about—the rest of it?"

I knew what Fiora wanted but I was damned if I would make it easy for her. "The rest of what?"

"Fiddler—please?"

"You're a big girl, Fiora. If you have to ask me whether you can trust Volker, then you damn well know what the answer is."

There was a long silence. "Tell me something I don't know," she said, her voice tight.

"I let Volker drive the Cobra."

That shook her a bit; I could hear a sharp breath. She knows how I feel about the Cobra. She ought to. We fought about it often enough.

"You liked him," she said.

"Christ, who wouldn't? But, Fiora—"

"Yes?"

"If you focus sunlight just right, you can burn holes in armor plate. No guarantees, woman. Not with him and not with Omnitronix. Still want me fiddling around?"

"I trust you. I need you. Danny—"

Something in Fiora's voice made me uneasy. She was Scots and fey, and Danny was her twin. I waited while she chose modern words to describe emotional connections more primitive than fire.

"Danny's in trouble," said Fiora, speaking quickly, coolly, as though to divorce her rational mind from the irrational source of her information about her twin. "It's bad trouble, Fiddler. I dreamed about him."

Fiora hung up without saying anything more. She didn't have to. The last time she had mentioned her dreams, the subject was me and Uncle Jake. She knew Jake was dead, and I was alive, before I did.

I was swearing as I hung up and went back to the Cobra. I drove straight south to Irvine Industrial Park. I was in no mood to wait for Volker to send me the key to Omnitronix.

The trip wasn't long enough for me to cool down completely, but by the time the turnoff came, I was once again susceptible to sweet reason. There's something about the average industrial "park" that encourages an unemotional approach to life. It's built into the place, like numbered parking stalls. For me, today, it was almost a relief, block after square after row of rational rectangles designed by earnest engineers who never dreamed of anything that couldn't be weighed, measured, and consummated in concrete. Reality solid enough to sink through lead.

After Silicon Valley, Irvine Industrial Park had the second greatest concentration of high technology in the world. It wasn't always that way. The park is as new as silicon chips. Fifteen years ago, Irvine contained only a handful of businesses scattered north and east of the John Wayne Airport. Today, there were 4,000 firms. I usually credit two factors for that ungodly growth—eucalyptus trees and tilt-up slabs.

Slabs are a peculiar construction method developed in the late 1960s on the flatlands of Southern California. Instant industry. You can erect a 30,000 square-foot two-story building in about three days. All you need is a crane, a pile of cement plates shaped like oversized playing cards, a steel framework, and a lot of bolts. Once the shell is complete, you can run up room dividers, cut windows and otherwise play with the interior. No matter what you do, though, the effect always remains the same—flat-roofed functional boxes, austere to the point of minimalist art.

That's where the eucalyptus trees come in. They're good for hiding tilt-up slab buildings. The trees start out as spindly shrubs in five-gallon cans, and in a few months they're four inches through and eight feet high. In six months the trees are as tall as a two-story slab, and their crowns murmur and dream in the dry winds. California, the land of the instant urban form, would be a lot uglier without eucalyptus.

Even with trees, Danny's Omnitronix wasn't much to look at. It was at the end of a quiet industrial cul-de-sac. The building's windows were clouded, as though they had not been washed for a couple of months. There was a small pile of throwaway newspapers scattered around the cement stoop. Some of the papers were so weathered that the print was unreadable. Five papers. Five weeks. Nobody had been home for a while. Or maybe it was just that nobody cared.

The company name was printed in black block letters on the glass door. The door was locked, of course, and the keys were in San Jose with Volker. Through the space between door and jamb, I could see that the dead bolt was in place. On the inner side of the glass there were copper wires, part of an alarm system that had been added after the building was rented out. Omnitronix had something that somebody was interested in protecting.

I cupped my hands against the glass to cut the glare of the afternoon sun. I saw a small pile of mail on the floor beneath the slot in the door. There was an ugly desk with a telephone on it. The dust was obvious even at a distance of ten feet and had been collecting longer than the newspapers scattered at my feet.

The telephone rang. I could hear the muffled bell and see the light beneath one of the buttons. The ring came five times. The light flashed for a while longer and then stopped. A few seconds later the sound came again, five more rings. Then it stopped.

I backed away and studied the rest of the building. There was the obligatory little strip of lawn, Japanese bunch grass, and a few wilting gazanias. There were also several circular stepping stones that invited me to explore the length of Omnitronix.

Halfway down the building there was a window strung with the alarm wires. Then the stupidity that ruined it all. The alarm box was right there out in front of God and everyone. Instead of being concealed on the roof or high on the wall—where a crook would at least have to carry a ladder to get at it—some idiot had put the box down at shoulder height on the wall. Made it easy to service, no doubt. Someone even had provided the name of the alarm company on the metal box, in case the crook had any doubt about which type of system had to be breached. All that was lacking was a four-color wiring diagram showing where to cut the wires. I wouldn't have been surprised to find it on the inside of the alarm box lid.

I didn't find the diagram when I lifted the lid, but whoever had already compromised the system by looping wires and alligator clips over the terminals apparently hadn't needed one.

There was no way of telling how long ago the work had been done. A week. A month. A minute. There I was, all tricked out for lunch on Rodeo Drive, not even a knife in my handmade boots. I would hate like hell to get inside and meet someone better dressed for breaking and entering.

Without making a lot of noise about it, I drifted the rest of the way along the side of the building, looking for an equalizer. The best I could do was a three-foot-long steel rod with a triangular handle on one end and a U-shaped fork on the other. The implement was made to turn on lawn sprinklers. Like a lot of other tools made by man, it could double as a weapon. I hefted the slender steel shaft and hoped I wouldn't need it.

Holding the rod close to my leg, I eased up to the back of the building. There were no windows. I stood, concealed by mimosa bushes, and looked around. The service bay along the rear of the building and the narrow little parking lot baked in the afternoon sun. Nothing moved but the wind. I waited for a while longer anyway, then stepped out of the bushes.

The back door was one of those steel roller numbers. The brass-jacketed padlock appeared intact until I bent over and examined it more closely. The lock came apart in my hands. Apparently somebody else hadn't wanted to wait for the keys. There was a bright crease in the brass next to the steel pin, where someone had put a heavy chisel and then slugged the lock. Either a good chisel or a bad lock, because it had only taken one strike to break it open. It was a neat job. The padlock could be put together again, as good as new in looks if not in function.

There is no absolutely quiet way to remove a broken metal padlock from a metal bolt on a metal door. I slid the bolt back and pushed the door up with the steel rod. I kept to one side, in case there was someone in the building carrying something with more range than a yard of slender metal.

There were no doors slamming, no shouts, no footsteps

retreating. No shots, either. I gave it a few more seconds anyway. Then I ducked inside.

The back room of Omnitronix was barren except for the four cardboard boxes stacked in front of the cargo door. I pulled the door up and down behind me, moved three steps to the side, and kept my back to the wall while I let my eyes adjust to the gloom. When I looked around again, I had the nagging sense of something not fitting. Then it struck me. Not only was the back room empty now, it had always been empty. The cement floor was unmarked, the walls were blank, the thin coating of dust on a work table along the wall was uniform, undisturbed.

Omnitronix was a ghost factory.

I went to the boxes. None of them was bigger than a file drawer. I flipped open the top one. Paper. Files filled with formal letterheads and torn teletype messages, machinery catalogs and spec sheets. A quick look at the other boxes showed more of the same. Standard entries in the paper chase.

The only thing I found that wasn't paper was a silver-dollar-sized black and gold disk. It was made of a metallic compound I didn't recognize. I flipped the disk like a coin. Both sides were blank. No faces. No numbers. I slipped the disk into my pocket.

I put the tops back on the boxes and moved away, wondering if the boxes had been left because someone's van was too full or if it was simply that the files were more trouble than they were worth. Of course, there was always the possibility that the thief hadn't left at all. That's why I was soft-footing it over the concrete holding a steel rod in one hand.

The door to the office suite was ajar. I lay against the wall next to the door jamb and listened. Dead silence. I was just reaching for the knob when I heard a dry metallic snap, a hum, and then a sharply punctuated clatter. In the second before I recognized the sound, I flattened against the wall and brought up the rod.

After about thirty seconds, the teletype stopped.

The silence was as surprising as the noise had been. I waited for a while longer, thinking about offices and ghosts and teletypes, the only sign so far that Omnitronix was alive. Not that a teletype meant much. A telex address is as anonymous as a phone booth. I know a con man who operated for years with a telex in his bedroom closet. The racket was annoying, but it saved office rent, and everybody else in the world thought that there really was a "First National Citibank-Haiti."

I waited another thirty seconds, then flicked the door open with the rod and moved into a little hallway. There was an office on the right, a smaller one on the left, and straight ahead was the reception area I had seen through the front door. The large office and the reception area were furnished by Abbey Rents. The smaller office was empty but for a closet holding a teletype machine humming to itself. Its two round, red status-button eyes stared blindly at me. A few inches of paper stuck out like a limp tongue. I tore off the tongue and read:

"Confrmd Del. this pm. one (1) 2" OC200,50c,39345 US 101, #12-1, Brlngme. Pymnt net 30 dys. Red."

That could mean anything, everything, nothing. There were four boxes full of similar junk waiting in the back. It looked to be a long night for me, sorting through files. I stuffed the paper in my pocket, closed the closet door and went on to the rest of the offices.

On my way to the reception area I glanced into the furnished office to make sure no one was looking for dimes under the desk. I didn't want to show myself in the front windows, so I merely stood in the hallway gloom and took a fast look. Nobody there. I went back to the furnished office. It contained one desk, one coat rack, one chair and one three-drawer file. All empty. The cleanup team had been thorough. There wasn't a scrap of paper left. There was nothing for me in Omnitronix but the cardboard cartons waiting by the cargo door. It was time to get them loaded and get the hell out.

Somebody else must have had the same idea.

He had slipped up behind me in the hallway where there wasn't enough room for me to swing a fist much less a steel rod. I got in one elbow chop and a fast look that told me all I needed to know. He was short and looked like a brick wrapped in a cheap black suit. He had a big gun and a long silencer. Both were black. The pistol was at least 9 mm with a large, open hammer, a streamlined action, and no name I could bring to mind. I'd never seen one like it. The silencer was the same. Black, smooth, bulbous, obviously not a basement job. It fit like an onion on a shish kebab.

He took my elbow shot, grunted, and gave me the butt of the gun behind my ear. My last thought was a prayer that Fiora wouldn't see me in her dreams.

4

I was half-conscious before I remembered that the man had used the butt of a gun rather than a bullet. That meant I was going to have to wake up eventually, so it might just as well be now.

I had plenty of time to regret my impulse toward consciousness. At first I couldn't see anything but the black memory of the gun. It had been the shape of a Browning High Power or a Smith & Wesson Model 59, but without the natural grace of either weapon. An ungainly pistol, top-heavy, as though it had been designed and executed by someone with primitive aesthetics.

But the gun sure worked. At least the butt of it did. A clean chop right behind the ear. No pain, really, just a numb sensation that had exploded through my skull, down my spine and through the backs of my legs, which had collapsed. No, it hadn't hurt then. It hurt like bloody hell now though.

As I grudgingly opened my eyes, the world revolved around my head. I wondered whether I had the serial number from the butt of the gun indelibly stamped on my skull. It seemed important to me for a moment, but I got distracted by the task of lifting my head off the scratchy, cheap carpet that covered the floor of Omnitronix Inc. It took me several tries because my head weighed more than the world, which was why the world was revolving around me rather than vice versa. Elementary physics, my dear Watson.

My eyes fixed on a piece of reality and tried to focus. White. Square. Dark lines. Smaller dark squiggles.

I blinked and peered. Groaning seemed to help more than anything else. The world snapped into focus. I was looking at a wall calendar, a gift from some Silicon Valley outfit whose logo was a futuristic aircraft with twin tail rudders and a bellicose fuselage. "EW for Peace" was the motto beneath the firm's name. Since "EW" stands for electronic warfare, I found myself trying to laugh. It felt so bad I decided I ought to try standing up. So I did. Several times.

By the time I dragged myself into a sitting position, the effort of standing up no longer seemed worthwhile. The exertion just made my head hurt more. I lifted my hand and tried to figure out how bad it was behind my ear. Braille has its limitations. Pain is one of them. In the end, though, I decided that not only would I live, I would eventually enjoy it again.

The guy in the cheap black suit could have given lessons to an anesthesiologist. I wasn't throwing up or caught in the black depths of concussion. The knot behind my ear was barely the size of a walnut. I'd bet that I hadn't been out more than fifteen minutes. I know dentists who aren't that precise with Novocain, much less with the more potent anesthetics.

I groaned to my feet, let the world orbit around me for a time, then walked carefully to the back door. I closed it behind me when I left, but I didn't bother to lock up. Whoever the brick-shaped man was, he had taken the boxes with him, the ones filled with the papers that were the only confirmation that Omnitronix had ever existed. The tilt-up building that had once housed one of Southern California's leading high tech export firms was ready for a new entrepreneur to drive the eucalyptus road to fame and the Fortune 500. Sic transit mundane.

By the time I woke up enough to realize that I shouldn't be driving, it was too late. The fresh air blowing by at eighty miles an hour was what had revived me. I cut it back to a decorous fifty-five. Even so, the open cockpit of the Cobra had me almost back to normal by the time I got back to Coast Highway again. The neighbor's Rhodesian Ridge-

back, N'Krumah, jumped on me at the front gate and tried
to incite a game of Frisbee.

For all his size, N'Krumah is a gentle soul. He sensed my
unplayful mood, especially after I threatened to hit him
with the steel rod I had carried all the way from Irvine.

After an icebag and fifteen minutes of wondering
whether alcohol was contraindicated for concussion—it
was, but I hurt too much to care—I was in the proper mood
to punch the buttons on the telephone. I caught Sharp at a
desk somewhere in the 213 area code. I was hoping to get
lucky and crash through with some explanation of what had
happened to me. You can't find out unless you ask, as every
reporter knows. Whether or not the mark answers is something else again.

"You got a partner built like a very short linebacker?" I
asked after I had introduced myself again.

"What in hell are you talking about?" asked Sharp, civil as
always.

"I'm talking about the guy who did a black-bag job on the
Omnitronix office in Irvine this afternoon. The guy who as-
saulted a citizen in the process, that citizen being me. The
guy I am going to describe in great detail to the inspector
general of customs or whoever it is that investigates the
commission of felonies in the pursuit of justice."

I paused for breath, wondering if I was making more
sense to Sharp than I was to me. Maybe the alcohol hadn't
been such a good idea after all.

Sharp took a moment or two to run my words through his
clever border brain. "It wasn't anybody I know," he said
finally.

Some cops are pretty good liars, but I tended to believe
Sharp. He wouldn't lie when the truth didn't do me any
good, either. Like every desert survivor, Sharp saved his
juice for the times it counted.

"You're probably telling the truth," I said pleasantly. "You
federal cops don't get enough practice with a gun butt to do
a surgical job of it."

Silence, during which I could practically hear Sharp

leaping for conclusions. The one he grabbed was the right one.

"I told you to stay out of it," he said, not bothering to stifle his amusement.

"Kiss my ass."

Sharp's laugh was short, derisive. "Didn't your Uncle Jake teach you not to swear at cops?"

I closed my mouth. I had known Sharp was going to put Jake and me together, sooner or later. I wish to hell it had been later.

"Jake had impeccable manners. That's what got him killed," I said.

"Yeah?" said Sharp skeptically.

"He let the other guy shoot first."

"I didn't think he was that dumb."

"Actually, he was that slow." I rubbed the icebag on the knot behind my ear. It hurt so good I almost groaned. "If it wasn't a friend of yours, who was it?"

I heard Sharp drag on a cigarette, then exhale with the effort of a man whose lungs were starting to get tired. He was too old to still be smoking. Anything over forty-five is too old. Anything over twenty-five, actually, but it takes a few years for the truth to sink in.

"What did he look like?" asked Sharp.

"An outhouse in drag."

"I couldn't say, Fiddler. I know a lot of people."

"Couldn't say, or won't?"

"Whatever." Sharp took another drag, his exhalation a sigh. "You aren't in shape to play in this league, Fiddler. For what it's worth, neither am I. Now just go sit on the bench like a good boy."

"Is that what you're doing, Sharp? Sitting on the bench? They didn't bring you in from the desert to get splinters in your ass. You're here because your handlers needed a shooter. Uncle Jake used to tell me how good you were with an M-1 carbine. He'd talk about the Lochiel Valley east of Nogales, where you used to knock Cessnas out of the air with one clip. Then you'd stand downwind of the wreck, inhale the burning grass, and laugh like a coyote."

Sharp chuckled and then drew a deep breath. I could hear the gentle wheeze of tired lungs. "There used to be room in the world for shooters," he said. "Now I'm just a customs cop on detached duty to the big city. Take my word for it, Fiddler. A pine bench is better than a pine coffin."

"Threat?"

"Not personally," he said. "I always kind of got a kick out of Jake. He was the only stand-up dope smuggler I ever knew. Maybe I feel I owe him a free piece of advice. Since he didn't survive his last mistake, I'll give the advice to you. Don't—"

I hung up before Sharp could finish. Good intentions I didn't want. Ditto for good advice. I took my glass of wine, my icebag, and my body to bed. The shot behind the ear must have been a bit less surgical than I'd hoped. I don't remember much about the rest of the day. I do recall leaving a message on Fiora's answering machine when I found that she had already left the office. Then I had another glass of wine, a little bit of cheese and bread and an apple. I sat while the last of the day bled into the sea, shades of red and gold and purple thickening into blue, then indigo, then iridescent black.

Usually the house's old glass helps to give me perspective on the day. Particles of energy moving faster than man can understand, bending and blending through glass a century old. But tonight the glass had no special effect on my view of reality. I was no closer to sorting out Volker and Danny and Fiora and Sharp and his steel-gray friend than I had been before I went to Omnitronix.

Oh, sure, Danny was involved in something illegal. Big deal. There are more laws in the world than anyone could know or obey. Natural laws were no problem. Break the law of gravity and go to the bottom of the cliff. With nature, enforcement is built into the law. But manmade laws were a different sort of reality entirely. Somebody was breaking human law every second of every day, world without end, amen. Breaking laws and making money and not a cliff bottom in sight.

It would have come as no great surprise to me if Volker

were doing that. He enjoyed the things money could buy as much as I did. But I doubted that his was a case of simple greed. Volker was charming, not innocent; complex, not transparent. If he were breaking the law, he was getting more out of it than a handful of silk shirts.

Danny, though, was a simple soul. Innocent as an egg. Transparent, too. Greed was enough of a motive for him.

And may their fondest wish come true.

The only thing that kept me from tossing the curse over my shoulder and walking away was that both Volker and Danny had a hold on Fiora. Whatever else she may or may not be, at bottom Fiora is as honest as the Scots hills she sprang from. She'll sail breathtakingly close to the legal winds on monetary matters, but she will never overstep. That's why she had called me in. When push came to shove, I wouldn't hesitate to break any law that threatened the woman I loved. She knew it. I knew it.

I wondered if Volker knew it.

I woke up sometime around midnight, the kind of wakefulness that means your animal warning system is screaming and pumping adrenaline into the bloodstream. I lay without moving. It's not smart to attract attention until you know what's out there tripping physiological alarms.

A small sound came, liquid swirls like tiny whirlpools, then delicate splashes.

I let out my breath and cursed. There was a prowler outside. Four-footed, though, not two-legged. But I slid out of bed quickly just the same, especially when I remembered that I'd forgotten to put the cover on the koi pond. It's a small pond, really, with just about a dozen fish, but I'm very protective of it.

I keep a special pistol in the nightstand just for this kind of situation. I grabbed the gun, threw a couple of pumps into it, and headed for the sliding glass door that opened out onto the side yard. As silently as I could, I slid the glass and then the screen open, expecting to see a couple of small gray figures with black masks perched on the rock ledge around the pond, trying to scoop thrashing, brightly colored koi from the water.

Southern California is largely a desert, even at the edge of the Pacific Ocean, and raccoons don't get too many chances at freshwater fishing. Captive koi are high on the raccoon's most-delicious list. It's a constant war of nerves. Every night, on their way to eat N'Krumah's kibble, the coons check to see whether I've put the wire mesh cover over the koi pond. If I haven't, the fish pay the price. That's the hell of it. If the coons would just bite me, I'd either stop forgetting or start eliminating coons. But the koi pay, not me, and I feel a certain responsibility to make sure they don't end up as a sushi appetizer before the raccoons' main course of Purina Dog Chow.

So I stepped through the door into the darkness with pistol in hand, ready to administer the kind of justice that a raccoon could learn from.

"Real cute," said Fiora. She was sitting on the rock seat beside the pond, a small pan of fish food at her feet. "A two-gun hero," she added dryly, in case I'd thought she was referring to the koi as "cute."

I looked at the raised pistol. "Two-gun?"

"Your pants, Fiddler," she said patiently. "You forgot to cover more than the koi."

I conceded the point with a smile and a little barb. "Never fear, pretty lady. You're safe. Only one of my weapons is primed."

I wandered over to the pond and tripped a hidden switch to turn on the recessed lights, illuminating the gently swirling koi, turning and twisting like bright leaves in a black whirlwind. The light also revealed Fiora's face, her slanting cheeks and shadowed mouth, hazel-green eyes dark as she looked at me while fish sucked delicately at her empty fingers. She was wearing a thin white blouse and jeans that were nearly old enough to vote, although they still fit her like high school. She wore both the silky cotton and the denim with extraordinary grace.

"The problem with this gun," I said, gesturing to the pistol in my hand, "is that once it gets pumped up, you have to fire it. There is no way, you should pardon the expression, to 'uncock' it."

As Fiora looked away her lips curved in a smile so swift that I almost missed it. I wished I had. That particular smile has always had a bad effect on my blood pressure. I took casual aim in the direction of the ocean bluff and tripped the pellet gun. With a cough, the lead wad disappeared into the night.

Fiora glanced up from the pond and knifed me with her dark eyes and regretful mouth. "I seem to recall you making the same complaint about your other weapon," she said gently. "Go put them both away, Fiddler. They distract me and—" She stopped and closed her eyes, refusing to look at me any longer.

"And?" I asked.

"And I have some more bad news for you."

The knot behind my ear suddenly began to throb, a bass drum trying to make rhythm out of chaos. I stroked the knot, listening to drums and other random instruments tuning up, the cello that was Volker's supple voice, the tuba that was the brick-shaped man, the hesitant viola that was Danny, and Fiora an alto soprano singing soft and wild, alone.

"Feed the fish," I suggested as I headed for the bedroom.

I was back in a moment, dressed in a pair of rugby shorts and a torn T-shirt from Hussong's Cantina in Ensenada. I brought an opened bottle of cold Eschol White and two stemmed glasses with me. N'Krumah had wandered over from next door, casualty of the kibble wars with the raccoons. He was drooling over the fish food, his heavy head draped across Fiora's knee, watching intently as she fed the koi a few pellets at a time. The fish rose and deftly sucked the small alfalfa-meal morsels from her pale fingertips. Just like old times, but the various creatures welcomed Fiora back more easily than I did.

"Here you go," I said, offering her a glass and pouring wine. I waited while she drank an appreciative sip, then a deep swallow that told me more about the state of her mind than anything she had said so far. "What's up, Fiora?"

"Two things," she said, looking at the wine. "First, Danny called. He wants me to come up to Cupertino tomorrow. He said it was important that he talk to me."

"He's heard of the telephone, hasn't he?"

"He said he had to see me in person, too. He had to give me something for safekeeping. No, he wouldn't tell me what it was," said Fiora, anticipating my question. Her voice was almost thin, less assured now than it had been this morning in her office.

I took a sip of the cold white wine and savored it. Eschol '81 was a high mix of Chardonnay and a bit of something else that added to the complexity, maybe Grey Riesling. I swallowed and looked at Fiora, who looked away from me the instant my eyes would have met hers.

"You don't need me to tell you that holding something for Danny at this point might be criminally stupid," I said, emphasizing the word *criminally*.

Fiora carefully fed the koi a few more pellets and just as carefully avoided looking at me.

"Sharp and his friend might read you your rights the next time through," I continued, telling Fiora things she already knew and didn't want to hear anyway. Not from herself and not from me.

"Danny's in trouble," said Fiora softly, talking to the colorful, swirling fish. "So much trouble he doesn't even know the half of it. He never dreams like me. . . " She pulled her fingers free of the importunate koi and looked up at me with eyes that were too dark to be called hazel. "I'm going to Danny."

"When?"

"At eleven. Danny's sending his plane for me."

His own airplane. My, my. Danny's a card-carrying success—and a world class simpleton. But I didn't say it out loud.

The koi had become impatient. They dashed in twos and threes to the surface and then spun and fled when no manna floated down from their goddess's hand. Their turns and powerful sweeping tails sent silver arcs of water beyond the pool, spotting Fiora's blouse and leaving dark splashes on her jeans. Her feet were bare, pale, oddly vulnerable in the shadow of the rock wall.

I sat beside Fiora and took a handful of pellets, trying to quell the feeding frenzy. The biggest fish in the pool, a five-pound orange and white *ikigama* named Lord Toranaga, glided up from his liquid domain and demanded tribute to his beauty and strength. I fed him, enjoying the cool mouthings and compressed power of a hungry koi. Toranaga is the only one of the fish I'd give a fighting chance with a raccoon.

"I'm going with you to Cupertino," I said.

I didn't look up from Toranaga's muscular grace, though I sensed that Fiora was watching me. She touched the back of my hand with her fingers, wet with water from the pond. I turned quickly, catching her off guard.

"Drop the other shoe, Fiora. Why are you really here?"

I watched Fiora's face in the shimmering, ghostly illumination of the underwater light. For just a second, I thought I saw a flash of panic. When she drew a deep breath, I was sure. Instinctively, I reached out to her, putting my palm against her cheek. She covered my fingers and gave them a squeeze.

"I think," she said, but her voice broke and she had to try again. "I think somebody tried to break into my office this evening." She spoke the words in a rush, getting rid of them as quickly as she could.

I poured Fiora a bit more wine. "Go ahead, honey," I said, letting my hand slide down to her shoulder. Beneath my fingers her muscles were knotted with tension. Body language, the quickest way to the bottom line. She was scared.

"I was working late, about six-thirty," Fiora said, her voice tight. "You now how those offices are in Century City. Everybody takes off at five. Well, I had some telexes to read so I sent Jason home and had him lock the outer door."

Fiora took a sip of the wine, wetting her lips. The way her tongue darted out to share in the moisture told me that her mouth was dry.

"The connecting door into my office was open, and I was

just getting ready to leave when I heard somebody rattle the knob, as though he were trying it," said Fiora, speaking so quickly I had difficulty understanding. "I thought it might be the janitor so I walked over to let him in, but when I got the door open, it was a little man, young, an Oriental with a wispy mustache, very compact, very strong, very surprised. He had a clear piece of plastic in his hand about the size of a credit card."

"It's called a 'shim,'" I said, cutting in, giving Fiora time to take a breath.

She nodded her head tightly, her muscles so tense that they barely shifted beneath my palm.

"I slammed the door in his face and shot the bolt," she said. "Then I called security. Then I had a little nervous breakdown." She hugged herself at the memory. "Was that right?" she asked in a small voice. "Did I do the right thing?"

I squeezed Fiora's shoulder. "You did just fine," I said as gently as I could, considering the fear-rage lighting up my blood. The idea of Fiora in danger and me fifty miles away with a knot behind my ear made my whole mental orchestra scream in discordant unison. "Where was the Beretta I gave you?"

"You know I don't carry it around with me. It's home in the kitchen drawer with my twine and telephone book," she said. She looked up at me and tried so hard to smile that her mouth trembled. "I leave the shooting to my two-gun hero, unless it's pellet guns and raccoons."

Fiora was the one who had bought the air pistol for use against the raccoons after one had offered to take her leg off below the knee. I settled that question by skinning the raccoon and using its mean hide to polish the Cobra. That had been a lifetime ago, when Fiora and I were still married and living together.

"Carry the Beretta," I said, giving her shoulder a squeeze. "For me, Fiora. Carry it." I could feel the tension radiating through the elegant trapezius muscle of her upper back. "Scary, huh?"

She nodded and bowed her head, inviting another reas-

suring squeeze. I took the knotted muscle between thumb
and palm and began to knead gently. She sagged a bit and
closed her eyes. We still read one another, the agreements
and needs, very nicely. Most of the time. She had opened a
door tonight and had a quick look at her own vulnerability.
She was still looking at it. Still scared. And she had come to
me.

I stood up, put down my wineglass, and shooed
N'Krumah back to his yard. Then I stood behind Fiora and
gently went to work on the knots. It took time and a lot
more gentleness than I usually have, but it worked. After a
while, I felt her muscles becoming resilient again, releasing
their tension.

"It was probably just your garden-variety cat burglar," I
offered, a lie almost as smooth as Fiora's skin.

"Did I get you to sign those papers?" she asked, her eyes
closed, her head rolling gracefully as she relaxed under my
hands.

"Which papers?"

"The ones for that real estate deal. You know. The
Brooklyn Bridge."

My hands hesitated, then I sighed. It had been worth a
try. I knew the burglar was connected to Danny's mess, but
her worrying about it would do no damn good. Fiora had
enough on her mind with her dreams and her idiot twin.

"Didn't I tell you?" I whispered, leaning over like a con-
spirator, "I gave up buying bridges when I started shaving."

Fiora laughed softly. "Can't blame me for trying. I sensed
a sudden, er, vulnerability in you when you started trying
to sell me on garden-variety burglars."

"Life is full of coincidences," I offered without much
hope.

She said nothing, but when her head rolled back against
my thighs, I saw the silent laughter on her lips. Quite a
lady. Her body was tied up with fear but she could still
smile.

I resumed working on the only thing within my control—
the female muscles that were slowly relaxing. The collar
kept getting in the way, so without thinking too much about

it until after I had done it, I reached around and flicked open the top button of her blouse. I eased the fabric off the knotted muscles of her neck. As my fingers gently kneaded, I felt a change in the texture of her, as though her deepest fear had begun to slide away, softening her.

Fiora sagged against my legs, letting me support her. "That's wonderful," she sighed.

"Best hands in the business," I said. "That's what my Little League coach used to say."

The diffuse light from the bottom of the pool gleamed in Fiora's smile. "I know some others who have made the same observation," she said dreamily. "There's no one like you, Fiddler."

I let my hands answer, stroking away Fiora's tension, enjoying the warmth and resilience of her. We fall into the patterns of comfort easily, both of us. We don't keep secrets from one another very well. When things feel good, we say so. It makes for a complicated relationship, but what's life without a few well-chosen complications? Dull, that's what.

I tugged delicately at the boundaries of the blouse. My hands were too big to fit beneath the fabric without straining it. Fiora undid two more buttons and shrugged the blouse off her shoulders until it settled in white folds around her elbows. She hung her head forward, presenting the back of her neck for me to massage. Light swirled as Toranaga rose. The twisting illumination transformed Fiora's back into pale curves and velvet shadows. She wore nothing beneath the blouse but the scent of lavender, and her skin felt smoother than silk, warmer, alive.

I slid my hands down her bare back and began to massage the flat lateral muscles just below her shoulder blades. Fiora feels the same way about exercise as I do—if she could phone it in, she would. But she can't, and flab offends her sense of self. So she swims several miles a week and keeps a tumbling mat in one room of her office suite. The result is magic to feel, strength beneath a very feminine softness. I had to work hard enough on her muscles to bring a bit of heat to my own skin. At least, I blamed the rise in temperature on the physical exertion.

"What's this about, Fiddler?" asked Fiora, her voice husky. "Do you know?"

"Not even the overture," I said.

"Nothing?"

"A few phrases here and there. Nothing solid, except—" I stopped, not wanting to feel her tighten up again.

"Except what?"

"It's something illegal," I temporized, "but you already knew that. We'll talk to Danny tomorrow. That's soon enough to worry. For now, just relax. You've had one hell of a day."

"Yeah," Fiora said, sighing. "Special agents and cat burglars, the Cobra and you. . . ."

She lifted her head and rotated it, trying to loosen her neck. I could feel the muscles sliding firmly beneath her skin. Not as tight as they had been, but not relaxed, either. I went back to work on the spot where her neck and shoulders joined. The fact that she had to support her head while I worked made the job impossible. At least, that's what I told myself.

"I can't do a proper job while you are sitting up," I said.

Fiora covered my fingers with her right hand and squeezed. With her other hand she held the unbuttoned blouse closed over her breasts. In the faint, shimmering light, I could see the outline of her nipples, firm and asking to be touched.

"You had some other place in mind?" she asked, her voice throaty.

I drew a breath, savoring the scent and softness of her skin, and enjoying the heavy, relaxed feeling she generated in me. "You still own half the bed," I said. "Or don't you remember the terms of the settlement."

With the grace that always fascinated me, Fiora stood and turned to me. She shrugged into the blouse but did nothing about the buttons that had been undone. White, soft cotton draped over her breasts and cast a shadow that invited my touch. She smiled dreamily, took my right hand, kissed the palm, and drew it into the shadow, closing her eyes as my fingers curled around her.

"I remember the terms," she said. "They were the only reason either of us went through with the divorce."

I undid the remaining buttons, then slid my palms down to her waist, holding her in the circle of my hands. When I moved my thumbs and stroked just inside the waistband of her jeans, she came up on tiptoe, arching her back as her arms met behind my neck. I bent to kiss her, then straightened, lifting her in my arms until our heights were equal.

Mutual pleasure is a powerful aphrodisiac, the most powerful in the world. By the time the kiss ended, both of us were breathing raggedly.

"Fiora . . . ?"

"Yes."

That night we made the kind of love that we seldom had while we were married. Driving, hot, and insatiable. Then again, smoother and slower and with our eyes open, both smiling and watching the other, as though we were trying to memorize every moment because we knew it might never come again.

5

Just like always, the sun rose, and Fiora rose with it. Just like always, I did not. I blamed it on my head. The serial numbers had faded to a tender little knot that I hadn't bothered to mention to Fiora. But I used my head as an excuse to roll over and get a bit more sleep. Sleep had been one thing that Fiora and I hadn't gotten around to.

By seven-thirty Fiora was already gone. She had left me a note that outlined our itinerary for the day and simultaneously confessed to slaughtering a bag of oranges in my honor (oysters not being a big breakfast favorite with me). She closed with a concise summation of our time together: "!"

Amen, lady. And neither of us had mentioned Volker all night. Maybe that European charm was not as overwhelming as I had feared.

I went out and did three miles on a dirt road that runs up Trancas Canyon into the burgeoning heat of the coastal hills. Then I did another mile on the hard sand below mean high tide, just as a little experiment. No fuzzy vision, no black spots, no cymbals banging in my ears. If you have to be cold-cocked, pick the man who looks like a brick in mourning clothes. There's no substitute for expertise.

I did some stretching just as the sun burned through the marine air layer and began to warm the deck. My body knew it had been in a lovely tussle recently. Every little ache was a new memory. I didn't want to miss a one of them, so I did a bit of t'ai chi, letting memories flow through my body to my arms and feet and legs.

T'ai chi is an arcane discipline that is fundamentally

58

tuned to the rhythms of the human body. The deep breaths and twists and turns covered me with sweat and made me as drunk as if I had been inhaling cognac. For a moment I felt like I could float with one of the seagulls that were holding station in the rising morning air over the edge of the bluff. If the bluenoses of the world ever find out how good a little exercise and plenty of oxygen make you feel, there will be a new Prohibition movement.

The night before hadn't hurt, either.

I cooled down, showered, and still had time to sit on the deck. I read the morning paper in the sunshine while I drank a quart of mineral water and listened to the gulls keening just beyond the bluffs at the front of the house. After a while, I worked up enough energy to get the quart of orange juice Fiora had left for me. The California Valencias were just coming on, sweetness and purity at the same time, and a color so perfect it made you believe in God. With her usual sense of style, Fiora had added a couple of fresh strawberries. The full, crimson berries had been permeated with the crisp flavor of citrus.

The sensual pleasures of the moment were so intense that I finally threw away the newspaper, filled as it was with the more unpleasant aspects of humanity, and enjoyed the brilliant morning on its own terms. News is a negative business. I decided this long ago, about the time I got out of it. As practiced today, its nature is essentially destructive, like a mediocre critic whose impulse is to demonstrate erudition by quarreling rather than by understanding. Maybe that's the legacy of adversarial journalism, of Watergate and Woodstein.

Which leaves me with nothing to read on mornings like this, when everything is transformed by brilliant sunlight, ripe fruit, and the call of gulls soaring on a silver wind.

About nine, I got around to packing—a change of clothes but no necktie, a pair of shorts, jock and T-shirt stuffed inside a pair of running shoes, toothbrush, comb, and handgun. Handgun? I looked at the gun balanced so nicely on my palm. Then I asked myself why I was bothering with clothes. I wasn't planning to spend the night with Danny, was I?

I sat down on the edge of the torn-up bed and thought about what my subconscious was trying to tell me. Truth was that even if I ended up overnight in Silicon Valley, they had stores there just like everywhere else. With cash, credit cards, and a smile you can buy anything you need. Well, almost anything. Ammunition you can buy off the shelf, but there's a three-day waiting period for something to use the bullets in.

The Boy Scouts have a point. I chucked in the pistol and two clips, and zipped up the ripstop duffel. Hiding the pistol gave me no twinge of guilt or pleasure. I have a concealed-weapon permit, the only status symbol recognized on both sides of the salt shaker. I have the permit because a man for whom I once did a favor is one of the people empowered to issue permits. But I don't habitually carry a gun for the simple reason that I don't habitually have any use for one. Nobody is trying to kill me, most of the time, and if I'm dumb or unlucky enough to get mugged, I'll gladly empty my pockets.

My skull, however, is another thing entirely. I like my brains right where they are. It wasn't just the Boy Scout knot behind my ear that was whispering *Be Prepared* to me; there was the open question about the Oriental who had been trying to shim his way into Fiora's office. There was a calculated aggressiveness in that act that made the orchestra in my head very restive. The garden-variety sneak thief is a smack addict looking for an IBM Selectric to hock. Junkies work in the middle of the night and usually have enough smarts left to bring a freight cart along for the heavy lifting. This guy had been trying to blend into the late workday traffic, nothing in his hands but a clear plastic shim. The only comforting aspect to the whole thing was that the burglar probably wasn't interested in Fiora personally, or he would have waited in her car in the parking structure.

While I'm a great believer in karate, judo, and other variations on the theme of unarmed combat, nothing is quite as effective in discouraging the unfriendlies of the world as a blue steel sidearm. The Detonics that was just below the duffel zipper was guaranteed to produce clean thoughts and cooperation in anyone looking up its barrel. The Detonics is quite a sidearm. The only thing unwieldy about it is the name. It is a palm-sized pistol with physical dimensions that make it more easily concealed than a snub thirty-eight. Semiautomatic, seven rounds, and a hell of a lot quicker to reload than a revolver. The Detonics probably will be the next sidearm approved and purchased by the Department of Defense. In other words, it is pretty close to state of the art. I thought about ordering mine in forty-five caliber, but that somehow offended my technical sense. The metric system is the way we all are supposed to be going, isn't it? So I went for the 9mm.

I lifted the bag and set out for one last errand before I climbed onto Danny-boy's plane. I had a man to see about a disk, the little black-and-gold number I had found in the box on the floor of Omnitronix.

When I got there, the Ice Cream King of Saigon was holding court over the telephone, pumping his wheelchair around his workshop, doing a dozen things at once, and spouting high tech gobbledygook into the phone at the same time. It wasn't gobbledygook to him, however. His workshop was the repository of some of the hottest high tech material around. RAMs and ROMs of stupendous computing power, VHSIC chips and plasma displays and audio systems.

Incredible doesn't cover it. The black-and-gold-and-silver stuff was scattered around on waist-high benches that were designed to accommodate a man in a chair. It looks like chaos, but I've never seen him hesitate over where any little item might be. When you get down to it, Benny Speidel, aka the Ice Cream King, is still a better computer than anything he or IBM can create.

Benny is a free-lance consultant, which is to say that he does just about what he wants to do and then sells the result to whoever is willing to meet his price. Benny's specialty is high tech cops and spooks gear, radio and satellite communications gear, bugs and debugs, electronic ears that

Benny says can hear a gnat fart three miles away. Surveillance stuff mainly. He designs them, builds them, and
then lets somebody else use them.

As such people go, the Ice Cream King is a moral man.
He recognizes that his talent for things technical is not to be
squandered on fools, knaves, and bureaucrats. He deals
with a very small group of clients, people he knows and
whose judgment he trusts—cops, private security people,
and even folks from the government. Not everybody in
those positions is on his mailing list, mind you. Some used
to be on it and got dropped. Some won't make it this side of
the Second Coming. Benny has definite ideas about who
does and does not wear a white hat.

I've known Benny for a decade, a few years less than the
amount of time he has spent on wheels. He earned those
wheels, as he says, by stupidity and bad luck. It happened
in 1970, in the place that is now called Ho Chi Minh City.
Benny had spent a half-decade there. He was the ambitious
sort who worked two jobs. In the daytime, he was quality-
control engineer at one of those civilian-contract plants that
kept the American GIs supplied with the comforts of home.
In Benny's case, comfort equaled ice cream. Every day, he
oversaw the production of about 5,000 gallons of chocolate,
vanilla, strawberry, and fruit-of-the-month. Good stuff, too.
If Benny had been given a free hand, he would have paci-
fied the whole God-forsaken Indochinese peninsula with
nuc mahm sherbet.

But the Ice Cream King had a night job, too, one that
paid gold into a numbered Hong Kong account and a promise of U.S. citizenship for the discontented New Zealander.
It was quiet work, technical consultation of some sort on a
communications system for some of the quiet elements in
the U.S. war effort. Messy work but honorable, so far as
Benny was concerned.

The other side must have thought so, too. They tried for
him a bunch of times, using the low tech but effective weapons that the black pajama brigade was famous for. Things
like the inner-tube bomb. That's an old-fashioned fragmen-
tation grenade whose safety handle is held in place with a

wide rubber band cut from a bicycle inner tube. Some young sapper snaps on the rubber, pulls the pin, and drops the grenade into your gas tank. The gas goes to work on the rubber, a process that may take a day or a week, depending on God's sense of humor. When the rubber finally dissolves, the handle pops up. Seven seconds later, *bango*.

Inelegant. Unpredictable, too. What if your mark doesn't happen to be in the car? Or worse, what if his friend is driving when God blinks and the rubber falls away?

Benny survived everything that the other guys threw at him for five years. Then a half-stoned, half-wit American sentry on a roadblock in Cholon thumbed the wrong button on his fully automatic, state-of-the-art, can't-go-wrong, space-age M-16. Half a clip poured out at a shattering velocity. One of the bee-sting slugs caught Benny below the sixth thoracic vertebra, cutting the cord irrevocably.

The experience left Benny with wheels, a state he finds inconvenient but preferable to some others he has seen. It is also an illustration of the First Law of Machines: "Machines do what you tell them to do, not what you want them to do." Benny is fond of citing that law and a corollary which we call the King's Corollary, when he refuses to do business with someone: "Don't trust assholes with state of the art." The King's Corollary also contains the implicit minor variant statement: "Assholes aren't always on the side you expect them to be."

Benny finished his phone lecture, which sounded as though it were being conducted in some foreign language, and chucked the cordless telephone onto a cluttered workbench.

"Assholes," he muttered, tossing his head until his black hair quivered. With his heavy beard and long hair, he looks faintly like a vengeful Rasputin. He pumped himself with one stroke to the other end of the long room, spun, and came back at me with the speed of a Double-A Class fuel dragster. Benny was more than capable of constructing a supersonic wheelchair, but he stayed with manual power because it was the only physical outlet he had. As a result, he had developed the barrel chest and oversized arms of a blacksmith.

"Anybody I know?" I asked mildly as I sat on a workbench and began twiddling with the silver-dollar-sized metal disk from my pocket.

"NSA couldn't find their ass with both hands and a mirror," snarled Benny. He stroked to the other side of the room, spun, and returned with a speed that made the tires whine soft complaints. "They built those bloody great antennae at Cobra Dane to listen across a couple hundred miles of water. Bloody great overkill, that's what. Those antennae could listen to cockroaches mating on Jupiter. So now the bloody idiots want to set up the same sort of system in the Bay Area to monitor outlaw radio sources."

"Sounds simple enough," I said, understanding my present role as straight man to the King. I knew selective monitoring of that kind was about as simple as constructing your average spacecraft, but you have to let Benny get things off his mind before he'll have room for your problems.

"Simple! The silly sods just want outlaw transmissions, not amateurs jacking off on their CBs. As though it's possible to tell one kind of radio transmission from another! But NSA insists there must be a way. They're pissing in their pants with fear that some muckracking news type will find out about the listening post and crucify NSA for spying on innocent civilians. Jesus save us from scientific illiterates and bourgeois moralists in search of headlines. *Assholes.*"

Benny has little of what I would call political finesse, a lack that I don't hold against him but which can sometimes make him difficult to be around.

"Why do you suppose the National Security Agency needs that kind of capability in the Bay Area?" I asked.

Benny made one last sweep of the room, then came to a stop and spun to face me. "I think they just discovered what every ham and hacker has known for years. There's at least one renegade Russian transmitter up there feeding semiconductor manufacturing data to a passing satellite. Big news, baby, but you'll never see it in print. Love thine enemy, right?" Benny snorted. "Sod them one and all. Ass-holes. You ever see the forest of antennae the Russians have on the roof of their consulate? Makes Cobra Dane look like a college FM station."

"No, Benny," I said, "I haven't. Remember, I'm a civilian. I make it a point not to pay attention to some other coun-try's 'diplomatic mission' in the Bay Area or to any of the other esoteric applications of high tech. I leave that to pro-fessionals like you." I flipped the metallic disk like a coin, hoping to lure Benny out of his dark pool like Toranaga ris-ing to food.

"Injured reserve, not pro," Benny shot back, but his eye followed the spinning disk as I flipped it again. "Someday somebody is going to come up with a coaxial connector and put the two halves of my spinal cord together again. Then I'll be glad to run you a footrace or make love to your ex-wife or any other little thing you have in mind."

I flipped the disk as though I hadn't heard Benny's refer-ence to Fiora. He knows how to bait me, and I know how to ignore him.

Benny sighed. "What do you have there that you're so in love with?"

"You tell me," I said, flipping the disk through the air to him.

He looked at it, turned it over, and spun it into the air several times with the quickness of an otter. "It's a silicon wafer, the kind they once used for semiconductor manufac-turing. Lay out a couple hundred integrated circuits, etch them into the silicon, and then cut them up and mount them in chips. Haven't seen one that small in a while, though."

I looked puzzled, which was easy.

"That's a two-inch wafer," said Benny patiently. "The standard for mass production in the U.S. nowadays is four- and five-inch wafers. You get more circuits to the slice, and while silicon is just sand, it isn't cheap to synthesize and prepare. Your toy is either an old slice or it's being used for some kind of custom work. Probably old, or else very poor quality, because it's already starting to come apart. Shoddy little piece, really," said Benny, looking at the disk disdainfully.

"Not too exotic, then," I said.

"Too old to be 'cutting-edge' and too new to be antique," replied the King. "It ain't worth shit. What can I tell you?"

"Only the truth, old man," I said, "which is what you just did. Does the name 'Omnitronix' mean anything to you?"

He shook his head. "Could be anything or anybody."

"You know a Customs investigator named Sharp?" I asked, deciding to try for a clean sweep. Sharp and the Ice Cream King didn't travel in the same circles, unless gossip of a high tech bust was making the rounds.

Benny shook his head. "Customs has a big push on right now, trying to cut down the illegal export of high tech gear." He snorted. "Not bloody likely they'll succeed. Most of their cops wouldn't know an integrated circuit if it was etched on their cock. I've looked at a few things for them. Mostly low-level fabricated equipment—chess robots and the like—that somebody was trying to slip out without proper licenses. I haven't dealt with anybody called Sharp. I can ask around if you want."

"Whisper, if you do," I said. "Special Agent Sharp is in the middle of something that he thinks is pretty hot. He doesn't want any civilian help."

"Told you to go shit in your mess kit, did he?" said Benny, grinning.

"Twice."

"Some people got no sense of humor," said Benny, a line he had stolen from me. "Maybe you should take his advice."

"Can't," I said. "Fiora's brother is involved. She's scared that he may finally have stepped into the cowflop right up to his charming lips."

"Has he?"

I sighed. "Probably, Benny. Probably. I don't know. There are some very spooky people around—an Oriental cat burglar, a European as handsome as Lucifer and as charming as hell, a steel-gray ghost, and a Border cop who knew Uncle Jake." I hesitated, listening to the chords quivering inside my skull. "Actually," I admitted, "if it weren't for the fact that Fiora is caught in the middle, it might be kind of fun. But she's too damned honest to play alone in this league and come out anything but dead last."

I wish I had thought of another way to put it. I really do. One psychic in the family is enough.

"That's why Fiora has such a hold on you," said Benny. "She's pure sunshine. You're a twilight type, caught between noon and midnight." He flipped the disk back to me. "You need any special equipment to play with?"

I stared. It wasn't like the Ice Cream King to be so forthcoming with his toys.

"Not for you, turkey, for *her*." Benny gestured with an open hand to the contents of his lab. "Maybe I could whip you up a handy wrist radio with a built-in 155 howitzer. Or a voice-activated drop-dead pill you can give to Sharp if he talks trash again."

I shook my head. "Nine millimeter is about as high tech as this affair is likely to get, I'm afraid."

"You after elephants or ants?" he asked.

"Don't know."

"You don't know much, do you mate?" Benny asked cheerfully. "Got just the thing for you, then. I was fumbling through some of my old Saigon stuff the other day." He rolled over to a drawer, opened it, and took out a small metal box. He opened it and shook out a handful of pistol cartridges. "Here," he said. "They've been in storage for a decade but the box was designed for the jungle."

I inspected the shells. They were standard 9mm Parabellum pistol shell casings with hemispherical bullets mounted like observatory domes on them. The slugs looked like what we used to call steelies when we played marbles.

"What the hell are these used for?" I asked.

"Killing people, back in the old days before America got religion," he said. The Ice Cream King didn't smile at the joke, because he didn't think it was funny. "The slugs are designed not to take ballistics marks. Any weapon you can fire them from is automatically untraceable. The agency used to have the slugs made up at some lab in France. A specialty item for close work. And I mean *close*. The slugs are a bad choice at ranges over six inches, but as the saying goes—no guts, no air medal."

There was a long silence as I looked at the cool metal in my hand. "I thought you made ice cream over there."

"Only a fool makes ice cream in hell," Benny said. His dark eyes were as flat as his voice. "Go ahead, take them. There isn't enough sunshine in this world to risk losing what little bit we have."

Fiora's XJ 12 Jag was in the parking lot when I arrived at the business jet tie-down area at John Wayne Airport. The Duke's airdrome lies at the edge of the industrial park that is the heart of the Southern California electronic commerce. Executive aircraft were lined up like sparrows on telephone wires. Some of them might even have been paid for.

Danny's plane was a surprise. I was expecting one of those plush tax write-offs done in velour and bad taste. But Danny's plane was a high-winged aircraft with a surprisingly thick fuselage and a pair of businesslike turbocharged engines. One of the engines was idling and the other was all but shut down, its three-bladed prop ticking over so slowly that you could almost read the labels on the metal. Fiora was already aboard, waving to me through the double cargo doors. I didn't recognize the make of the aircraft. It wasn't a Lear or a Citation, which was what I'd have expected of the up-and-coming Danny Flynn. This plane had a blunt utilitarian look about it that was almost startling amid the other sleek executive craft.

I jogged across the tie-down area, my travel bag banging me on the leg. Three steps up, and I was inside. The interior of the plane was everything the exterior advertised: proletarian decor and solid seats that could slide out easily to make a sizable cargo bay. Maybe Danny was learning to think like a cost accountant, buying a plane that could make deliveries as well as take 38-D mistresses to Reno for the weekend. Then I remembered that most of Danny's customers were in Europe. This might be a handy little aircraft, but it wasn't in the transatlantic class.

Fiora touched my shoulder and smiled, offering to take

my bag. Instead, I tossed it beneath one of the seats. The cockpit door popped open, and a dark-haired Latin-looking man walked into the cabin. He wore aviator's glasses, a white shirt with epaulets, and an irritated look around his mouth.

"Miss Flynn, are we ready now?" he asked coolly. "If we want to make your luncheon appointment, we'll have to move it."

Executive pilots are supposed to have better manners. Maybe he'd already made a pass at Fiora and gotten his nuts frozen off with one of her executive smiles. Or maybe he was just a prick.

"Am I late?" I asked Fiora. "Sorry, hon. I thought this was a private audition, not a cattle call."

The pilot slid me a look through his green-tinted aviator's glasses that was intended, I suppose, to make me feel like an insect in the presence of gods.

"My instructions were to pick up Miss Flynn," he said slowly. "Nothing was said about a boyfriend."

I watched two peach-colored flags rise on Fiora's cheeks. If flyboy's flaps hadn't been trimmed yet, they would be soon. I winked at Fiora. Flyboy couldn't see, but she could. She shut up and gave me the kind of look that said she was on hold but she wouldn't stay that way indefinitely. I turned back to the pilot, smiling the kind of superior male smile that is guaranteed to piss off the Pope. "If you don't think you can get this ungainly bastard to the Bay Area on time, kid, I'll be glad to show you how."

The pilot looked at me for another second, mumbled something impertinent and clinical under his breath, punched a button in a control panel beside the twin cargo doors and watched them slide closed.

"Take your seats," he said curtly. "Use the belts until I tell you otherwise."

Hell of a bedside manner, this one. He was about the right age to have learned to fly somewhere in Vietnam, and it looked like he had given up any aspirations of making first officer on a United DC-10 FriendShip.

Fiora was beginning to fume, but I shot her a look to

remind her that she was on hold. We sat down, one on either side of the little aisle, and strapped ourselves in. Captain Queeg of the airways watched us, then moved back into the cockpit and sat down. At least he knew how to handle the plane. With one hand he picked up the revs on the windmilling props, with the other he snapped a couple of toggles on the instrument panel. The sound of engines revving came through the metal walls. He got on the radio, demanding ground control clearance.

"Who does that prick think he is?" demanded Fiora, turning on me.

"He's really a hell of a nice guy," I said calmly.

"Bullshit," she snapped. "He came on to me like a kid with his first erection. Never heard of the word *no*. You know the line! There aren't any repulsive men in the world, just frigid bitches." Her green eyes sparkled with the kind of energy that propels her into battle every day in a world dominated by men.

I tried not to smile. I really did. But memories of last night kept making the corners of my mouth turn up. Frigid? Not likely, friend. Poor flyboy had done the one thing that is guaranteed to make Fiora killing mad; he had assumed that anything as small and pretty as she was had to be a toy.

I took Fiora's hand, lacing my fingers through hers. "Be grateful he's so damn dumb," I said soothingly. "Because now he'll believe it when you go and talk to him and make him feel that he is the most gorgeous, most efficient and skillful man you have ever laid your beautiful green eyes on."

"Fiddler, I don't do 'Sweet Young Thang.' I gave it up for good when I got out of Harvard Business School."

I smiled and rubbed my mustache over the back of Fiora's hand. "Think of it as revenge. Don't lay it on too thick, though. I want him to feel good about you, but not so good he comes back here and tries to chat while I'm reading the pilot's manual."

"The pilot's manual?" One delicate eyebrow arched upward. "Am I missing something?"

"Not for long. When flyboy gets out onto the taxiway, go up and ask him for the pilot's manual. Tell him you're thinking of buying a similar plane for your company and want to know the specs on this aircraft."

Fiora's tawny eyebrow descended into a small frown. She studied me for a minute, thought about asking what I was up to, the shrugged elegantly. The smile she gave me told me that she remembered last night as vividly as I did. "Whatever you say, Fiddler. For a while . . ."

Ground control held us just short of the right runway, behind an old Stinson, a Piper Cub, and a Gulfstream II. Fiora unbuckled and swayed up the aisle to the cockpit door, wearing a bright, innocent, girlish smile. To me she looked as innocuous as a mongoose gliding toward a snake, but the Latin lover had an unbreakable sense of his own allure. He went to the slaughter with less fuss than the bag of oranges Fiora had juiced for breakfast.

Fiora rested her hand on the skin just below the pilot's short sleeve, leaned over so that he could get a whiff of expensive perfume, and smiled down at him until he almost forgot to let loose of the throttles. When she had his attention, she murmured her request in his ear, so close to him that her breath ruffled his hair. After thirty seconds or so of this treatment, he smiled like a used-car salesman and handed over a bag that had been lying on the cabin floor beside him.

Fiora swayed back down the aisle toward me. She made a mark in the air, signifying another kill, and handed me the travel bag.

"Some day, my love," she murmured, leaning down, touching me, giving me the same treatment she had just given flyboy, "you'll have to ask me to do something hard."

"Okay. Go sit over there and be ugly."

Fiora strapped herself in just as the plane was cleared for takeoff. Before the wheels lifted, she had her briefcase in her lap and had begun to sort through papers. I had the pilot's bag open and was doing ditto.

As I'd expected, the bag was stuffed with maps, manuals, operating instructions, and maintenance certificates, all the documentation a pilot needs to travel from here to there and back, all the information I needed to find out where "here" and "there" were and how often this aircraft and pilot had made the trip.

I began to read with equal parts interest and growing unease. The more I read, the less equal the parts became.

6

The first batch of papers told me less than I needed to know. The operations manual did confirm that the plane could be used as an executive aircraft or for small-to-medium freight shipments. It could handle up to 6,000 pounds of whatever would fit inside those double doors. Hell, that was a big enough payload to make this aircraft a likely prospect for marijuana smuggling, if it came to that, although I'd never seen any indication that Danny was that tough or smart or crazy.

Despite its ungainly looks, the plane was smooth. I barely noticed when we powered out onto the runway and lifted over the airport fence, giving a few seconds of reality therapy to the folks in their million-dollar houses beneath the John Wayne Airport noise footprint. I took one look at the Pacific Ocean—still there, still blue—and then returned to the papers in my lap. We were out over the Catalina Channel when I discovered that the flyboy's real name was Charles Francisco Ortega, born in Brownsville, Texas, thirty-six years ago. He had most of the single- and multi-engine ratings available from the federal government. A bit overeducated for an executive chauffeur, but maybe flyboy's attitude problem got in the way of corporate relations.

The pilot's passport intrigued me, but I had to wait until he was occupied clearing the Los Angeles Center air traffic control system and picking up the Santa Barbara locator. Then I opened the dark blue folder and flipped through it. I'd been right about the aircraft's transatlantic capabilities. There were no European stamps on the passport, just a colorful rash of Mexican immigration and customs stamps.

Flyboy had been in and out of Mexico City's Benito Juarez
International Airport about once a month for the last year or
so.

The pattern of the flights was the same each time. Touch-
down in Mexico City, where pilot and aircraft checked
through customs and immigration, stayed twenty-four
hours or less, and headed north again. Flyboy was unusually scrupulous about his dealings with U.S. Customs.
Most private pilots, assuming they even bother to clear
customs, pick some convenient spot like Lindbergh Field
in San Diego, or even LA International. But Pilot Ortega
had followed the letter of the law, landing at the first available customs port of entry, Calexico.

Unusually scrupulous behavior always sends little sour
notes screeling through my brain. Or it might just be the
fact that Sharp was a customs agent from Calexico, the dirty
little desert city just across the border from Mexicali, the
capital of Baja California Norte. Calexico is the cesspool of
the misnamed Imperial Valley, one of the more unpleasant
places on the North American continent. Calexico is a place
I happen to be kind of fond of, in a perverse sort of way, but
even in my fondest moments I know how small it is. Finding two people who spend time in Calexico is like finding
matching socks in the dark. Not real likely.

I filed that uneasy coincidence with the other dishar-
monies sawing away in my brain. I didn't know if I could
make the Calexico connection harmonize with anything. It
was just one of those little bytes of information I play around
with in my spare time. The only difference between my
mind and a computer is that a computer knows what's going
to happen next.

I prowled through the rest of the papers, taking care that
I stayed out of flyboy's line of sight, but I didn't find much
that would subtract from the chaos of phrases, flats, and
shrill notes in my mind. The pilot made the Mexico trips
alone. There were several airport tax receipts for one aircraft and one pilot, no passengers. There were a couple of
hotel bills, as though he were saving them until he filled out
his expense account.

Cacophony. No way flyboy fit the classic profile of a weed smuggler. In Mexico City he stayed at the Fiesta Palace, which is a renowned tourist trap, ate a meal in the rooftop restaurant, drank a bit at the bar, and didn't pick up anything but the tab. Unless he was loading up with weed at Benito Juarez, which is the equivalent of loading up on the apron at LAX, flyboy probably wasn't in the marijuana smuggling business. At a glance and a guess, his flight times didn't allow enough time for a stop at some dirt strip in Michoacán for a load of grass. Then there was the fact that he checked in with customs as religiously as a Muslim prays to Allah.

Flyboy was a sloppy bookkeeper. Chits and papers were stuffed into the plastic envelope along with flight inspection certificates. But he was thorough. There was lots of fascinating stuff stashed away. Some of the fuel chits were six months old. I began sorting through them, putting them in sequential order. The pattern jumped out pretty quickly. Fuel up at John Wayne, fly south, and refuel again before leaving Mexico City. A couple of times he took on more fuel in Calexico. Topping off probably, as he usually took 150 gallons in Mexico City and then only 75 in Calexico.

I tried to make music out of it. Not a chance. I fiddled with it anyway, trying to imagine all the illegal things flyboy could do between John Wayne and Benito Juarez, with Customs stops in between. All the things I imagined were so improbable that I gave up. You can be too smart, too cute, when you're looking for the melody line. You start inventing things that will never play in Peoria.

With a sigh, I stuffed everything back into the plastic bag. Fiora was wrapped up in some fancy spread sheet, adding figures here and calculating new profit margins there. I told the cacophony in my head to take five, kicked back the seat, and watched California slide beneath the wing. I estimated we were at about 12,000 feet. The Pacific blue had been replaced by the dense green of oak trees scattered over the sere foothills south of Carmel. I could see the broad, shimmering sweep of Monterey Bay ahead, then the Santa Cruz Mountains with redwoods covering ragged ridgelines.

The orchestra refused to take five. It kept trying to take a Scots idiot, a Mexican flyboy, and a European charmer and make something harmonious out of them, with an Oriental cat burglar thrown in as a leitmotiv. It didn't work worth a damn. I fell asleep and dreamed of Volker driving the Cobra. And then, in the irrational way of dreams, it was Danny driving the Cobra. A nightmare. I'd never let him drive it. The Cobra was just too much power to give to Fiora's hapless twin. He couldn't handle it. It was running away with him, going flat out, blue hell roaring up to a cliff, leaping, falling while Danny screamed—

I woke fast, only to find it was the plane, not the Cobra, that was losing altitude. I looked out. Silicon Valley's practical geometries fanned out below. My ears popped, and the last of the nightmare slid away. We were descending toward the Santa Clara County Airport in San Jose. Flyboy must have gotten a straight-in clearance, because he set the prop-jet down without chopping back on the throttles. His manners might have lacked polish, but his flying didn't. He put us down so smoothly that Fiora never lost her place in the spread sheet.

A Hertz Thunderbird waited for us at the executive terminal, and a message from Danny with directions to a restaurant somewhere in Cupertino. I loaded Fiora and her spread sheets in the car, got on Interstate 280, cut over to the Junipero Serra Freeway and headed north. As I drove, I talked to myself about the decline of the American car. Fiora ignored me, as I had known she would. I ignored the ignoring, as she had known I would. It's a comforting thing, knowing.

"The Ford Motor Company ought to be ashamed of itself," I said. "Any resemblance between the engine of this Thunderbird and the power plant of the Cobra is an oversight soon to be corrected by the Environmental Protection Agency and the Department of Transportation.

"Now, I try not to be too much of a reactionary about such things, but I'm troubled by the ineluctable fact that the displacement of the two engines—the T-Bird and the Cobra—is roughly equal. The mileage is different, though. About five miles to the gallon different. I'm not going to tell you which car would win an economy run, except that it will *not* be the T-Bird.

"And the power, that feeling of something happening? Well, mashing down on the accelerator of the Bird is like stepping in fresh cow puckey. Something happens but it isn't what you could call exhilarating."

Fiora shifted the spread sheet in her lap. I changed the subject several times, trying to lure her into conversation. Normally I wouldn't have disturbed her work, but she wasn't working. She was looking at the papers, yet she was making no entries anywhere, no notes, no nothing. There were two deep frown lines, just about where her eyebrows came together. Whatever she was thinking about wasn't financial manipulations.

In the end, I left her to her frowning thoughts and concentrated on one of my favorite places, Silicon Valley. I like the area because it, too, is inventing itself and revising the future every damn day of the year. All that the valley's tilt-up treasure houses lack are eucalyptus. Up here they use juniper and cypress.

The restaurant Danny had chosen was called La Petite Ferme. It sat on a small knoll just off the freeway. This place was right out of Beverly Hills, only since they were so far north of Hollywood they had to try harder. The Mexican kid in the red jacket had the door open before I could decide whether he was a bandit or a valet. I took one look at his unsmiling face and voted for valet. Thieves usually enjoy their work.

The redwood steps matched the parts of the building that were not glass. None of the restaurant had had time to weather yet. It was one o'clock, hot, and dusty beneath the prickly oaks. As we climbed the steps, Fiora touched my arm.

"Try not to be too hard on Danny," she said, looking up at me through worried green eyes. "He—" She looked away, then back at me quickly. "He'll never be as strong as you, Fiddler. And he knows it."

Danny had never given me so much as a glimmer of that

feeling. I thought he simply disliked me. But I let it slide. It was enough that Fiora had finally admitted that Danny didn't walk on water. Unfortunately, the admission had cost her too much to make me feel good. The frown lines were deeper, bracketing her lovely mouth. I sighed and squeezed her hand.

"I've never gone in for pulling the wings off butterflies."

Fiora tried to smile. "I know. It's just that you're so damn competent."

I shook my head but said no more. It was an old argument and a new day. I'll take the day, and to hell with the argument.

We walked into the cool shadows of the little French farmhouse built of redwood and double-thick smoked glass. The maître d' greeted us like his oldest friends, or at least like his oldest customers. Maybe we were. The Little Farmhouse hadn't been around long enough to grow a shadow.

Danny's table was the best spot in the restaurant. It was on a small, raised veranda with big, open french doors that overlooked the tawny hills and black oaks. Fine crystal and sterling silver and bone china, cane-backed chairs with silk brocade seats. Very nice. It must have cost Danny a couple of yards just to get in the door. A waiter stood over Danny as attentively as a heron fishing a shallow pond.

And lounging in one of the cane-backed chairs sat Daniel Flynn, handsome Danny-boy with his USC fraternity pin, blow-dry haircut, and dark green Brooks Brothers summer suit. The suit was fine, but not Danny's best color today. His face was as white as the china plate in front of him, except for a spot of color high on each cheek. But then, the plate couldn't drink a bottle of Schramsberg Blanc de Blancs, which is what Danny had done. The boy was flying, and not a plane in sight.

Yet it took only a look to see that it was fear, not wine, that burned beneath Danny's pale skin.

With a waiter at one elbow, a wine steward at the other, and the maître d' aching to be of some small service, Danny looked as lonely as any man I've ever seen. He was pouring his own wine, fast, and staring out the open french doors toward the tanned foothills, looking as though he would burst into tears or come apart all over the expensive place setting.

No wonder Fiora had been so distant. If she was participating at some psychic level in the emotions burning beneath her twin brother's face, she must be dying inside. Then I realized that I had put my arm around Fiora and drawn her close to my side in a protective gesture that was as futile as it was inevitable. For an instant she leaned against me, something she rarely did. Any doubts about whether I was going to play first violin in this mad orchestra vanished as I felt Fiora's weight against my hip. If Danny-boy was going to play a tragic concert, for once in his life he would play a solo, not a duet for twins.

Danny was so caught in his inner turmoil that he hadn't noticed our approach. Fiora called his name once, softly, too softly for him to hear. Yet he turned toward her instantly, leaping up, knocking over his empty champagne glass and chair in the same instant. The color flooded back into his face. For just a moment, he was the old Danny, almost pretty in a way, a yacht-club prince with eyelashes as long as his sister's and eyes that were luminous and kind, almost childlike.

"Twin!" said Danny, smiling and dragging Fiora away from me. "Where have you been? I was worried."

Fiora kissed her brother on the cheek, hugged him, and then asked precisely the question that had turned coldly in my mind. Had Danny turned into a dreamer too?

"Why would you be worried about me?" asked Fiora.

Danny's smile slipped, as did the color in his skin. Gone was the ambience of sun and sea. "I was afraid—that is, uh, I thought you were, uh—"

Danny looked almost desperately at me, but I couldn't help him. That was the hell of it. For all my supposed competence, I was as much use as an empty gas tank when it came to Danny. It had always been that way.

Danny looked away, closed his eyes, and got a grip on a usable half-truth. "I was worried you'd change your mind about flying up. And you know how I hate eating alone."

Fiora gave her twin another quick hug and then held him at arm's length so she could inspect him. She saw nothing in his face to comfort her. "You knew I'd come," she said quietly.

Danny had the grace to look guilty, because the same couldn't be said of him if the roles were reversed. He forced a smile. "Don't look so worried, twin. This is a celebration. I'm within one phone call of closing the biggest deal of my life. For once, I'm going to be as successful as a certain twin sister I know."

Danny smiled when he said it, but the implicit envy spoiled the effect. Fiora had always felt guilty because she was at least three times as bright as her brother. Danny had just enough smarts to exploit that guilt on a regular basis. Every time he did it, I had to grit my teeth until my jaw knotted to keep from calling him by name. Several names, in fact.

"Money is a lousy way to measure yourself," Fiora said sadly. "You're always a success with me."

"Right," I said, because I could say that through clenched teeth. Then, "Lunch," another word that didn't require a loose jaw to pronounce.

Danny resisted being steered back to the table, even when Fiora took his arm.

"No, no, now wait a minute," he protested. "I'm the host here. Let me do things." He turned toward the waiter who was smiling a bit uncertainly, as though he, too, had caught the strain in Danny's voice and his jerky gestures. "More champagne, immediately. And I mean real champagne, not this California shit."

I grimaced and tightened the jaw a few more notches.

"Okay, ex-hubby," said Danny, coming down hard on the *ex* with his first real smile of the day. "You're no good on marriage, but I'm told you're a damned expert on wines. What would you suggest?"

Fiora's hand closed around my arm in a silent plea. "Danny," she said. "I asked Fiddler to be here."

She said nothing more. She didn't have to. I was the only

argument Danny had ever lost with Fiora. He had never forgotten it. Or forgiven.

That's okay. It was mutual to the last full stop.

I put my hand over Fiora's, feeling her tension vibrate through the contact. I could think of several better—and cheaper—champagnes for Danny to swill, but knew he would reject them. So I did what he wanted me to do. I named a bottle of hundred-dollar champagne, figuring that would be about tops for La Petite Ferme's wine cellar.

"Is that the best in the house?" demanded Danny of the waiter.

"One of them, yes, sir," said the waiter smoothly.

Danny looked disappointed to find out that I was right. "Put it on ice," he snapped. "Then put the second best bottle on ice. No more cheap shit, hear me? I can afford the best."

I cranked up the old jaw another notch. Danny with a bottle of wine in him was a working definition of "nouveau riche." Fiora's fingers tightened enough to leave marks on me, but she didn't say anything. If she tried to rein in her twin, he'd turn ugly and take it out on her.

That was when I'd start keeping score. No free ones for Danny Flynn. He'd used them up years ago.

The three of us sat down. The chairs were a lot more comfortable than the silence. We studied the menus the way linguists once studied the Rosetta Stone. Fiora still held onto my arm. I didn't know whether it was to comfort herself or to restrain me. Both, probably.

Eventually the waiter was back with a bottle and a sterling ice bucket. He held the bottle out for Danny's inspection. Danny went through the whole ritual with lots of emphasis and no conviction. As much wine as he'd had already, he would be lucky to sense the difference between piss and vinegar. He didn't care, though. He had ordered the most expensive wine in the house.

As the waiter poured Fiora's glass, Danny said curtly, "Don't forget the phone call."

"Yes, sir," the waiter nodded. "The very moment it comes, sir."

Whatever it was about, it had obviously been discussed previously. Several times, to judge from the waiter's suppressed sigh.

"I'm waiting for a call from Volker," Danny said, looking sideways at me when he said Volker's name. It was clear that Danny enjoyed the fact that I knew about Volker and Fiora. "As soon as the deal is finished, he'll let me know, and I'll officially be rich."

"Where is Volker?" asked Fiora.

I was surprised that she didn't know. I looked at her, trying to figure out if she cared. If she did, it didn't show. But then, she was good at hiding emotions—until she got in bed.

"He's at the Irvine warehouse," said Danny carelessly. "Checking on a delivery or something." He shrugged, telling us he was beyond worrying about such trivia.

"Tell me about this big deal," I invited casually. I held the delicately fluted crystal glass up to the sunlight and watched little bubbles climbing up through the pale amber wine. The champagne was yeasty and complex. But Schramsberg was, too.

"It's a whole bunch of stuff," said Danny. "All kinds of electronics gear. Millions of dollars worth, in one order," he said. "How do you like that, Fiora?" he asked, then knocked back half a glass of champagne. "Millons of dollars," he repeated, licking his lips.

It was all right until he laughed. The sound was like a slack bow bouncing across the strings of a cheap violin.

"That's great," Fiora said, smiling, meaning every word with every bit of hope in her body. "Who's the customer? Maybe they need help with their books."

"Foreign," said Danny shortly, looking at his wine with sudden, intense interest. "There's a lot of demand for U.S. equipment of all kinds. We're the best in the world." He laughed again, ragged strokes of sound. "Free enterprise strikes again. Now if Uncle Sam would just get the hell out of the way, we'd all be rich. Kick the Japs and the Frogs and anybody else who gets in the way. Run their asses right into the dirt. We'd be in the driver's seat again. Nobody can invent and build like Americans do."

My mind flashed back to what Volker had said about delivery dates and bureaucratic red tape. Danny was playing a patriotic variation on Volker's theme—down with useless regulations. It probably made Danny feel better about what was otherwise a philosophy of pure, unenlightened self-interest. But I knew better than to point that out. What the hell. People believe what comforts them, at least people like Danny. I didn't know what Volker believed, but I doubted that comfort and the Fourth of July were part of it.

"Speaking of Uncle Sam," I asked, watching Danny through my wineglass, "did Volker tell you about the government men who came to see your sister yesterday?"

"What?" he asked hoarsely. *"What?"*

The color left Danny's face as my words penetrated the layers of alcohol he'd wrapped around himself. I swore behind my teeth. I still didn't know what the problem was, but there was no doubt any longer that it was seriously criminal. So why did I feel like a boy with wings in one hand and butterfly body in the other?

Fiora shot me a hard look, but it lasted only a second. That was as long as it took her to realize that Volker had kept her brother in the dark about Sharp and the customs investigation. Her face went as pale as Danny's. Unlike her twin, she didn't ask questions or offer alibis. She faced reality the way she always did—head on, right now, no flinching and no prisoners. If Danny had only had half of Fiora's guts and grace, we all would have been a hell of a lot happier. But he didn't, and we weren't.

The first course arrived at that moment. The vichyssoise mirrored the restaurant, bland but beautifully presented. The silence was dense at the table while the waiter served, refilled wineglasses with precise, elegant motions, and then slid back into place at the edge of consciousness like the good piece of furniture he was.

Danny's hand shook as he raised the wineglass to his lips. He didn't stop swallowing until he was sucking on air. I took a sip, but it didn't change the tarnished taste in my mouth as I resumed plucking off Danny's brilliant, fragile wings.

"Don't you want to know why the government men wanted to talk to Fiora?" I asked, trying and failing to keep the edge of disgust out of my voice. Nothing irritates me like crooks who bank on luck and then whine when luck fails. If you can't do the time, don't do the crime, as Uncle Jake used to say. Before he died, he'd done his share of both.

"Somebody—" Danny's voice broke. He took a swig out of Fiora's wine. "Somebody probably forgot to file for the customs export licenses, I guess," he mumbled. "So many goddamn forms, you're bound to forget one or two."

"Why are you so sure the men were from Customs?" Danny looked blank. "You said they were."

"No. I said they were government."

Danny shrugged. "Same difference."

"Not quite. I get the feeling you and Omnitronix are on an IRS shitlist, too."

"No way!" said Danny hotly. "The only trouble we're in is with those jerk-offs in Customs! And they're so dumb there's no chance of them catch—"

That is what is called guilty knowledge, and it approaches what a federal prosecutor probably would call criminal intent. Danny was smart enough to shut up suddenly. In the silence, you could almost hear the sundered wings fluttering down. I didn't look at Fiora. Again, Danny had put me in the position of hurting her. She was more than human enough to shoot the messenger who brought the bad news.

"Look, Danny," I said, speaking gently to him because he was so damned fragile, and Fiora loved him. "I don't know the lyrics but the melody is clear. You're in trouble. Maybe we can help, maybe not. If we can't help, I'll find someone who can. I promise you." The last words were for Fiora, but Danny didn't know that. He had his eyes closed and a death grip on Fiora's wineglass.

"Nothing's going on. I'll be all right," he said quickly, not noticing or not caring about the contradiction built into his words.

"Danny," said Fiora.

Her voice broke my heart, but not Danny's.

"Danny," she said again, "let us help you. Fiddler can —"

"No!" snarled Danny. "I'm as good as he is, and I'm going to prove it!"

Déjà vu settled around me, cold and bleak. The poor, sad son of a bitch. Just bright enough to sense how dumb he really was.

"Tell Fiddler to go away," said Danny to his twin. "We don't need him. All that happened is that some bureaucrat stumbled into a legitimate business deal, and you make it sound like the end of the world."

The idea of Sharp being described as a bureaucrat would have made me laugh if I hadn't lost my sense of humor already. Occupational hazard of wing pullers. Fiora turned and looked at me with eyes as green and hopeful as spring. I wanted to kill Danny for putting her and me on opposite sides of hope.

"You have a good attorney?" I said, my voice slightly warmer than the bucket of ice at his elbow. "A criminal attorney, Danny-boy. You're going to need one."

Fiora's fingers touched my lips, telling me that she knew why I was mad but would I please shut up anyway. I went back to strengthening my jaw muscles and counting champagne bubbles.

"Please, Danny. Fiddler knows the kind of men who interrogated me. They aren't stupid. They aren't bureaucrats. It might be a good idea to talk with an attorney. For me, Danny. Please?"

Danny sighed and fiddled with his long-tined dinner fork. "Everything's just fine," he said. "Volker will call, and everything will be fine. You trust Volker, don't you?"

Fiora took a sip of wine. Danny had emptied her glass as well as his own, and until we quit sending out hostile vibes the waiter would stay away from the table.

"I'm sure Volker knows what he's doing," said Fiora.

"Yes," sighed Danny. "He's real smart. Just as soon as he picks up that last shipment, everything will be fine. You'll see."

"What's the last part of the deal?" asked Fiora, her voice very soft, very reluctant.

Danny was even more reluctant.

"C'mon, Danny," I said, mocking him. "If everything is kosher, you can tell us about your coup." My voice said there would be ice-skating in hell before Danny pulled off anything more important than dirty underwear. It worked. I knew it would. Wings coming off one by one.

"We just have one last piece of equipment to ship," he said defiantly, "and then you'll see."

"Is that going to Mexico, too?" I asked. A guess, but a safe one, considering the flyboy's trip sheets.

Danny shot me a look of surprise. "How did you find out about Mexico?" he asked. "I just found out about it myself the other day."

More wings. God, Danny wouldn't last five seconds with someone like Sharp.

"Volker may have said something about Mexican banks," I said, shrugging. I didn't look at Fiora. She didn't look at me. At the moment, we both probably loathed me equally.

"Yeah," said Danny. "Money. Ortega is supposed to take the merchandise to Mexico City tonight and pick up the last of the payment."

The thought of money brightened Danny's life. He smiled that childlike, gentle smile, delight and hope and all the good things he could imagine evident for just an instant in his green eyes. Fiora had often tried to describe that smile to me, but I'd never seen it before. For an instant I understood why even hard-headed Fiora could not demand too much of sweet Danny Flynn.

"That reminds me," said Danny with a smile, instantly sensing the change in the emotional atmosphere at the table. "Would you hold on to something for me, twin? Just for a few days."

"Sure," said Fiora, smiling in return.

I touched her arm. "Fiora. Wait." I turned toward Danny. He didn't try to smile at me. "Yesterday I told Special Agent Sharp that Fiora wasn't involved in whatever was being investigated. *I want it to stay that way.*"

Danny hesitated. He had already gone to his coat pocket and produced a letter-sized manila envelope secured with a clasp. Before Danny could make up his mind, the maître d' appeared carrying a cordless telephone.

"Your call, Mr. Flynn," he announced.

Danny dropped the envelope like he had been bitten, grabbed the phone, and stalked off mumbling about privacy. The maître d' ushered him across the room, speaking in clear tones about private offices and pleasing clients.

"Danny's so scared, so alone," whispered Fiora. "What are we going to do?"

"One thing we are *not* going to do is to accept that," I said, pointing to the envelope poised on the edge of Danny's salad fork. "When the federal government issues a piece of paper called a criminal indictment, they might list accepting that envelope under the heading of 'overt acts.' Danny is in a hell of a lot of trouble. It won't help if you land in the shit as deep as he is."

"He needs help, Fiddler."

"That's what lawyers get paid all that money for—helping."

The waiter cleared away the nearly untouched vichyssoise. By the time he had brought the plates for a fish course, Danny still hadn't come back. The look on Fiora's face said that the rest of the lunch was going to be as much a waste as the first part had been. As one, we picked up our forks and pushed fish around our plates.

There was a small commotion across the room. I looked up in time to catch Danny's expression as he shoved past the maître d' toward the front door. Danny looked like he had been lobotomized. He didn't even glance our way as he ran outside.

I ripped open the envelope. A handful of brilliant crystals poured into my palm. Diamonds, hard and perfect, taking light and breaking it into all the colors of men's dreams. I dumped the beautiful bad news back into the envelope and took off after Danny.

No one was going to leave Fiora holding the bag if I could help it, not even if the bag was full of diamonds.

7

I hit the front door of La Petite Ferme and jumped from the cool dark to brilliant sunlight so quickly that I was almost blinded. I glimpsed Danny at the foot of the stairs, just climbing behind the wheel of a Porsche 911 that the parking attendant had delivered. I was about to call Danny's name when a movement out in the small parking lot stopped me. Before I knew why, my reflexes had pushed me back into the shadow of the door.

I looked again, and thanked the vestigial animal brain that lurks beneath layers of rationality, the part of the human animal that learns avoidance through pain. The man who had coshed me with the black automatic was sitting quietly in a car parked beneath a dusty oak tree. His blocky outline was as distinctive as the ugly gun he had used.

Just as I was wondering how in hell he had traced me, I realized that he wasn't watching me. Danny was his quarry. That wasn't much comfort. The tactical situation wasn't encouraging, to say the least. I'd be a fool to think that the bricklike man wasn't armed. As for me, all I had in my boot was my foot. My pistol was still in the duffel bag, which was in the trunk of the T-bird, four slots over from Brick. No help there.

Then I heard the 911 rev hard as Danny ham-footed his way through first, then second gear. At the same time I heard the deeper note of Brick's Volvo starting up. Danny squalled out of the parking lot, barely keeping the red-and-black Porsche from spinning around and biting its own ass. Brick did a lot better. He slid out of his parking slot and into traffic by the numbers. No fuss, no noise, just a precision

88

machine at work. The man, not the car. He knew he didn't have to sit on Danny in order to keep track of him. Flashy red-and-black cars handled by incompetent drivers are easy to follow.

For an instant I was tempted to follow Danny. Then I heard him accelerating down the highway and realized that by the time I got into the game, the play would have moved out of sight. I had to settle for memorizing Brick's license number as he went by. When I turned to go back into the restaurant, I bumped into the waiter. He had followed me to the door. There was a worried look on his face. Not surprising. He had just seen two-thirds of his $300 lunch tab split on the check.

"Bring me a bottle of Chardonnay, cold and unopened," I said. "If you can't find one under $30, bring mineral water instead. Any place that doesn't stock a decent Chardonnay for that much can't be trusted at any price."

I settled the tab right there. It wasn't the first time that I'd bailed out Danny-boy. He went through life stiffing people. Not that he meant to, particularly. He just didn't think. "If it feels good, do it" was as close as Danny came to introspection.

Fiora looked up as I came to the table. Her skin was too pale, too tight, her high cheekbones standing out clearly. Her eyes were almost black. She was near tears, but not entirely from sadness or fear for Danny. Frustration and anger were part of the emotions seething just beneath her smooth surface. She was mad at herself for being suckered by her twin. I knew it wasn't the first time, though, and it wouldn't be the last.

I was only half right, and that half didn't matter. But then, I'd never claimed to be clairvoyant.

Silently, Fiora watched as I took the manila envelope and balanced it in my palm. I thought for a wild instant of just dumping the whole thing into the ashtray and walking away. Then I sighed. Not that easy, Fiddler. It's never that easy. I held out my hand to Fiora.

"Let's go. We'll find someplace where we can count Danny's troubles one by one, privately."

Nobody left the parking lot as we did. Nobody pulled out of a side street and latched onto the T-Bird. The motel I found was like all big new motels. Flavorless. That's why I had brought the Chardonnay, to take away the taste of being had one more time by Danny Flynn. I used the corkscrew on my pocket knife to open the wine. As I poured it into SaniSure plastic glasses, the rich scent of good Chardonnay expanded into the stale, air-conditioned room.

Fiora took a sip, let out a long breath, and leaned against the headboard of the queen-sized bed. I sat next to her, wishing I had nothing to do but admire the elegant woman in the jade green silk pants and blouse. Wisps of hair had fallen from the businesslike twist she always wore when she was upset, as though by controlling her restless hair she could control everything that was coming apart.

Because I wanted to reach for Fiora, I picked up her purse and pulled out the manila envelope. In the upper left-hand corner, like a return address, were the words "Kim Van Kieu." I recognized the words from a long conversation I'd once had with the Ice Cream King. Vietnamese. A name, yes, but more. The title of an ancient epic poem depicting the rape and brutalization of a woman who in the end triumphed through wit, guts, and perseverance. The Vietnamese had come to see the epic as metaphor for their own bloody past and tyrannized present.

I stared at the words for a long time, wondering if they were being used as a motto or as someone's name. The rest of the words on the envelope were less enigmatic. "Fine Jewelry for Love and Investment." There was also an address in San Francisco.

I opened the envelope's metal clasp and gently shook my hand. A jeweler's packet slid out. Leave it to Fiora to do what Danny had been too lazy to do himself—repack the diamonds correctly after he had looked at them.

The packet was folded in the centuries-old manner, a long paper rectangle divided into thirds, the stones in the center, paper tucked and turned in neatly. It was a convenient, safe way to carry stones that were both very small and very valuable. The packet had been sealed shut with a dab of red wax and imprinted with a highly stylized Chinese ideograph. The paper itself was textured and heavy, with a high linen content.

The seal had been opened impatiently, its elegance destroyed. I could see Danny ripping open the packet and all but spilling the diamonds in haste to count his treasure, becoming a bigger man with each diamond he saw. Poor, sad Danny Flynn. Like the stones in my hand, he had beauty and no brains at all.

In silence, I examined the diamonds. Twenty-five stones. Eight of them were at least five carats each. Seven more from one to four carats. The rest from one-half to one carat. All of them were as perfectly matched in color as diamonds can be. When I moved to the daylight pouring through the north motel window, the diamonds showed their true nature. They literally blazed. Double D and flawless, I'd bet, though I'd left my loupe at home. Some of them might have had a very small imperfection somewhere in their inhumanly beautiful depths, but I doubted it.

I closed the drapes and went back to the bed, my fist clenched around the diamonds, wondering who Danny had had to kill for that kind of wealth. Fiora watched me with eyes the color of emeralds, waiting for me to tell her what she already knew. I hesitated, then stretched out on the bed beside her and began thinking out loud.

"Color grades are tricky," I said. "One notch either way on the wavelength of refracted light can mean thousands of dollars a carat. Even so, these are dynamite. Double D, D, nothing worse. I don't have a jeweler's scale, but I'd guess between sixty and seventy carats total. Half a million dollars, give or take 30 percent."

Fiora closed her eyes. "Danny . . ." It was a long, sad word, full of love and regret and frustration.

Then she reached for the telephone, called her office, and told them to cancel her appointments for the rest of the day and tomorrow, too. She gave Jason the motel number in case some important client couldn't take no for an answer. Pragmatic as hell, and a lot more beautiful.

Fiora hung up and turned toward me. "What are we going to do?"

Pragmatic and scared. Her voice trembled just enough to tell me how hard she was fighting for control. I wondered if she dreamed even when she was awake, but I said nothing. Her almost mystical sensitivity and inexplicable closeness to her twin were things I finally had come to accept without questioning. I took her hand, kissed her palm, and wrapped her fingers around the glass of wine. She hesitated, then took a small drink.

"For openers, you're not going to keep the diamonds. I am." I watched Fiora for the signs of rebellion I knew so well and had learned at such great cost. But her honey-colored eyebrows didn't shift into a frown. She simply nodded, touched my mustache with her fingertips and watched me with green eyes that were afraid to hope. "I'll do what I can, love," I said, knowing she didn't want to ask. "But don't expect miracles. Danny outdid himself this time. Your dreams didn't include jailhouse bars by any chance?"

I regretted the words as soon as they were out of my mouth. Fiora made a small sound and shook her head. Then she shuddered. I took the wineglass from her, set it aside, and held her as though she were about to come unraveled. I tucked her against my body, rocked slowly until the shuddering passed, and silently cursed myself for being so stupid as to mention Danny and dreams.

After a time, Fiora's body relaxed against me. I pulled the jade clip out of her hair and eased my fingers against her scalp. I rubbed slowly, knowing that she loved that the way a cat loves sleeping in the sun.

"What are you going to do about Danny?" she asked, rolling her head against my hand, increasing the pressure of my fingers against her scalp.

Actually, I had in mind to find Danny and beat the truth out of him one unsavory word at a time. But I didn't see any advantage in telling Fiora that. Nor did I see any point in bringing up the brick-shaped man and the Volvo. Fiora had enough to worry about without telling her that a cosh artist was following her twin around.

"There are a couple of loose ends that I want to tie up here," I said. "I'll take you to the airport and—"

"No. I'm staying." Fiora's arms came around me, holding me with surprising strength. "Whatever you do, be careful," she whispered, telling me more about her dreams than I wanted to know.

"I'm always careful."

She laughed raggedly. "That's how you got your scars, right?"

My only answer was to hold Fiora as tightly as she was holding me. My gift for getting into other people's trouble was one of the things that had driven Fiora and me apart. Now she was asking me for help, and it was dangerous, and she knew it. She didn't like that, and I knew it.

Her body shifted against mine, a single, subtle movement that made my breath stop. "Fiddler . . . ?"

I didn't say anything. I didn't have to. She felt my answer before her question was finished.

I left Fiora sleeping deeply, no dreams to disturb her serenity. I didn't want to disturb her either, so I tucked the diamonds into the breast pocket of my blazer, checked my pants for change, and went to the motel restaurant to make my calls. The first was to the Ice Cream King. A long time ago he had compromised the security system on the California Department of Motor Vehicles computer. I gave him the tag number on Brick's Volvo. Benny put me on hold and did a little computer-to-computer communicating with the DMV in Sacramento.

The average citizen can get the same information for seventy-five cents and a return envelope. But you have to wait a week, and the DMV sends a little notice to the holder of the license tag stating that somebody has made inquiries after his identity.

I much prefer using Benny. It's cheaper.

It wasn't long before I knew that the Volvo was registered to Omnitronix, only this address was in Silicon Valley, not Irvine. Despite that, I somehow doubted that the cosh artist was Danny's personal bodyguard. Possible, but not probable. If Danny had a bodyguard, he'd flaunt him like a showgirl with a five-carat engagement ring.

But if Danny, the putative owner of Omnitronix, hadn't given the brick-shaped man a car and a gun in the guise of corporate fringe benefits, then who had? Volker? Not a comforting thought. Volker, the man with the built-in sunshine and the reflexes of a hunting cat. Volker, who had charmed two twins and one ex-husband. Not equally, though. Danny may be blind, but Fiora dreamed.

And I heard uneasy, perfect chords forming in my mind, the orchestra settling in to play in earnest.

I went back to the room. Fiora was still asleep, beautiful and serene. I hoped she would stay that way. I unzipped the duffel and pulled out my shoulder holster. Next came the 9 mm. I checked the pistol's clip and dropped the gun into place beneath my right arm. Being left-handed has a few advantages. Most pros watch your right hand, a simple matter of overwhelming odds in favor of someone being right-handed. I've surprised more than one man that way and a few women, too.

I left Fiora a note telling her that I had the diamonds with me, I would call her later, not to worry, if Danny could be pulled out of the fire I'd do it, and, yes, I'd be careful while I was dicking about in the flames. I said it all in three words, too.

Hertz had thoughtfully stocked the glove compartment with a map of the Santa Clara Valley. I followed it to the Silicon Valley address of Omnitronix.

This office was more impressive than the one in Irvine. The puffy white clouds that were beginning to build over the Santa Cruz Mountains were reflected in the mirrored glass sides of the four-story office building. That glass is becoming one of the most overused architectural devices in California, but I still like it, trees and clouds and sunlight gleaming back at me. It certainly fits the California environment better than the shit-brown brick facades that are coming into vogue.

I circled the parking lot twice, but I didn't see Danny's flashy Porsche. The Volvo wasn't there either. I hesitated, then decided to take a run at the office. Maybe I'd find a few file boxes there, boxes brought up in a Volvo from an empty office in Irvine. I'd like to know what was worth beating a stranger senseless to hide.

The building directory was almost humorous. Besides Omnitronix, there was Micro-Computer Devices International, Software Unlimited, Megabytes, CompuFuture, and a half-dozen other firms whose names were state-of-the-art gibberish. Omnitronix had the penthouse and a glass door that let me see rooms nicely furnished with rented teak and mahogany veneer. No storage area, just two offices and a reception area. Nobody home, and no back door with the padlock sawed through.

On the next floor down, I tried to buttonhole a pretty young secretary who was hurrying down the hallway. Before I could open my mouth she pointed to an open door up the hall and said, "In there, but I wouldn't get close to the greasy little monster, if I were you." She didn't bother waiting for the elevator. She slammed through the stairway door and kept on going. Her heels made sharp, diminishing clicks in the silence.

"There" was the office of ByteMarks, Unltd. Apparently someone in this building had a sense of humor after all. Not too classy, but in the never-never land of engineers you take what humor you can find. A long-haired, barely postpubescent type wearing a Dungeons and Dragons T-shirt burst into the hallway from the open office.

"Did she come this way?" he asked anxiously.

"If she was wearing blue slacks, white blouse, and red blazer with face to match, yes. At the rate she was going, she'll be in the parking lot by now."

"Oh shit." His voice broke, making him sound like a boy trying out his father's vocabulary. "It was just a couple of little pinches. Not like I meant anything. I'll bet she crashed the program too, just to get even. Now I'll never get those damn invoices out before quitting time!"

He tried several variations on the theme of fertilizer, then ran his hand through hair that must have itched to be washed. "Wait a minute," he said. "I'll bet you're Miller, aren't you? Oh, damn. I am sorry, Mr. Miller. I suppose this is no way to give a good impression to a prospective investor in ByteMarks. Please, come in. I can assure you I run a very professional operation here. I'm Gary Felkner. I can answer all your questions."

That's the kind of offer I'm not likely to pass up.

He led me into an office that contained an empty secretary's chair and a desk strewn with papers. "I don't think I really need a secretary, anyway," he said. "I can always get my Mom to take care of that stuff. What I really need is a partner, which is why you're here, I hope."

I didn't argue as he led the way into another office. This one was full of bins and boxes and bowls of esoteric silicon chips, thousands of semiconductors, row on row, rank on rank, the kind of subtly ordered chaos that reminded me of the Ice Cream King's workshop.

"Nice," I said, but I made my voice carefully unimpressed. Another trick left over from newspaper days. Make them want to tell you. Give them an excuse to strut. Especially when they're as young as Gary.

He looked at me and sighed. Another clod to initiate into the wonders of Gary's ByteMarks, Unltd. "This is the future," he said calmly. "This is what you want in on. Chips, bugs, insects. Call them what you will. The stuff in these bins will control billions of mundane lives out there."

There was mockery in Gary's voice, but not malice. It was the little boy in him, just getting his first doses of testosterone. I put his age at twenty-two, but he had the oily skin and thin beard of a late bloomer.

"Listen, I did almost $2 *million* last year out of my folks' garage, so they made me get a place of my own, but Mom comes over and straightens things up every week or so."

I've known people who do $2 million out of their garages, but I don't know many who can still con their mothers into cleaning their rooms. "What's the key to your success?" I asked, deadpan, earnest.

"I'm smart," Gary said. "That's what you'd be buying a piece of. That and my inventory. I don't need your money as much as I need someone who can organize an expansion. I'm not very good with people."

His voice said that he didn't particularly care.

"Parts are something else," he continued. "I can figure out what parts are going to be in high demand, and corner a supply of them." He reached into a carton and produced a handful of semiconductor chips. "Like these," he said. "Multitronics 8500s—64k chips, good stuff but not the cutting edge. They work fine in everything from word processors to avionics systems, and they're worth $52 each, according to the Multitronics catalog."

Gary tossed me a chip. I inspected it—a flat, black plastic rectangle half the size of a matchbook with twelve gold wire legs and a round plastic window in the middle of its body.

"I get $100 apiece for them," said Gary.

"From somebody who doesn't know how to do business with Multitronics?" I asked.

"Nope. From dummies who don't know their way past a parts catalog. Multitronics can only produce a given number of these chips. To keep all their customers happy, Multitronics puts everyone on a quota. No one receives more than five hundred of these chips a week. That's cool, if they only use five hundred a week. But say you have a DOD contract to meet, and you need a thousand chips, you'll be glad to pay me $100 a chip to make up the difference."

"How are you getting yours? Multitronics employees? Padded quotas? Illegal runs in the plant itself?" I asked, naming a few of the more common ways the gray market supplied itself.

Gary stiffened, then relaxed. "You've done your homework, partner. Mostly I pay $65 apiece to the parts managers of Multitronics customers, who order full quotas but only use two hundred chips a week. Strictly legal, so long as their bosses don't find out they're making a couple hundred a week on the side. Sometimes," he admitted, "I get a big order myself, too big for the managers to eat. So I have a source in the Multitronics testing department who can walk out with a lunch pail full of the little beauties. I only have to pay him ten or twenty bucks apiece. The markup is a lot better for me, but it's much more dangerous."

I smiled my most crooked smile. "It's called receiving stolen property. The cops don't think much of it."

"Hell, most cops wouldn't know the difference between a chip and a pork chop," said Gary, but his smile was uneasy. Underneath all that hustler was a good boy gone to silicon and adrenaline. "It's the damned security guys from Multitronics you have to watch out for. They caught a friend of mine buying stolen chips, took his money away, and then beat the shit out of him. A dead loss all around."

"How about foreign sales?" I asked.

He shrugged. "Sure. Half my customers are in France, Germany, and Switzerland."

"Aren't there export restrictions?" I asked, getting to the bottom line.

"We take care of that with the Three-Suiter Trade," he said. "Everybody in the business owns at least one piece of Samsonite three-suit baggage. You get a big order from Germany, and you pack in a thousand EPROMs, with space left over for a small rock group. Then you get on Lufthansa at SFO and away you go."

"What about German customs in Frankfurt?" I asked.

"There's no German law on imports, only a U.S. law on exports."

"What about U.S. Customs, then?"

"They just can't keep up with the flow. I'll bet 5,000 pieces a week go out of the Valley that way."

I made a mental note to introduce Gary to Sharp someday. It might shake the kid up a bit to know that the gray market was not an entire mystery to U.S. Customs.

"I'm not stupid," said Gary, as though he read my qualms. "I always make sure the guys I'm dealing with aren't Russians or anything.

"But, hell, even if I do make a mistake or two, what of it? Chips are like matches. This country can afford to give them away, so long as we have the match factory."

"Suppose there are other parts brokers around who don't have your sense of patriotism," I said, leading the witness.

He shrugged and picked at his scraggly beard. "There're guys around who don't give a damn who the customer is. You read about them going to prison every once in a while, in the *Electronics News*. Some of them you never read about."

"Like Omnitronix."

Gary hesitated, looked sideways at me, and tugged at his beard as though urging it to grow. "You've done your homework," he said again.

"I always check out the competition."

"Yeah. Well, outfits like Omnitronix give the gray market a bad name. They've shipped a lot of fabrication equipment—mask makers, etchers, silicon saws, photolith stuff. I mean, sooner or later even the thickest fed is gonna catch on, and then the shit will hit the big fan."

"Why? Lots of people ship gray stuff."

"Yeah, but not many of them ship the whole factory."

I heard several chords in my mind, blending and growing, condensing into minor key music. Modern music, the kind that makes your teeth ache.

"Where are they shipping it?" I asked.

"Switzerland. At least, that's the word around the Valley."

Sure. Switzerland needs wafer scrubbers the way a snake needs track shoes. But there was no need to point out the obvious.

"How much would a factory like that be worth?" I asked.

"Look, Mr. Miller. If you're thinking of buying into Byte-Marks and then going out on the cutting edge of gray marketeering, forget it. Omnitronix might make $10 to $20 million on the deal, but no one in the Valley will touch them. They're all alone, and word has it the government is closing in."

Poor Danny. Some envious gray marketeer had already snitched him off to the feds. Even this greasy kid knew about it. Maybe Gary had done the snitching himself, in the name of God, country, and profit margins.

"Do you know the Omnitronix people?" I asked, flipping the $100 gray market chip into the air and catching it.

"I see Flynn from time to time. He's the president. He

has a European money man named Volker. That's it. They fired their secretary a few months ago."

"Nobody else? Just two men?"

"Hell, Mr. Miller. I ran this company myself for two years. All you need is a computer."

I doubted that the bald-headed Brick was a computer in disguise. Which left the question of how the hell he came into use of the Omnitronix Volvo. I flipped the Multitronics chip back to Gary, turned and walked out the door, leaving the boy wonder with a few questions of his own.

In the hall, I passed a three-piece suit worn by a man with a puzzled expression on his face.

"Miller?" I asked.

He nodded.

"In there," I said, jerking my finger over my shoulder toward the offices of ByteMarks, Unltd. "Sounds like a hell of a deal to me."

8

I shoved the Thunderbird out onto the Bayshore, heading north against the grain of the increasing rush-hour traffic. It takes an hour to get to San Francisco. I spent it with the windows rolled up, the air-conditioner at half-speed, and the stereo nailed to the lower threshold of pain, decibels of Mozart pouring from a classical station. The whole philosophy of Detroit luxury cars is to separate you from your environment. The Bayshore, into its fourth decade and rough as a wagon road, is an environment worthy of being separated from.

I wished the music in my head had half the elegance and coherence of the sounds filling the car. I'd underestimated Danny-boy's capacity to get into trouble. He had always been inept, but he never had been criminally foolish. Now he was dangerous to himself and anyone who happened to be around when his experiments with reality all blew up in his pretty face.

Music was condensing in my head, an overture that sounded like Stravinsky on an LSD roller coaster. One un-melodic line was Danny. Another line was Volker, a man with enough charm to light the dark side of the moon and enough hardness to do a flying dismount twelve feet down onto a broken foot. The counterpoint was sung by Fiora, caught between Danny and me, Volker and me, herself and me, the past and the present calling to her in an off-key chorus, demanding that she sing along with everybody at once, tearing her apart.

Thoughts scattered and re-formed, phrases of music slid-ing into place. Danny, smiling Danny, owner of a company that was illegally exporting a semiconductor chip factory. Piece by piece, machine by machine, fragments fell together into a symphony that began in stupidity and greed and was swelling toward harmonics that would shatter him like glass.

A whole factory. One piece at a time. Christ. No wonder the Customs Service wanted to bust Danny's ass into a thousand pieces.

Volker was the brains; Danny was the all-American patsy; and the brick-shaped man was the muscle. Judging from what Danny had said at lunch, the end was one movement away, a single piece of equipment that would make the rest of the pieces interlock.

Was there any time before the final movement? Time to rewrite the score, to slide Danny out of the auditorium, out of sight? Otherwise he would spend a lot of years looking through federal bars, a miserable existence for a pretty, towheaded kid. I didn't like Danny very much, but I wouldn't wish hard time on anyone as soft as he was.

And Fiora. Watching Danny turn thin and sour in prison would kill her, if sharing his dreams didn't do it first.

Of course, having Volker carted off to jail might have hurt Fiora, too, if he hadn't involved her precious brother in this scheme. She wasn't a woman to forgive much. Still, Volker would survive jail better than Danny. And maybe he'd play his own version of the victim so convincingly that Fiora would buy it. Yet I reminded myself that when Fiora was scared, she came to me, not Volker. As much as I had enjoyed Volker and his reaction to the Cobra, I'm a practical man. Also a jealous one.

There was another aspect to this modern symphony that nagged at me; who the hell was on the podium? Who had orchestrated everything so that a whole factory would be shipped to Mexico? And from Mexico, where would the factory pieces go? Mexico needs a semiconductor factory even less than Switzerland. Japan had factories of its own. They stole our blueprints and engineers, not our fabrication equipment. France? Perhaps. God only knew what would appeal to a Frenchman. Germany? Perhaps. But both of those countries could obtain factory equipment from the United States legally.

That would leave what is politely referred to as the Eastern Bloc. They would buy whatever technology they could. Period. They had the brains and the resources and the sheer brass to steal a factory a piece at a time. But I found it hard to believe that Danny could ship restricted machines and shitlisted parts, month after month, nearly two years now, and not have the feds all over him like a bad smell. Whatever I may privately think about some government cops, as a whole they simply aren't that inept. It was possible, sure, but it wasn't very damn probable.

The overture began to fragment, phrases in search of coherence, jarring silences where some unknown musicians should have been. I had a lot to do before I could redeem my promise to Fiora, and only two strings to my violin— Danny and the diamonds.

The address from the manila diamond envelope was close to Fisherman's Wharf, in a big brick cannery building that had been gutted, sandblasted, and then filled with small, tasteful shops. Definitely not for the usual run of tourists. This was aimed at the white-wine-and-Brie set. The parking spaces were wide enough for Volvos, the car favored by quiche-eaters.

It was coming up on three-thirty. The weekday crowds had already begun to thin out in the candle shops and kitchenware boutiques, but there was enough foot traffic strolling about that I faded easily into the shadows. I bought a crab cocktail and a chunk of sourdough from a sidewalk stand a few doors down from the jewelry store that had supplied Danny's diamonds. I leaned against a wall amid an outbreak of potted trees, my profile disguised by greenery. As I ate, I watched people go by, making sure that nobody was watching me.

It took about ten minutes for my animal brain to do its primal little trick. I let myself be absorbed back into my surroundings before I really saw the bald, blocky man coming toward me from the opposite corridor. I turned away as the cosh artist passed by and walked into the jewelry store like someone who had been there before.

As he entered, I heard the bell over the jewelry store door jingle a brass warning. The man reached behind him and reversed the elegantly inscribed card so that it now read: CLOSED. Adrenaline slid into my veins, tuning my body to concert pitch. I unbuttoned my blazer and walked closer.

An exceptionally beautiful Eurasian woman emerged from behind the scarlet curtain that closed off the rear portion of the shop. She must have known the brick-shaped man, because recognition showed on her face an instant before fear sprang up like a shadow veiling her beauty.

The man spoke as he opened his suit coat like a Brooks Brothers flasher, showing her the gun. The woman's face changed again, no expression now, a carved statue. She turned without a word or objection, sliding through the brocade curtain. The man followed.

I gave it a long ten count, then stood in front of the espresso shop that was the tiny jewelry store's nearest neighbor. I inspected the display of herbal teas and imported coffees in the window, standing as close as I could to the jewelry shop window without silhouetting myself. Glass makes a fair medium for conducting sound waves. I could hear a pair of voices, male and female, from behind the brocade curtain. Sound, but no meaning, just the clear feeling that the man and woman weren't agreeing.

I eased along the outside of the jewelry shop until I was at the door. I listened again. They were still arguing. Still sound without meaning, although now I was close enough to realize that both of the people spoke with pronounced accents.

Slowly, I pushed the door of the shop open, first an inch, then two, until I could see the metal arm that held the brass bell. For once in my life, I could do without music. I reached up through the crack made by the open door, closed my fingers gently around the bell, and softly pinched the clapper against the metal. Silenced bell in hand, I opened the door just far enough to slide into the shop. I closed the door with equal care, released the bell, and felt sweat trickle down my ribs beneath the leather holster.

I quietly shucked out the gun. For the first time since yesterday, I felt like I was on equal footing with the bald-headed man. Then I moved to the counter and listened closely, trying to isolate the voices that came from behind the scarlet brocade. I'm no linguist, but I have a good ear. The man's accent was East European. The woman's was Vietnamese—and something more, a breathy thickness at the end of English syllables that was almost French.

"You will tell me about the machine," said the man, "or you will die." His words were as basic and blunt as his body.

I couldn't see what effect he was having on the woman but he had me convinced of his sincerity. This wasn't your average businessman out to make a killing in the free market. At least, not the kind of killing capitalists usually made, not even in the cutthroat world of Silicon Valley's gray market.

A cold feeling settled in my gut. I didn't need much more confirmation about that match factory's ultimate destination. Did Danny know?

A little friendly civilian mayhem is one thing. World class nut-cracking is another. There are only a few countries that play the kind of hardball that was in progress here. Iran was one. One or two African nations. And Russia. The Third World was a limited market. But not Russia.

The overture resumed, but instead of faltering for lack of players, this time the theme came smoothly, perfectly, minor chords more Oriental than Occidental. An image flashed in my head, a great shrewd bear standing on back legs and sniffing the winds of change.

The sound of an open hand striking flesh was louder and even less enigmatic than any words that had been spoken behind the brocade curtain. Then there was a muffled scuffling, as though the woman had begun to resist the blocky man.

There would never be a better time. I moved up to one side of the curtain, where a long sliver of light ran between the wall and the scarlet cloth. The first impression was of a workshop, orderly and filled with the tools of the jeweler's trade—polishing wheels and gem microscopes and engravers' implements. Beside one of the workbenches stood a pair of pressure tanks that fueled a small furnace for melting gold. The furnace was so hot it glowed.

The man stood with his square back to the curtain, his bald head gleaming as he bent over five feet from me. He was dragging the woman toward the burning furnace with one hand. In his other hand, he held the ugly pistol he had used on me the last time we met. The silencer was still in place, a black onion on a thick skewer.

Though the woman was barely five feet tall, she had strength, the raw animal strength that comes from fear. She didn't waste breath on whimpering. She tried to break the man's Adam's apple with the side of her palm. He parried the blow with the hand that held the gun. Even then, not a cry came from her lips. For an instant the contest was even. Though the man was vastly stronger, he could not control the woman with one hand.

When she started to scream, not from fear but in a calculated effort to attract attention, the bald man hesitated, plainly wanting to end the struggle with a gun butt laid behind her ear. But unconscious women don't talk much, and he was focused on burning some answers out of her. He laid the pistol down on the bench and clamped his hand over the woman's mouth.

That was the first mistake I'd seen him make.

I came through the curtain. He still had his back to me as he bent the woman's arm behind her and turned her toward the furnace. With measured force, he hit her just below the breasts, knocking the wind out of her, making a scream impossible. Then he twisted his fingers into her long black hair and forced her face toward the glowing furnace.

I grabbed him around the neck with one arm and straightened him. His reflexes were fast, but I had expected them to be. I blocked an elbow at my ribs as I yanked him off-balance, stiffened my arm into a bar across his throat and began to choke him in earnest. He released the woman. As a reward, I let him breathe a bit. Then I raked the front sight of the Detonics across the thin skin just above his eyebrow, drawing a veil of blood across his eye. I screwed the muzzle of the gun into his ear, stretched him up on his toes, and held him there.

He went very still. The woman staggered to the workbench and gasped for air as her paralyzed diaphragm began to work again. She straightened slowly, turned, and studied the blocky man and me as though there wasn't much to choose between the two of us.

The blocky man began to settle forward, bit by sneaky bit, trying to drag me with him as he regained his balance. I put a little more pressure on his carotids, shutting down the blood flow to his brain. He stopped moving.

"Lady, I'm on your side, so relax," I said, digging the muzzle a little deeper into the man's skull. "Go out and lock the front door. Then we'll have a little talk with our friend here. I'm sure he has an explanation for all this. Don't you?"

When he didn't answer, I shifted his weight onto my hip, as though I intended to throw him onto the searing furnace. His face changed as hers had when she had recognized him—no fear, just a kind of psychic shutdown that nothing short of an enormous amount of pain could penetrate.

I might have broken him, I suppose, but the problem with torture is that by the time you bring someone to the point of conversation, they'll tell you anything they imagine you want to hear, whether it's true or not. As a method of getting to the truth, torture is overrated, especially when you're dealing with professionals. And there was no doubt that the man was a pro.

So, for that matter, was the woman. She picked up the silenced pistol from the bench and started to bring it to bear on us. She still hadn't recovered fully, though. In slow motion, she brought up her thumb and snapped off the safety on the pistol.

The blocky man decided he was already dead, so what did one utterly mad risk matter? He twisted his head suddenly, letting the muzzle of the gun slide into the blood flowing from his eye. Simultaneously he gave me another elbow shot, stuck his chin in the crook of my arm, and

slipped straight down out of my grip. Then he ran. I could
have killed him three times before he got to the door, but I
saw no real advantage to it.

The beautiful Eurasian had no such scruples. She tracked
the man's scrambling progress with lead slugs that coughed
delicately out of the ugly silencer. One slug chewed the
floor at my feet. Another buried itself in the doorjamb. The
third slug went into the ceiling as I grabbed her wrist with
one hand while wrenching the pistol out of her determined
little fingers with the other. Not that I really minded her
putting a hole in the bald man. I simply wasn't sure that she
would have stopped with him.

As I separated her from the gun, the brass bell clanged
merrily, telling of one man exiting, center stage, at a dead
run. By the time I got to the window, he had vanished
around one of the thousand corners built into the trendy,
boutique-ridden building.

I spun around toward the woman, expecting her to have
vanished through the shop's back door. There wasn't one, so
she was still with me, standing just in front of the scarlet
curtain. The only sign of her close encounter with a red-hot
furnace was her unusually pale color and her tumbled black
hair. She wore an elegant silk tunic top in patterns of gold
and indigo and ebony. Her slacks were black, rough silk,
and expensive. She watched me with haunting amber eyes.

The woman's face was extraordinary. But there was more
than beauty there. She seemed truly ageless. She might
have been thirty or seventy. I had seen the same look once
on the face of a beautiful woman who had borne relentless
physical pain for two decades. The woman before me had
known mental rather than physical anguish, but it was just
as real and just as enduring.

"Who are you?" she asked. Her voice was like her eyes—
patient, unflinching, haunting.

"I'm the guy who just saved you from a third-degree facial," I said reasonably.

"You don't know me. Therefore you saved me for your
own convenience."

Hard to fault that logic. "My name is Fiddler."

Her eyelids fluttered once, suggesting that she recognized the name. Her mouth remained motionless, waiting to see if I'd noticed.

"Where did you learn to shoot this?" I asked, holding up the alien, ugly gun.

She smiled very slightly. Suddenly I was glad I was holding the only weapons within reach.

"The pistol looks like a Tokarev TT-33. It is a very good pistol, although the silencer makes the balance awkward. We used to steal them from the Viet Cong. . . ." She paused and looked inward again, smiling even less this time.

"Go on," I said.

She shrugged, an elegant Gallic movement of her shoulders. "I would have enjoyed killing a Russian with a Tokarev."

There are times when I'd really rather be wrong. This was all of them rolled into one. *Russian.*

"Do you know this Russian's name?" I asked, my voice as disgusted as my expression must have been.

"Valerian Korchnoi," she said, handling the Russian syllables with the ease of someone to whom Russian names aren't strange. "He's a Soviet agent."

"Accredited?"

She nodded. "He works at the Soviet consulate in San Francisco."

I wanted to doubt her so bad my teeth ached, but every word she said filled up another hole in the theme, added another player to the orchestra, circled closer and closer to the man who had to be conducting it. She spoke in the clear tones of truth as well as ideology. Soviet microprocessing is such a faithful copy of U.S. technology that the parts are virtually interchangeable. Only the electrical current needs are different. We use 60 cycles and the Russians use 50. And, as the Ice Cream King never tired of pointing out, the Soviets have a bigger consular staff in San Francisco than they do in New York, the putative head of trade and diplomacy in the United States.

But there was a big difference between polite research of

unclassified technical material by diplomatic attachés, and clobbering civilians like me behind the ear and trying to stuff pretty women into furnaces. Either the Cold War was warmer than I thought or the Soviets were highly motivated to conclude the Omnitronix deal.

"Do you have a name?" I asked, more rudely than I had intended. I wasn't above wanting to shoot the bearer of bad news myself.

"Kim Van Kieu," she said.

Her eyes watched me, trying to read my response. It must have been fairly clear.

"Does my name amuse you?" she said. "It is a very old Vietnamese name."

"Not everyone is named after an epic," I said.

Her pupils flared, dark pools of interest in the center of her unusual amber eyes. "You are better-schooled than most of your countrymen," she said. "But Kim Van Kieu is nonetheless the name I use. It is on my refugee card. It is the name on my business license. If the city of San Francisco and the government of the United States say my name is Kim Van Kieu, how can it be otherwise?"

"All right, Kim Van Kieu, how do you fit in with an all-American moron named Danny Flynn?"

Again, the darkness expanding in her eyes. "Do you know anything about diamonds?" Kieu asked.

"A bit," I said, knowing that my pupils must have expanded every bit as much as hers had. It shows better against gray, too. One of those disadvantages Anglos have to live with.

"Did you look closely at the diamonds Danny had?" she asked.

"Excellent color, no visible imperfections, one half to five carats."

"Did you count the facets on the small ones?"

"No."

"Soviet cutters put an extra facet on their small stones. That is how I knew Danny was doing business with Russia even before he did."

"How did you get involved?"

She hesitated, then said, "Danny brought two diamonds to my store for appraisal. They had extra facets. He didn't believe me. We have had several arguments."

"You and Danny had more than a business relationship." It wasn't really a question.

Kieu studied me with her dark amber eyes. They had great depth, great intensity, when she allowed it. "They had to convert their Russian diamonds into U.S. currency to pay for the machinery," she continued. "I was Danny's appraiser."

"What did Korchnoi want from you?"

"Danny."

"What about the machine?"

"What machine?"

"Shit, lady," I said, disgusted. "The machine that Korchnoi was going to fry your face over."

"Why do you not believe me?" she said softly. Her amber eyes looked downward, demure innocence in the sweep of her eyelashes and the slight trembling of her lower lip. "Is it that you do not believe in Russians?"

"Oh, I believe in Russians, all right. And machines."

"So many Americans would doubt the Russian involvement," Kieu said, sticking to her tangential answers with admirable will. "I suppose it is natural. It is four generations since your civil war. You have never seen blood flowing in your streets because of politics. Everything is very polite and agreeable in this country."

"If you believe that, you and Danny must have made as pretty a pair of deuces as God ever saw."

"Do you treat everything as a joke?" she asked.

"No, but I pick my causes carefully."

"What are your causes?" she asked.

Kieu's amber eyes were intent, searching for a point of agreement or a weakness in me. The two were the same thing to her. Leverage in an unending tug-of-war.

"I believe in individuals, not causes, and certainly not in big groups like nations. Groups that big don't need me."

"Families?" she said quickly. "Do you believe in families?"

I stared at her cautiously and said nothing. After all, what did I have to say on the subject?

She shook her head. "Vietnamese believe in one thing and one thing alone—blood. That is why they are good at small conspiracies and family businesses but not wars, nations, or corporations."

"I share your aversion for corporations," I said, "but I'm afraid I never met a cousin I liked."

"Then you are not Vietnamese," she said.

"Does that matter right now?"

"Only to a Vietnamese."

I looked at Kieu for a long moment. Like Korchnoi, I wanted to know about the machine, whatever it might have been. Unlike Korchnoi, I didn't have the stomach to fry the information out of Kieu. And she knew it.

"Did Danny give the diamonds to Fiora as he threatened to?" Kieu asked.

I didn't answer. I didn't have to.

Kieu frowned. "It was not very wise of him to involve his sister. But then, Danny sometimes is not very wise, is he?"

I thought of Fiora, sleeping alone in the motel. She had called her office, telling them where she was. Anyone who cared enough would be given the motel number. After that, it was no trick to get to Fiora. I knew she didn't have the diamonds, but no one else knew it. And I had left her there, asleep.

"Stand over there, against the wall," I said.

Kieu never hesitated. She was very good at reading voices, and mine had told her that I had found something worth frying her over. I punched in the motel number with one hand. The other hand pointed the Tokarev at Kieu, the safety still off.

The phone rang three times, five, eight, eleven. I hung up and tried the desk.

"Room 23 doesn't answer the phone," I said with a calm that was no deeper than my skin. "Any messages for me?"

"Yes sir. Miss Flynn left an envelope."

"Open it."

There was a hesitation, the sound of tearing paper, and then the desk clerk cleared his throat. "Danny called."

"That's it? No number? No address?"

"No sir."

I hung up and went to stand behind the woman called Kim Van Kieu. "You're taking me to Danny."

9

The address Kieu gave me was for an apartment complex in Mountain View. I decided that I wanted company. Hers. I waited while she shut down the furnace and put jewelry in the safe. I followed her through the shop, paused while she locked the door, and then took her left arm just above the elbow. The compleat gentleman, that's me.

By the time we got to the Thunderbird, I knew I was being followed. It wasn't Korchnoi; his bulky silhouette was imprinted on my hind brain. This man was slender, barely five-and-a-half feet tall, and moved with speed and silence. He might have been sixteen or sixty. At fifty feet, without wrinkles and gray hair, it's hard to tell.

Kieu noticed the man, too. She was good. Her glance passed over him without hesitating, as though he were just one more potted plant. He walked past us, then stopped and looked into a shop window. It was no accident that we were reflected in the same window. Kieu's signal was small, utterly normal. She reached up with her right hand and smoothed back her hair. The man waited until we were beyond the window, then turned and followed us through the crowd.

It was all very orderly and calm. Then I saw several more Vietnamese disperse through the crowd, going back to whatever they had been doing before the CLOSED sign had appeared in Kieu's shop window. I wondered what would have happened if she had used her left hand to straighten her hair.

Not everyone went back to business as usual. As I pulled out of the parking lot, I glanced in the rearview mirror of the Thunderbird. A Vietnamese man was climbing into a highly polished Camaro that had pulled up to the curb. Either they were not terribly sophisticated about surveillance or they weren't worried about taking a burn. Or maybe it was just Kieu's way of telling me that I should behave myself. I didn't know, and I didn't care. I was a hell of a lot more worried about a telephone ringing in an empty motel room than I was about any variety of Asian tail.

"This is not the way to go," she objected.

I ignored her. We went west a couple of blocks before I found what I wanted. I made a right onto a one-way street, accelerated a half-block, and waited for the Camaro to follow. As soon as it was committed to the one-way flow, I threw the T-Bird into a 180-degree turn and headed back against traffic.

Horns and shouts, raised fists and middle fingers greeted me. I returned the greetings. The only car that didn't seem to care was the Camaro. The driver and passenger ignored me as I swept by. If I needed confirmation that they were following me, that was it. I gave the Camaro the same greeting I had given the other cars.

I made a quick left at the nearest intersection, and then another fast turn, heading east. I drove hard without making a lot of noise, caught a couple of lights on the yellow, and then headed back toward the Bayshore. I didn't see the Camaro again.

If Kieu worried about losing her pals, her face didn't show it. She lowered the sun visor on her side and spent a lot of time fussing with her hair. No matter what she did, though, no high-gloss Camaro popped up to be reflected in the little vanity mirror.

"Relax," I said. "As long as Danny's apartment is at the address you gave me, I'll be like a kindly older brother."

Kieu gave me another long look, another long silence, and settled in for the ride.

The Giants were at Candlestick Park, playing another futile game in the world's only wind tunnel with built-in bleachers. Traffic in the area was heavy. Between that and the bone-numbing harmonics in my head whenever I thought of Fiora and empty rooms, I was fully occupied. I was almost to Burlingame before I had enough attention left over for a well-mannered fishing expedition.

"Have you lived in the U.S. long?" I asked.

"Too long," Kieu said, glancing at me as though I had stolen her thoughts. "You call us 'refugees,' but we call ourselves 'exiles.' There are a half million Vietnamese in California, perhaps 100,000 of us here in San Francisco. But exile is still a lonely place."

"And you can't go home again," I said.

There was a bitterness to Kieu's smile that was a perfect counterpoint to my thoughts of Fiora and Danny. I had left Fiora one message. She had left me another. Danny.

"I have killed too many Viet Cong to go home again," Kieu said simply.

"Were politics always so important to you?" I asked, looking sideways at her. She must have been damned young to be out in the streets of Saigon trolling up Tokarevs and death.

"My family was not political," she said. "But they were Catholic. I was born in Hanoi. I was only a year old when the country was partitioned in 1954. Catholics died by the thousands at the hands of the blessed revolutionary saint, Ho Chi Minh." Kieu made the name an epithet. She looked older now, much older. "Three brothers and I are the only ones from my immediate family who survived the journey to Saigon. Two of those brothers died fighting the Viet Cong. They were brave soldiers, despite what American journalists said."

"If your brothers had half your guts, I'm sure they died as bravely as any man," I said, remembering her silent struggle against Korchnoi's much greater strength.

Kieu looked at me as though seeing me for the first time, measuring my words. There was an intensity to her that was unsettling. She was stretched too tightly between past and present.

"Your third brother," I said. "Is he the one who followed us?"

Kieu shook her head, then looked away. She said nothing.

I wondered, then, who her guardians were. "Is your brother still in Vietnam?"

"No. He is one of the 50,000 Vietnamese men who have been sent to Russia as slaves to repay the war debts of the Viet Cong."

Then, before I could say anything, she shook her head.

"Keep your easy words about war and loss. You are an American. You do not know what it is to be conquered and enslaved."

Kieu's expression said she was through talking about her family. I decided to approach the question of her Vietnamese keepers from another angle.

"You must be very lonely without a family," I said.

"I have my work."

I remembered the jewelry I had seen in Kieu's shop as I waited for her to lock up. Delicate, elegant, yet somehow powerful, curves of precious metal complementing carefully chosen gems. One piece in particular stood out in my mind, a large triangular emerald ring whose magnificent color had nearly concealed the deep inclusions and internal fracturing of the stone. It had required breathtaking confidence to set such an emerald. The chance of shattering it as the prongs tightened into place was enormous. The gamble had reaped stunning results.

"The jewelry you make is very beautiful," I said honestly. "But however beautiful, gems are cold."

"Like me? Is that what you are saying?"

That wasn't what I was saying, but before I could explain, she laughed—a harsh sound that had no humor.

"You must ask Danny about that. He may enlighten you."

Kieu returned to her brooding silence. She was like that emerald—color and brilliance and the appearance of crystal hardness. But jewelers know emeralds are the hardest stone to hold. Sometimes they come apart in your palm for no better reason than the heat of your touch subtly warming the molecules, expanding them just that tiny increment that allows the natural flaws to overcome the crystal lattice that holds everything together. To work an emerald, you have to be willing to destroy it. Kieu and I hadn't come that far—not yet.

We said nothing until Palo Alto. At her direction, I left the Bayshore, moved over to El Camino Real and drove south into Mountain View. The evening traffic was light. She directed me to a cluster of apartments just off El Camino. Danny's Porsche was parked in a carport behind one of the two-story buildings. I parked beside it, took Kieu's arm and let her lead the way.

The sign in front of the apartment building had said something about a forest. The motif was carried out with transplanted, head-high black pines and a thin, heavily chlorinated stream that ran between concrete banks for about fifty feet before disappearing down a drain to be recycled.

The glaring spotlights aimed at the pines cast odd shadows against the clusters of two-story buildings, making me uneasy. Kieu, too, seemed haunted by something. Her face was strained. She pointed to the door of a corner apartment on the ground floor. There were no lights on inside. I knocked on the door. No response. I tried to open the door. Locked. Kieu produced a key from her purse.

Her gasp as the door swung open told me she had recognized the smell as quickly as I did. Cordite first, a chemical bite in my nostrils. Then the smell beneath it, unpleasant and cloying. I shucked the pistol out of my shoulder holster and groped for the light switch. As I flipped it on, I stepped aside, quickly pulling Kieu with me. I leaned against the exterior wall, waiting for a shot to come.

But all I could think of was Fiora.

No shots came, no sounds. No nothing. I slid around the corner and into the apartment. Danny was propped against the divider that separated the kitchen from the living area. Half-sitting, his legs in front of him, unblinking, eyes open. He could have been drunk or stoned except for the blood smeared over his shirt front and the lack of definition at the back of his skull. The hole in his forehead had spoiled his flawless face and made a bad joke out of his $35 razor cut.

I went through the apartment like an avenging angel. Fiora wasn't there. Neither was the killer. No one was waiting in the closet or shower or jammed under the circular bed. Nobody home at all, especially not Danny Flynn. I went back to what was left of Danny.

First the sickness came, then the rage. *God damn Danny's ineffectual soul.* He had no right to die and leave me with his blood on my hands. What in Christ's name was I going to tell Fiora? What pretty lies could I dream up to cover the ugly truth of her miserable twin with his miserable brains blown all over a Silicon Valley apartment?

And then the worst of it sank in. I wouldn't have to tell her at all. She would have known when her twin died, just as she had known his pain when he was alive. Somewhere out in the night Fiora was crying for the lost half of herself—and I wasn't there to hold her.

Kieu moved, reminding me that I wasn't alone. Her face was as pale as it had been when Korchnoi had tried to burn her. I went over and shut the front door. Pretending I had never seen Danny before, I approached the body and got down on a level where I could study it. He had been shot twice. Once would have been enough. The first shot had hit him in the chest, opening up an artery. The second shot was a coup de grace in the middle of his forehead. The heavy, low-velocity slug had left behind a round, bloodless hole in front and a churned-up mess in back. From the look of it, I guessed the caliber to be 9 mm.

I turned back to Kieu, who hadn't moved. Her face was pale and drawn, her amber eyes fixed on Danny, her tiny hand clamped over her mouth. I stood up, feeling anger and impatience like a hot drumroll in my blood.

"Can it, lady," I snarled. "Anyone who hunted Viet Cong through Saigon sewers isn't going to puke over a fresh corpse. And don't tell me you loved Danny, either. He was too soft, and you're too hard."

Kieu's eyes closed. A delicate shudder moved over her body. Then she dropped her hand, opened her eyes, and knelt next to what had once been Danny Flynn. She touched the distorted face with two fingers, closing the green eyes. It was an act of surprising gentleness.

"I did not love Danny," she said, looking at me with dark amber eyes. "But I did not hate him, either. He was only a fool." She murmured a few phrases in her native tongue, sliding tones and surprising consonants. Then she crossed herself and sighed. "Though he meant nothing by it, his foolishness could have killed many of my people."

Kieu's voice was soft and distant, speaking more to herself than to me. When she turned toward Danny again, she looked a thousand years old.

I wondered how Fiora looked.

"Get out of the way," I said quietly, kneeling again beside Danny.

He hadn't been dead long enough for rigor to set in, but he was too cool to be anything but a corpse. I rifled the inside pockets of his camel hair jacket. It was crusted with blood from the chest wound, but the wallet was still there. I went through it quickly and found nothing unexpected, certainly nothing that would be worth killing for. I replaced the wallet and went through his pockets as best I could. Change and car keys, chewing gum and breath candy.

I stood up and inspected the rest of the room. There was an empty folder spread out on the counter of the room divider, next to the telephone. Empty folder. Dead man. What had been in the folder? Was that what had been worth killing for?

I went around the divider, looking for the contents of the empty folder. Papers were scattered across the kitchen floor as though Danny had thrown them over his shoulder when the first slug hit. I gathered up the pieces, pink rectangles and yellow ones, cream and white, thin and thick, flimsy copies and originals. Most of the papers were bills of lading and delivery orders, documents that related to equipment purchased in the past several months.

It was pretty much as Gary had said: a factory going out the back door piece by piece. I saw reference to wafer saws and scrubbers, engravers and etchers, all the machines used to make silicon wafer chips and then to sketch the intricate conductive gridworks on them. The papers showed the delivery address to be the Omnitronix warehouse in Irvine. Thin strips of unlined paper were stapled to each receipt. The strips were telex messages identical to the one that had come clattering into Omnitronix just yesterday, a few minutes before Korchnoi had fitted a gun butt behind my ear.

I studied the telex messages, ignoring the voice in my brain screaming *Where is Fiora?*

Decoded, the strips of paper were shipping confirmations wired ahead by the equipment manufacturer when the shipment left Silicon Valley. All were pretty much in the same shorthand, with the original delivery order beside it. The code itself was easy, more a shortcut than an attempt to hide information. There was a manufacturer's model number, an abbreviated description of the machine, and then the street address of the Irvine warehouse.

But the telex that had come in yesterday had had a different address. I knew it by heart, having run it through my mind time and again: 39345 US 101, #12-1, Brlngme. Not Irvn. Brlngme.

Burlingame. A city about fifteen miles from where I stood.

The missing machine wasn't missing after all. It just hadn't been shipped to Irvine. Had Danny had a last-minute realization of just how deep in the shit he had gone? Had he rerouted the last machine, double-crossing Korchnoi and earning a death sentence?

Even as the thought came, it sounded flat. At lunch, Danny had been looking to get out from under pressure, not to add more. He simply didn't have the *huevos* to take on Korchnoi.

Then who had? And what was at 39345 U.S. Highway 101 in Burlingame? A house? A vacant lot? Another factory?

I looked at Kieu. She looked at the papers crumpled in my fist. Then she carefully looked at nothing, her eyes fixed on some personal crossroads in space and time. It was the look she had given Korchnoi, the Russian who was so cer-

tain that she knew where the machine was that he was willing to hold her face in the furnace until she talked.

Danny wasn't strong enough to take on Korchnoi, but
Kieu was. I was glad I wouldn't have to depend on anything
as fragile as an oxygen furnace to get information out of Kim
Van Kieu.

I realized that I was staring at the phone while my unconscious yammered at me, trying to get my attention. The
phone was splattered with blood, even though the counter
itself was clean. Danny must have been talking on the
phone when he was shot. He had dropped it as he fell, and
it had hung loose beside him, rolling against the divider as
the second shot was fired. Then the killer had calmly hung
up the phone and left.

The thought that Danny might have been talking to Fiora
when he died made me want to kill something. Anything. I
wrenched my mind away from the possibility, knowing that
I would only make things worse if I slipped the leash and
started administering justice before all the evidence was
gathered.

"Out," I said to Kieu, jerking my head toward the front
door.

I stuffed the papers into my breast pocket, pulled out a
handkerchief and wiped the wall switch and doorknob on
the way out. I loaded Kieu into the Thunderbird with a
force that told her all she needed to know about my temper.

"Where are we going?" she said.

Without answering, I started the T-Bird and eased out of
the parking lot with my lights out, putting distance between me and the apartment building. Whoever Danny
had been talking to on the phone might have wondered why
the conversation ended so abruptly. He might have been so
upset that he called the police and complained. Word of
gunshots gathers cops like shit gathers flies.

A block behind me, a car cruised into the apartment
parking area. For a second the car was backlighted by a
street lamp. No light bars on the roof, no siren lumped in
the rear window. But there were two men inside. The car

came on purposefully. I turned right, accelerated, and left my lights off.

Just as I turned again, I caught the flash of headlights in the mirror. The car with the two men had turned as I had turned. I speeded up, turned another corner, and found myself in one of those damned residential cul-de-sacs so beloved of suburban designers. I was trapped. I made a U-turn and parked by the curb. With one hand I yanked out my gun. With the other I jerked Kieu across my lap. I buried my fingers in her long hair and held her face against my neck.

"For the next few minutes we're going to look like very good friends," I said, my lips against her ear and my whole attention focused in the driving mirror.

My words might have confused Kieu, but she understood guns very well. She lay quietly against me, just one more girl gone bad in the front seat of a Ford. The car turned into the cul-de-sac. At first I thought it might be Kieu's shadows again, but it was a Plymouth, not a Camaro. I was not exactly relieved. Lots of cops drive unmarked Plymouths.

The driver of the car saw the cul-de-sac. Slowly, the Plymouth went by the mouth of the little street, as though the driver were searching for a street name or an address. Though the car didn't turn in, it was close enough for me to catch a glimpse of the two men. They looked official, whatever they were, but otherwise hard to place. They seemed to pay more attention to the building numbers than they did to us. Then again, I seemed to be paying more attention to a lap full of woman than I was to the Plymouth cruising by. I watched the car go on down the street, turn, and disappear. I waited for five minutes by the clock, holding Kieu and the gun. The car didn't come back.

I had the feeling that I wasn't going to have to drop money in a pay phone to let the local cops know they had a homicide on their hands. The men in the Plymouth had fairly reeked of official confidence. I made a mental note to dump the Thunderbird at the first opportunity. Even if they hadn't noticed it, somebody else in the apartment complex might have.

I lifted Kieu off my lap and holstered the gun. In a few minutes I was just one car among hundreds.

"Where are you taking me?" asked Kieu.

Her voice was neutral, almost uninterested. The strain of the last few hours was getting to her.

I didn't answer. The orchestra in my head was playing an off-key threnody, music for a dead twin, prelude for a symphony of horror. But it was the living twin who concerned me now.

Ten minutes later I pulled into the parking lot of the motel. The room clerk was so used to the family trade that he gave me a hard look. First I had come in with a blonde. Now I had a Eurasian on my arm.

I traded in the T-Bird at the motel's Hertz counter. All Hertz had that was capable of zero to sixty in less than two weeks was a red Mustang with a four-speed. Too damned conspicuous, but I took it anyway. Kieu stood by me the whole time. The fact that I hadn't let go of her arm might have had something to do with it. I didn't let go until I had herded her into the room and thrown the bolt closed behind me.

"Did your people come after Fiora?" I asked.

Kieu's face didn't change, cold and featureless, like my voice.

"We can do it easy or we can do it hard. But it'll get done, baby. *Did they come after Fiora.*"

"There would be no reason to," said Kieu finally. "Fiora doesn't have the machine."

Fiora wasn't here, but she wasn't dead in Danny's apartment, either. I hoped she was sitting on the beach somewhere, alone, trying to believe in a future without Danny Flynn. Maybe I could help her. Knowing the reason Danny died might help the rational part of Fiora's mind accept what could not be changed.

"Who killed Danny and why?" I asked. "Did he have the machine?"

"No."

"What's so important about this machine that it's worth murdering for?"

Kieu said nothing. Her expression said she planned on keeping it that way.

"I don't care about the machine, whatever the hell it is," I said. "But I'm going to be able to tell Fiora why her brother died tonight. One more time, Kieu. *What's so important about the machine.*"

Kieu studied me for a long moment. As I watched, her face settled into shadows and lines, receding down a tunnel into the past filled with hatred and death.

"It is a key," she said softly. "Without it, all the other machines the Russians have bought are absolutely worthless."

Chords vibrated through my mind, grim and forbidding. The threnody was becoming a dirge for bassoons and brass. No wonder Korchnoi was willing to cook one woman and probably murder one man. The key to Russia's $20 million semiconductor factory had slipped from Russian hands.

"Was Danny holding them up for more money?" I asked.

It tempted Kieu, but in the end she refused to play that tune. "No."

"Did Danny know you were going to steal the machine?"

Kieu treated the question just like the fully loaded gun it was. She ducked it completely and, in doing so, answered it.

"What are you going to do with the machine?" I asked, walking toward Kieu.

"The Russians will never get it," she said. Her words were simple, but her voice vibrated with hatred.

"What you're saying is that Fiora's brother died because you want revenge for your brother who is a slave laborer in Russia."

"It is not just for my brother that we do this," Kieu said quickly. "It is for all the Vietnamese people, for all the people of the free world. Every chip that factory makes would go into planes or trucks or machines to make war."

This time her whole small body vibrated with the depth of her emotion. I wondered if she had ever used those depths for anything besides hate. Love, real love, with her might have been exceptional.

But I doubted that any man had ever known it or ever would.

"You can stay with me until I find out where Fiora is, or you can go," I said. "Your choice."

"May I use the phone?" she asked politely.

I handed it to her. She dialed, then had to speak to the operator to give a room number. After a moment, she resumed speaking, this time in the sliding tones of Vietnamese. She hung up after a brief exchange.

"I will wait in the lobby," she said.

Kieu started for the door slowly, as though expecting me to stop her. She shot back the bolt, opened the door, and then turned back to look at me.

"I regret the death of Fiora's brother. What Danny was doing was very wrong—but we did not kill him. Nor did we mean for him to die."

Quietly, Kieu closed the door behind her.

10

I looked at the closed door and tried to think. Two thousand years of war in Indochina had come to a new home. Poor Danny. His idea of a hard fight was fourth and one at the goal line. Poor dead Danny. God rot all fools, including me, the fool who had left Fiora alone when she most needed me. Where in hell was she now?

But it was too late for anything, including regrets. Replaying the mistakes wouldn't rectify anything. Think, Fiddler. Damn you, think.

If the machine were as crucial as Kieu said it was, I probably owed Sharp and his silent partner a telephone call. I'd have to play with that idea for a while, though, listen to what it added or subtracted from my own personal orchestra. There wasn't as much cacophony as there had been. Too bad. I'd liked cacophony better than the jangled, untra-modern, antimelodic piece that was sawing away in my mind.

The phone rang. There was only one person who knew about this room besides Kieu. I picked up the receiver.

"Fiora?" I asked.

I could hear a ragged breath and then, "Fiddler . . ."

There were tears in her voice, tears and something more. She was afraid.

"Oh, Fiddler, I'm sorry I got you into this!"

Before I could answer, I heard a brief struggle as the phone changed hands.

"Fiddler," said a new voice. Volker's voice, as cold as January.

For an instant, before the adrenaline roared into my system, I was afraid. No one could be that cold. No one. Then I almost laughed aloud at my innocence. If the stakes were high enough, I could be whatever *I* had to be to get the job done. And the stakes were high enough.

"Volker," I said, my voice an echo of his. Mirror images feinting, waiting, music condensing around us, atonal, feral, predatory. "Or whoever you are. I'm here."

"You already know, don't you?"

I said nothing, waiting for him to tell me what I already knew. Fiora.

"You are like me," continued Volker, cold chords of assurance resonating in his voice. "You still do not want to believe that, do you?"

I'll believe whatever I have to, you bastard. But I said it only to myself, a final uncivilized theme added to the music, a summation. The first movement was over, all themes introduced. Only the variants needed to be played.

"You know about Danny," continued Volker, pausing only fractionally, telling me he was listening intently to any physiological clues I might give away—quick breaths or a quavering voice. "You know about the OxyCon." Pause. "You know about the Vietnamese. You may even know what they hope to do with the machine." Pause. "No questions, Fiddler?"

I waited, saying nothing. I had nothing to say that Volker wanted to hear. As long as he had Fiora, he was the conductor.

"Do you know what I want, Fiddler?"

I waited.

"Let us both be civilized about this. After all, so much is at stake. For both of us. And for Fiora," Volker added softly.

And then he waited until I spoke.

"Until a moment ago, I didn't even know the machine had a name," I said, listening to the vicious echoes of my voice in my own mind. It wasn't a voice to curl up and sleep with anymore.

"You know where the machine is," said Volker.

"Wrong," I said flatly. And it was the truth. I didn't know.

I was guessing. I wasn't going to hang anything I loved on a ticker tape guess.

"Fiora can hear me, Fiddler. Think about that before you make me force your cooperation."

"Does Fiora know what you did to Danny?" I asked. My voice was soft but the tones carried a certainty of violence. Like his. My goddamn image looking out of a mirror. I didn't like the view one bit. There are possibilities and parts of myself I'd just as soon not be on a first-name basis with.

"I did nothing to Danny," said Volker. "There are some things that I cannot control. Fiora's brother was one of them."

There was a minor chord of defensiveness to Volker's voice. And descant regret. The bastard had a voice like a cello, all shades of emotion—but no true feeling. *Inhuman*.

"She no longer smiles at me, Fiddler. I have nothing more to lose."

That I could understand, believe, and fear.

"Stay in the motel," said Volker. "I will call before nine o'clock tomorrow morning. Then we will make arrangements for transferring the machine."

"I don't have the OxyCon," I said.

"Then Fiora will die."

Before I could say anything, I was holding a dead phone in my hand. I held the useless receiver for a moment, then dialed the front desk. They told me that Kieu had just left. Two men in a car had picked her up. Obviously she had friends closer than San Francisco, which was nearly an hour away. Friends in Burlingame, perhaps?

I thought about what I knew and what I did not, hope and fear and facts. Danny was dead. Kieu was an unknown quantity. Volker—ah, Volker. You should not have stolen Fiora. Or is it simply that I should have taken your offer, taken Fiora for a month or two while Danny died and an OxyCon caromed between Vietnamese hatreds and Russian empire-building?

But I hadn't. I was stuck with a reality where Fiora's life would be traded for an OxyCon. My kingdom for a horse. And where was Volker's weakness, the overlooked horseshoe nail that fell out and brought a kingdom tumbling down? I waited, straining to hear the theme of Volker's weakness. Nothing came but silence and the knowledge that his only vulnerable point was a machine I didn't have and had no certain way to get. I could call the cops, of course, local, state, federal, spooks. I could call them all.

And then Volker would kill Fiora.

I knew it. He knew it. That's why he hadn't even bothered to mention it earlier. I might be driven to include the cops, but I hoped not. All cops have their own priorities, and those rarely harmonize with the needs of the victims. Lots of innocents are buried alive and then die because local cops hate to deliver ransoms without making a try for the bad guys. Lots of counterintelligence agencies, including the FBI, hate to force the security issues until every last drop of information has been wrung out.

Either way, local or national, Fiora became tangential. Like Danny.

I checked my gun automatically, started for the door, then stopped. I doubted that Volker had overlooked the obvious. On the other hand, it wouldn't be the first time that a brilliant mind had been brought to foolishness by a simple thing. I went back to the phone, dialed, and waited for the Ice Cream King to pick up the other end. He answered with a snarl, telling me that he had been asleep. Had I been in a better mood, I would have relished catching him asleep. As it was, I guess I was rather abrupt.

"Where can I buy a two-inch OxyCon 200, 50c? Tonight."

Benny knew me better than to ask questions. He simply answered my worst fears. "You can't."

"Why?"

"Fifty c means 50 cycles. That's a custom job for the Eastern Bloc."

"Why?"

"They use 50 cycle current. We use 60 cycle. You won't find a 50c OxyCon on anyone's shelf. Have to be built from scratch."

"*Shit.*"

"What's wrong, mate? You got a lot of wafers that need baking in a hurry?"

"If I did, would I want an OxyCon?"

"Depends. If you want quality stuff, reliable chips, then you have to cook the little buggers just right. You can make circuits without OxyCon, but not good ones, and not many."

"Like that two-inch wafer I showed you this morning?"

"Just like it."

"Any way to fake an OxyCon?" I asked.

"No."

"Just like that? 'No.' Maybe you could throw in a 'Let me think about it.'"

"How bad do you need it?"

"The way you need another spinal cord," I said, only realizing how brutal the words were as I heard them echo. "Benny, I'm sor—"

"Forget it. It's Fiora, isn't it?"

The man is uncanny. "How did you know?"

"She affects you that way. Me, too. What can I do for you besides build an OxyCon? Because I can't do that, Fiddler. Not by nine tomorrow morning."

That's the King. No questions about what the hell is going on, no protestations of undying friendship, just *What can I do?*

"Stay close to the phone."

I hung up before he could give me good advice. He'd already given me what I would use if I could—assassin's bullets from a French lab. But not yet. First the machine, then the man.

A red Mustang isn't ideal for skulking side streets, but it was all I had. I swung onto El Camino and drove north for Burlingame. Cool damp air from the Bay thickened around the car, too thin for true fog and too thick for air. El Camino Real runs up through the old commercial districts of former agricultural towns and then branches into bedroom communities for The City, as San Francisco is called by those who take it and themselves seriously.

I toured past twice-billionaire David Packard's little factory on Page Mill Road, and past Watkins-Johnson, such a super-secret operation that it pays its public relations department not to return phone calls. Watkins-Johnson makes communications gear mostly, custom stuff that catches signals that bounce off satellites or microwave receivers that link Rapid Deployment and Delta/Blue Light and superspook outfits with their headquarters in Crystal City and McLean and Fort Bragg. Out there where the A-Teams are rear echelon. Out there so far on the cutting edge that there's nothing ahead but the abyss.

Now, in the middle of the night, these places look just like Frito-Lay and Granny Goose and Nabisco—sprawling, well manicured, and quiet. There is a community like the Silicon Valley in the Soviet Union, Zelenograd, just outside Moscow. Zelenograd shares its protected and secure circle with the Russian aerospace workers. Volker and Korchnoi can move freely through Silicon Valley. Only the wind moves freely through Zelenograd.

I preferred to live free. I wondered whether Volker had a preference.

I wondered if he thought about it at all. There was an intellectual ruthlessness to him that equaled his charm. Had he seduced Fiora, a tough and bright and passionate woman, simply to put a tighter lock on Danny? Or had Fiora come to Volker from nowhere, a beautiful song sliding through the cold of his mind, so that everything still human in him had said *I must have this woman*.

It had been that way with me.

But Volker wasn't me. Close, very close, but not identical. He could kill Fiora. I couldn't. A small difference when you consider the myriad possibilities of countries and cultures, but it was the only difference that mattered to me.

I found a twenty-four-hour supermarket and discount store in San Mateo. Twenty minutes later, I had spent a hundred dollars on a pair of black jeans, a black sweatshirt, EZ-Off oven cleaner, Gerber folding knife, bolt cutters, and a palm-sized flashlight. I changed in a Denny's rest room, shot down a couple of cups of coffee for the caffeine, and locked most of my stuff in the trunk. The 9 mm went into the glove box. In California, armed burglary is worth ten years, no questions asked and no plea bargaining.

I got back in the car and drove the Mustang hard. Highway 101 was a freeway through most of the Bay Area but in a couple of spots business routes swung off the four-lane and into town. In Burlingame, just south of San Francisco International Airport, the business route ran down through an industrial area that looked as old as World War II. Some leftover Quonsets and one-story buildings with arched roofs still showed in the mercury vapor lamps along the street. The rest of the area was more recent—machine shops and air-freight outfits and lumber yards.

Compared to the rest, 39345 Highway 101 was quite modern. The address belonged to storage rental units. Rank on rank of one-story concrete-block buildings cut up into individual suites ranging in size from two hundred to one thousand square feet. Each unit had its own overhead rolling steel door with individual lock. In California, storage areas are used for everything from antique cars to truckloads of *sinsemilla*. The storage spaces were sort of an industrial variation of the safe-deposit box: no official curiosity so long as you keep the rent current.

This rental yard took its job seriously. Ten acres, mostly well-lighted, and surrounded by an eight-foot chain link fence that was topped with two strands of razor wire. Very discouraging to the usual round of junkies looking for a quick smash-and-grab.

I cruised the area once at normal speed and then drove down the road for five minutes. I came back a second time, a bit more slowly, driving like a guy who had just closed the local taproom and then gotten lost in his own front seat. I stopped at the front of the storage yard, looked around with exaggerated furtiveness, fumbled in my pants, and then pissed against the chain link fence. While I did, I got a good look at the razor strands. I saw no unexplained wires that could either alarm or fry me, and spotted a few numbers on storage doors. Number 12 was not one of them. The way my luck had been running tonight, 12 would be under the brightest light on the lot.

I walked around a few minutes, shaking my head and staggering from time to time, the picture of a drunk trying to get it together enough to face the California Highway Patrol on the freeway. I hung around long enough to confirm what I'd already guessed. The Vietnamese didn't trust razor wire and lights and locks to keep their treasure safe.

There was a four-door Chevrolet parked in the otherwise deserted parking lot of a tortilla factory a half block away. The car was lined up so that anyone inside had a clear view of the only vehicle entrance to the storage lot. The car's windows hadn't fogged over, though the metal of the car gleamed with condensed moisture. Somebody must be inside, body heat warming the windows enough so that the fog didn't condense. I was willing to bet the warm body—or bodies—turned out to be Vietnamese, but I wasn't going to get close enough to inspect. For my purposes, it didn't matter who warmed up windows.

The good news was that I didn't see a dog in the yard. Neither did I see a sign warning of a dog. A sign is no guarantee that there is a dog to back it up, but nobody in the security business can turn a dog loose at night without warning the dog's potential victims. I've always felt that was taking the protection of the innocent burglar to an unwarranted extreme. On the other hand, there was the second-story man who collected damages from the homeowner whose dog had eaten the burglar's ass for a midnight snack. Put up a sign and be suit-proof. No sign, no dog.

Gratefully, I jammed the EZ-Off into my hip pocket. I've never had to use the stuff. I never want to. Yet it's the only thing that's foolproof on guard dogs. Mace just pisses them off. As for pistols, even silenced ones—have you ever tried to shoot 90 to 120 pounds of black, leaping dog in the darkness? Just one shot, mind you, and no noise. If you miss, you scream. If you hit but not well enough, the dog screams. EZ-Off in the eyes makes no noise, can't miss, and the dog just wilts. You have to shoot them later, I'm told. By then, presumably, it will be safe to make noise.

Yes, I was damned glad not to use the oven cleaner. But I'd do it to a thousand dogs if they were between me and Fiora. Like the cops and Volker, I had my own priorities.

I climbed back into the Mustang and drove off, weaving just enough to keep up the image. Nobody in the Chevrolet stirred. Probably asleep. God knows it was a quiet night. I drove on down 101 for almost a mile, then cut over onto a side street and began making my way back to the yard. A half mile away from the storage yard, I stopped, took the screwdriver and flashlight, and removed the bulbs in the taillights and in the dome light. Then I drove by Braille and memory until I found a hiding place, a shadowed carport behind a filling station.

The storage lot extended from the highway all the way through the block to the street I was on. As I'd hoped, the rear of the lot was not lighted as well as the front. I found some shelter along one edge of the fence where I could work without being visible from the street. The night had gotten damper. Shreds of fog were starting to settle around the street lamps, blurring the hard edges of light and darkness. Even two miles away, the jet airliners on the runways reverberated like thunder as the moisture amplified their engine noise. I could feel the folded Gerber in my hip pocket, the smooth handles of the bolt cutters in my right hand. And the fence, cold and rough, sweating chill moisture in the night.

The razor wire was tightly strung. It vibrated when I put the cutters to it. I let the wire settle down, then made a quick cut next to one of the stanchions. The first strand was hardened. Rattles shivered down its entire length before the cutters bit through. The second wire was easier. I moved the razor edges aside. But I was impatient. I cut myself even through the gloves I'd bought.

The whole secret to work like this is to take it slowly. I repeated that fact at least one hundred times in the next ten minutes while I watched from the shadows, making sure I hadn't tripped a silent alarm on the fence. Nothing came, though. No security guard, no alarm-company patrol unit, and no local cop. Not even any sound from the Chevrolet, which I could see if I changed positions a dozen yards. Nothing was attracted to me but the fog, which settled around me cool as death.

So I went over the fence. It took me about fifteen seconds, and I was drenched with sweat when I hit the other side. I slid into the nearest shadows, yanked the EZ-Off out of my pocket and waited. No sniffing sounds came toward me through the night. No feral growls. No snick of claws on cement. No dog.

Keeping to the shadows, I eased through the storage lot. There were a dozen buildings, serially numbered. Each storage slot was numbered as well. Twelve-one was the first slot in the building that was closest to the back fence. The overhead light was at the other end of the building. Luck evens out, sometimes.

Most of these storage yards have been built in the past five years, usually as short-term investments. Fiora had lectured me about them, telling me that they were really temporary land uses while an area was in transition. The investment packagers who'd put together the storage yards had cut every corner they could while still maintaining the appearance of security. Why not? After five or seven years, short-term depreciation, the whole thing would be written off and razed.

These storage units were no different, thank God. The metal doors were impressive as hell, and the padlocks were new brass, very shiny even in the bad light. But the framing timbers around the doors were only two-by-fours and the locks would have been easy to jimmy. Even more important, the door to 12-1 was so ill-fitting that I could see the steel plates of a contact alarm. Whoever opened that door without first keying off the alarm would be in for a bout of deafness.

I swore but wasn't really discouraged. I hadn't expected it to be easy. I had the forces of law on my side—the law that required builders to ventilate anything people were going to be walking around inside of. There are three ways to comply with the law: windows; a fancy, machine-driven air-circulation system; or a hole covered with some kind of metal grate to keep out the mice.

The hole was below the roof line, under the eaves. I tried it without the light first, but couldn't see anything. I put my palm over the flashlight, opened a space between my second and third fingers to allow a tiny pencil beam of light to pass, directed the light through the grid and got ready to run like hell. Nobody yelled. Nobody stirred. If there was somebody baby-sitting the machine inside, he was either asleep or dead.

I played the light around inside and blessed the avarice of builders, who had built the little boxes with ceilings so low I'd have to walk barefoot or bend over or both. The storage bay in 12-1 was fifteen feet deep and six feet across. It was also empty, except for a single shipping case pushed against the corner farthest from the big door. The bare, rough pine that made the crate was new. The nails were big and shiny. The whole thing reminded me unpleasantly of a pauper's coffin, except bigger. Four feet square and perhaps six feet long.

I looked around the rest of the bay. I saw just enough of the edge of the bay door to confirm my guess that there was a contact alarm attached. There was one other thing in the room, too. I looked as long as I dared, but couldn't quite figure out what the hell the other item was. It looked like a furnace filter standing close to the box. Whatever it was, it wasn't a random piece of junk. The Vietnamese were a tidy lot. Not so much as a dirty footprint on the cement floor.

I snapped off the light and faded back into the shadows, feeling frustrated and more than a bit angry. The OxyCon oven was considerably larger than the microwave-sized item I'd hoped for. No way to ease in there and sneak out with the machine on my back. No smash-and-grab this time. It was a truck job or nothing at all.

While my eyes had readjusted to the dark, I thought of all the variations on the theme of getting one OxyCon by morning. I could approach Kieu and offer to buy the damn thing. I doubted she'd sell for love or money, though. Danny's death hadn't moved her to tears. I didn't see how

Fiora's would. I could only guess what Kieu intended to do with the machine. None of the guesses added up to holding Fiora alive in my arms again. As for the cops, nothing had changed there. They had different priorities. Like Volker. Like me.

I did a quick tour of the shadows around the storage yard, letting variations on the theme grow in my mind. Each of the twelve separate buildings had twelve storage bays, six on a side. Some had advertising signs on them, indicating that they were being used as low-rent work spaces by everything from cabinetmakers to Roto-Rooter operators. A number of the bays were unoccupied. Their doors bore stickers saying: FOR RENT.

I came back down the opposite side of building number 12. Bays 1 and 2 were occupied. So were the rest of the bays, except for 11 and 12. The latter shared a common back wall with the bay that contained the OxyCon in 12-1. In my head, I began making a list of things I would need. I made and remade the list, knowing that only one thing was wrong with it: Come nine o'clock tomorrow, I still wouldn't have the OxyCon.

So I tried arranging the list another way as I headed back to the opening I had hacked in the razor wire. No matter how I lined up the elements, though, one fact came out the same. Not enough time. No way, Fiddler. No way in hell.

I leaped up, grabbed a handful of fence, and clawed my way over the top. I landed lightly, knees flexed, everything by the book—except for the gun screwed into my left ear and the other gun gnawing on my right rib.

Nine o'clock had never looked more impossible.

11

Hands up, asshole," said a voice.

"Move and you're dead," said another voice.

The first voice, the one that came from the direction of the gun in my ribs, belonged to Sharp. His Oklahoma twang, then his low chuckle were unmistakable. I didn't laugh with him, though. From the corner of my eye, I had recognized the other man I wanted to see least in the world—the gray, featureless man from Fiora's office. Another player added to the orchestra pit. It was getting crowded there. My secret hopes for a quiet round of chamber music were going quickly.

"Take your pick," I said. "Hands up or don't move. Which one of you is the head honcho?"

"That's easy," said the gray man. Then he chuckled.

I didn't move. I noticed right away that Sharp didn't shoot me for not putting up my hands. The gray man seemed to be in charge. It was almost a relief. Almost. I've been arrested a time or two, but this was out of the ordinary. I felt like a pork chop between two hungry wolves.

Sharp frisked me very quickly, but thoroughly enough to have included the tops of the boots he remembered I wore. He took the Gerber and the tools.

"I thought I told you to stay home," said Sharp under his breath as he pocketed my Gerber.

"You should have listened, cowboy," said the gray man.

Since he still had the gun screwed in my ear, I didn't argue.

They holstered their guns and pointed me in the direction of the street. We kept to the shadows. They, too, seemed to know about the Vietnamese surveillance. There was a Plymouth sedan parked at the curb, lights out but engine running. A third man stood at the front door, waiting. The man had medium short hair, no mustache or beard, a neutral shade of windbreaker and jeans. He moved like an athlete, but was otherwise as nondescript as the gray man who had stuck the gun in my ear.

"Where's your car, Fiddler," said Sharp.

Not a question, really. A command. "Over behind the service station."

"Keys." Sharp held out his hand.

I dug out the Hertz key ring and turned it over to Sharp. He flipped it to the man who stood by the Plymouth.

"Why don't you get it, Sharp," said the gray man. "Don and I will take care of this clown."

Sharp gave him a look that cut deep, even in the dark. "Joint case, joint custody. Remember, Innes? That's what the attorney general said." There was steel in Sharp's voice. "And we aren't taking Fiddler down to the Federal Building, either."

"What did you have in mind?" Innes said softly, but there was an edge of impatience and anger to his voice.

Score one for Sharp. It was the first show of emotion from the gray man known as Innes. I watched the verbal shoving match with real interest, trying to forget the fate of the pork chop no matter which wolf won.

"Fiddler's a civilian," said Sharp. "You know it and I know it. He's either clean or too smart for you, because we don't have shit on him. As of this minute," Sharp shrugged, "he hasn't broken any federal laws that I know of. Why don't we all go get a cup of coffee?"

"He's messing around with a high-level federal case," said Innes. "That's called interfering with a federal officer."

"Balls. He'd be on the street again before you finished filling out forms. Innes, I know this old boy. You pull your usual chickenshit federal god routine on him, and all you'll get is more trouble than he's worth." Sharp turned away. "Get in the car, Fiddler," he said, opening the front door of the Plymouth.

I slid into the front seat like a good old boy. Sharp sat behind the wheel. Innes had no choice but to take the backseat or my lap. The other man hesitated, then walked toward the garage and my Mustang. Sharp pulled away from the curb. He waited four blocks before he snapped on his headlights.

Nobody said anything during the drive down 101. Sharp pulled into the parking lot of a twenty-four-hour coffee shop, where the old highway rejoined the Bayshore Freeway. We got out, went inside, and headed for a back booth. I slid in on one side, positioned myself in the middle, and forced the two of them to sit side by side, facing me. The waitress brought three coffees and disappeared while Sharp fished a pack of cigarettes out of the pocket of his shirt.

Sharp lighted up, exhaled a long stream, and closed his eyes as he rubbed a blunt hand through his salt-and-pepper hair. He looked a hell of a lot older than when I had seen him yesterday morning. He clearly didn't do as well on allnighters as he had when he used to chase Uncle Jake along the border. The bags under Sharp's eyes were as pronounced as the deep creases in his desert-tanned face. He was going to be an old man, someday. Soon.

Innes was about the same age as Sharp, mid- to late forties. But Innes was in better shape; probably because he wasn't a smoker. His brown-gray hair was well cut, his face almost patrician. He had the look and manners of an eastern Anglo-Saxon, but he wasn't an Ivy League type, more New Jersey than New England, clearly more FBI than any other kind of cop I could think of, but not as narrow as most cops. I suppose counterintelligence work broadens you. Innes was shrewd and self-assured, but he wasn't a man used to walking ridgelines and listening to the long silences of open country. He wasn't a Westerner. Sharp was. I wondered whether that was one source of the obvious friction between them.

Sharp took a long drag on his cigarette. "Well, did you find it?"

"Ask me something a lawyer would want me to answer," I said. "Admitting to trespass isn't on the list."

Innes made an impatient sound. The corner of Sharp's mouth lifted in a small smile. "This here guy," Sharp pointed with his thumb at Innes, "don't deal in anything less than high treason. Trespass and burglary are a way of life for him."

"You sound jealous," I said.

Sharp took another drag, tipped back his head, and blew out a long dirty plume. "It makes his job easy sometimes," Sharp said. "And sometimes it makes it hard. I once served a no-knock search warrant and got my ass whipped by a cocksman who happened to be screwing the suspect's wife. I went back to doing things by the book."

Innes took a sip of coffee and grimaced. He shot me a look out of very intelligent, very hard eyes. "What do you know about the death of Danny Flynn?"

"Is Danny dead?" I asked, sipping coffee.

"You know he is," said Innes. "He was shot yesterday afternoon about six. You were seen leaving his apartment about an hour later."

I made a mental note to revise my estimation of the two guys I had seen in the cul-de-sac. They had made me in the dark, clear back at the parking lot.

"How do you know when he was shot?" I asked. "There hasn't been enough time for an autopsy."

"I was talking to him on the phone," said Sharp, ignoring Innes's hard look. "Flynn was trying to roll over so we could scratch his tummy when somebody came in and blew him to hell. The killer used a silencer, but I could hear the shots. That's how close he stood to Flynn."

I closed my eyes and felt older than Sharp looked. Danny had finally understood that this was one scrape he couldn't smile his way out of. But the understanding came too late. He must have panicked when the machine turned up missing, so he decided to save his tender little ass by snitching off Korchnoi and Volker. Only Korchnoi had killed him— and Volker had taken Fiora as insurance against what he knew I would do to whoever had murdered Fiora's twin.

"How did you know where the machine was?" I asked.

"Danny," said Innes.

"Bullshit," I said quietly. "Danny didn't know."

Sharp chuckled, but it wasn't a pleasant sound. "You're gonna love this, Fiddler. Go ahead, Innes, tell him why Danny Flynn died. Then Fiddler can go home and tell Danny's sister and we can go back to watching fog and shadows."

"Listen, Sharp—" began Innes.

"*Tell him*," said Sharp.

I looked at the two men. Innes was as uncomfortable as a man sitting on a very pointed fence. Apparently Sharp obeyed Innes sometimes, and sometimes Innes gave in to Sharp. The rest of the time they pushed and shoved and snarled at each other.

"Sharp, you're dealing way over your head," Innes snapped. "You're getting into areas that have 'top secret' stamped all over them."

"Ah, crap." Sharp mashed out his cigarette. He turned to me, disgust in every line bracketing his mouth. "The FBI has known about the OxyCon for six months. This manufacturer tipped them when an order for a shitlisted 50-cycle machine came in. The Bureau's counterintelligence corps decided to roll up the pipeline all the way to its beginning. To do that, they had to let the machine be delivered."

I waited, wondering why Sharp was so disgusted. It was common practice to stake out the bait in hopes of catching the real predators. Hell, Sharp had spent a lifetime doing just that, following dope from Mexico to cutting rooms in LA, wrapping up buyers and sellers and middlemen from one end of the thousand-mile pipeline to the other. So why was he riding Innes for doing the same thing?

"When the Feebees started their own investigation, they cut my sign right away," continued Sharp. "I was working a smuggling case out of Calexico and was about two steps from throwing Flynn's candy ass in jail, but the Feebees wanted more than Danny Flynn. So here we are, Innes and Sharp, Feebee and Customs, God's own shotgun marriage." He made a disgusted sound and reached for another cigarette. "But the longer we're married, the less I can figure out what I ever did see in him in the first place." Sharp looked sideways and drawled, "He don't take orders no better than a blind mule."

"Sharp, take that country boy act and shove it up your smart ass," Innes snarled.

Sharp smiled, lighted his cigarette, and shut up. His mother hadn't raised any dumb ones.

Innes wasn't stupid, either. He realized that Sharp had found out what I knew by letting me ask a few questions. That's the hell of asking questions; you have to give away a lot in order to get an answer.

"All right, Fiddler," Innes said. "You're not bad, for a civilian."

Sharp's laugh was soft, mocking.

"You've gotten a lot further a lot faster than we expected," Innes continued, ignoring the laughter. "So you know that the OxyCon is one end of a very long, very complicated thread that we've been unraveling. If you'll agree to stay the hell out of the way, I'll pay for your coffee, give you back your car, and wave good-bye. Otherwise," Innes shrugged, "I'll just tuck your butt into a federal can for the duration." He smiled. "Protective custody, Fiddler. After all, one witness has already died."

Sharp turned and watched me with pale, narrowed eyes. Smoke trickled from his nostrils and curled up from the cigarette held between two scarred knuckles. I remembered what he had said about why Danny died.

"Tell me why Danny died, then I'll go."

"Sharp—" began Innes.

"So divorce me, baby," said Sharp, his voice as hard and worn as his face. "Because I'm gonna tell him. He'll be a lot less trouble that way. And God knows we have all the trouble we need right now."

Innes muttered something straight from Jersey sewers, but he didn't interfere. Apparently he had learned during the shotgun marriage which things were worth arguing over and which weren't. It was a valuable thing to learn. Fiora and I hadn't managed that until too late.

"You ready, Fiddler?" asked Sharp, his eyes narrowed against the rising smoke.

I didn't answer, because Sharp didn't expect me to. He was already talking, telling me why Danny Flynn had died.

"See, the Feebees wanted to give this little surprise party when the bad guys picked up the machine and tried to sneak it out of the country," said Sharp. "It would have been a dandy party, too. But they got too clever. When things started to go sour, instead of cutting their losses and grabbing what they had, the Feebees decided to get complicated."

Innes made an impatient noise, telling me that we were getting to the crux of a long-running argument.

"The machine never got delivered to the bad guys," Sharp finished. "It ended up over in this storage yard. The top end of the pipeline, the end Innes was sweating to get his hands on, is out of reach. Instead of Russians with fancy titles, all we've got now is a bunch of Vietnamese that nobody gives a damn about. But do we wrap it up? Do we grab the goddamn machine and get in the wind? Shit, no. We sit on our thumbs and wait for someone to come along and take the machine away from us the same way it was taken from the Russians."

"That's not possible," snapped Innes. "We're covering that machine from every angle."

"You think the Russians weren't?" asked Sharp sarcastically, killing the cigarette with a single blunt motion.

"Look," said Innes, oozing patience between clenched teeth. "We've been over it a hundred times. We can still salvage the operation. When we're done, the Soviets will be right in front of the fan, and we'll turn that mother on to full power."

Wrong. Fiora would be the one in front of the fan. But I didn't say anything. There was the feeling of international power politics about all of this, and like a smart coon sniffing around a koi pond, I realized it.

"I thought that keeping the machine here was the important thing," I said, looking into the muddy depths of the coffee, "not smearing shit over everyone in reach."

Sharp's lips thinned into a hard smile. Innes's eyes narrowed. Bingo. The bottom line. Sharp was an old hand, a border cop whose job was as clear as spines on a cactus: Grab the goods and the smugglers and let the politics go hang. Innes came from the new school: Grab it all, and be sure you have a reporter along to spell your name right.

I knew, even as I thought it, that I was being unfair to Innes. If he could get the Russians, more power to him. In the long run, it was the only efficient way to solve the problem of high tech smuggling. That was a forebrain thought. The hindbrain hadn't forgotten Fiora, a woman being used like a five-dollar chip in a no-limit game. For a moment I considered telling Innes about Fiora. The moment passed quickly. I wasn't sanguine about the prospects of Fiora surviving an international power struggle waged between Volker and Innes.

"We are in a position to monitor the Vietnamese negotiations with the Russians very closely," said Innes, his voice neutral. "When all this is over, we'll be able to demonstrate the scope of Soviet espionage efforts in Silicon Valley. It has already been decided that this case will not be handled quietly. We will force the closure of the San Francisco consulate here. Do you remember when the French expelled forty-six Soviet diplomats?"

"Yes," I said. My voice didn't sound like me. The more I heard, the less I wanted to hear. Fiora, my beautiful woman, caught in the fault zone between two continental plates. Fiora, ground to nothing at all in the massive, ponderous movement of international politics. The thought shouldn't have shocked me. It wouldn't be the first or the last time people died for being in the wrong place, wrong moment, wrong everything.

But this time it was Fiora.

"What the French did in 1983," continued Innes calmly, "will look like a love feast compared to when we start trucking Russians out of San Francisco, New York, and Washington."

I didn't say anything. I didn't look at anything but the dregs of my coffee settling down the stained sides of the cup. Then I saw that my knuckles were white from the death grip I had on the mug. Very carefully, I set it down. I had a lot to do between now and nine o'clock. I couldn't get any of it done if I was sitting in handcuffs somewhere.

"Hooray for our side," I said. I stood up. "I'll tell Fiora that her brother died for his country."

Sharp's smile was quick and cruel, the smile of a hunter.

Innes looked at me for a long moment. He was a good enough cop to know when something was going on. But he was also a man in an international fault zone. Like Fiora. Pressure from both sides, squeezing. If Innes lost this game, he wouldn't die—but he'd wish he had.

"Does this mean that you're going to leave everything to our resources and expertise?" asked Innes dryly.

Outside the glass window, shadows and fog reigned supreme. Dawn wasn't even a possibility. I could see the red Mustang by the curb where the other FBI agent had parked it. He was sitting at the counter now, drinking coffee and waiting for his boss to utilize him as a resource or an expert.

Two other men had joined him. I had the feeling there probably were a half dozen more back in the woodwork somewhere. Everyone was wearing jackets or windbreakers or long shirts that covered the guns in holsters in the small of the back or under the armpit. The sleepy waitress was filling sugar jars, and the cook was wiping grease from the stainless-steel order wheel. They would have been shocked to know they were in the presence of more pistols than you find in the average pawnshop. None of them were Saturday Night Specials, either. These were .357 Magnum and Walther P 38. They belonged to the kind of men you don't underestimate, if you expect to survive.

For all the good it did Fiora, they might as well be Boy Scouts throwing marshmallows.

"Tell me, Innes," I said. I knew I should shut up, but there was a wild kind of anger clawing at me, demanding to get out. "Is one of the Soviets Danny died to expose a blocky man with no hair and a silenced Tokarev?"

The pupils of Innes's eyes dilated as he examined me with new interest, no doubt wondering how I knew about the Tokarev, the silencer, and all the rest.

"Sounds like Korchnoi," said Sharp. "He's the chief cultural attaché at the consulate here."

"Is he the most important one?"

"He has the highest rank on paper."

Innes and I looked at each other. Both of us knew that with the Russians, titles and power often didn't march in sync. Chauffeurs were also KGB officers.

"That should make a nice clipping for Fiora's scrapbook," I said. I threw fifty cents on the table, price of a bad cup of coffee. "Give me the keys, and I'll be on my way. With luck, neither of us will ever see the other again."

Innes hesitated. Sharp looked at me. Innes looked at Sharp. Sharp shrugged, but for all the casualness of the gesture, his eyes watched me with the unblinking interest of a hungry snake.

One of the agents from the counter approached. He wore a pair of glasses. Nothing unusual, until you looked closely and saw what looked like hearing aids attached behind the ears. As surveillance radios go, this one was pretty good. But a Sony Walkman would have been a bit more in touch with the times. Nobody would look twice at someone sauntering down the street wearing his own electronic cocoon.

The agent motioned Innes away from the table. They conferred for a moment with their backs to us. Sharp yawned and stretched like a man coming to the end of his endurance. He rubbed his hair and muttered random obscenities. But his eyes were clear, feral, a hunter's eyes. He looked at me and smiled. It wasn't a comforting gesture.

Innes returned to the booth. He didn't sit down. Something was stirring out there that needed his attention, shadows sliding through shadows, making the skin beneath his holster itch.

"Good-bye, Fiddler," said Innes. "You better hope we don't meet again."

I looked at Innes for a long time, wondering whether all FBI agents had their facial hair removed by electrolysis. It had probably been twenty-four hours since Innes had shaved, but somehow the stubble didn't show on his face like it did on Sharp's or, I supposed, on mine.

"Why should we meet?" I said. "You don't need any amateurs. You've got plenty of men, and they all have guns and
badges and radios. What more can you ask?" I smiled. It
must not have been a nice smile, because Sharp came to a
point. Innes didn't like it either, but he let it go.

"Just so I don't find you crawling around in storage yards
in the middle of the night again," Innes shot back.

I shook my head. "No way, baby. No way in hell."

Innes hesitated, clearly pulled between me and the
urgency of whatever the agent had told him. Abruptly,
Innes turned to Sharp. "If Wonder Boy here screws up, it's
your ass."

Sharp shrugged and yawned. He took a long swallow of
his coffee.

"Wrap it up, Sharp," said Innes impatiently.

Sharp studied his coffee cup for a moment. There were a
few stray grounds in the bottom of it. He examined them as
carefully as any man ever examined tea leaves.

"Tell you what," Sharp said finally, yawning again. "Let
me have a car. I have a couple of calls to make. I'll use the
phone over at the Customs office at the airport. I'll catch up
with you later."

"How do you know where we'll be?" Innes asked. "We
may have to move fast."

"That's why Uncle gave us radios," said Sharp. "If you
leave me a car, it'll have a radio, right? Then I'll just use that
little old radio to call you, and it will all be real simple."

Innes started to object.

Sharp stood up suddenly. "Just give me a goddamn set of
keys, will you? I'm getting real tired of this my-cock-is-big-
ger-than-your-cock game."

Innes glared at him for a moment, then surrendered the
keys to the Plymouth.

"Thanks," Sharp said, as he pocketed them.

"My pleasure," said Innes.

Both of them meant it. They were tired of living with
each other. Sharp stalked out the door of the coffee shop. By
the time I had the keys to my Mustang, the Plymouth was
gone. I watched the FBI climb into cars and vanish. I

stayed put at the booth for a few minutes, watching everyone drive into the seamless night. I walked out to the Mustang, listening carefully for a door to open, footsteps to
follow. Nothing but fog and the cool feel of the Mustang's
door handle against my palm.

I stood for a minute, thinking of ways to persuade Volker
not to kill Fiora.

Nothing came to me. A dirge filled all the spaces of my
brain. That and rage. There was a lot of that banging
around. I got into the Mustang and sat there for a couple of
minutes until I spotted the surveillance car. It was parked at
the curb on a side street where the driver could eyeball the
coffee shop parking lot. I could even see him backlighted by
a bare bulb above the door of a machine shop.

I started the Mustang, pulled across the road, and onto
the side street. I parked directly opposite the Plymouth.
Then I shut off the lights, dragged the Detonics out of the
glove box, locked the door behind me, and crossed the little
street. Not much of the dirge was left, but anger was; a
drumroll of sound like adrenaline in my blood. Somewhere
nearby a rainbird sprinkler worked rhythmically over a
lawn, delicate counterpoint to the rushing in my arteries.

I yanked open the passenger door. "Your place or mine,"
I said as I slid onto the seat. It wasn't a question. It was
more in the nature of a command.

Sharp sat upright, sighed, and pulled out a cigarette.

"Your place, Fiddler," he said after a moment. "I don't
have one in this end of the world. But my car, OK? It's a
damn sight less flashy and Uncle pays for the gas."

"I've got some gear in the trunk," I said, sliding out
again. No light came on as I exited. Sharp had been busy
removing bulbs, too.

I emptied out the Mustang and went back to Sharp. Neither one of us spoke. He didn't need directions to my
motel, and I didn't feel like making cute conversation.

Sharp drove like a man with an immunity to speeding
tickets. Which, I suppose, he had. The Plymouth was a
quality machine, as was everything else the FBI used. The
car had a big engine. Even better, someone had thoughtfully

removed the smog control equipment from the V-eight. That, plus professional quality suspension, made it a mean pursuit car. Sharp ran it up to eighty and held it there like a gambler crossing the Mojave on his way to Vegas.

We pulled into yet another parking lot. Sometimes I think the road to hell is paved with parking lots. I took out my gear and headed for my room without waiting for Sharp. I unlocked my door, walked in, and heard Sharp slam it shut behind me. I turned around.

"OK, Fiddler, school's out. Tell me what Innes doesn't know."

12

I didn't have to think about my answer. I'd known what was coming since I'd spotted Sharp in the Plymouth. Innes might have believed my kiss-off. Sharp hadn't. In some ways I was like my dead Uncle Jake, and Sharp had known Jake the way a hunter knows his prey. Short of love, there's no greater knowing, no greater intimacy. That, too, Jake had taught me. Sharp was my prey. I was his.

I picked up my violin and began to play, hunting through variations to find the one that would snare a border man called Aaron Sharp.

"How would you like to get a shotgun divorce?" I asked. "And while you're doing it, how would you like to make the biggest case of your career, up to and including a personal citation from the President?"

"I'd rather have a good quail dog," said Sharp dryly.

"You may have to shoot some people," I added, ignoring his comment about the dog.

"Innes?" asked Sharp, narrowed eyes watching me.

"I had in mind a Russian or two."

Sharp shrugged. "These days you take what you can get."

He looked at me. I looked at him. Slowly, the wariness and fighting edge left him. Truce. He pulled out a cigarette, lighted it, and took a long drag. I didn't move.

"What's in it for you, Fiddler?" asked Sharp, sending out a dense stream of smoke. "And don't wave the flag at me. If it was the flag, you'd have bowed out the first time you saw Innes's credentials."

"Call it revenge."

His pale, shrewd eyes measured me again. "For what? You didn't like that candy-ass Flynn any better than I did."
152

"He was Fiora's twin."

Sharp hesitated, smoking, thinking about it. Then he shook his head slowly. "Not good enough, Fiddler."

I hadn't really expected it to be, but it was worth a try. "Do you know a man called Volker?"

Sharp nodded. "Blond, quick, a player. Owns Omnitronix."

"He's Russian, not German."

Sharp nodded.

"He's KGB."

Sharp's eyes narrowed, and the cigarette glowed as though he had taken a quick breath. He waited with the patience every hunter learns.

"Volker has Fiora," I said. "He'll trade her for the OxyCon."

With a sigh, Sharp took out the cigarette and measured its glow. "Shit Marie," he said, sighing again. Then he shook his head. "No matter how pretty the little lady is, I just can't give that machine to the Russians. Sorry, Fiddler."

"I'm planning on walking out of there with Fiora *and* the OxyCon."

"So are the Russians, I'd bet."

"Then they'll lose. Either Fiora walks away or no one does."

I tried to keep my voice level but something in the timbre alerted him. He heard the truth of what I said and something more. Something predatory.

"I read your file," said Sharp slowly. "The divorce wasn't contested. So what's Fiora to you, Fiddler?"

"I've asked myself that question at least once a day for ten years."

"Any answer?"

"I'll kill for her, Sharp, and she's not even mine. Is that an answer?"

"It's the only one that matters." He swore softly beneath his breath, a tangled, oddly musical mixture of English and Spanish. He ran his hand through his hair, then gave me a look from pale eyes. "Why didn't you say something to Innes?"

"Innes has his job to do," I said. "He'd be sorry if Fiora was killed, but it wouldn't matter all that much to him. Like Danny."

Sharp chuckled dryly. "Yeah, Innes is a cold son of a bitch. It's the only thing about him I like." Sharp took a last drag on his cigarette. "I suppose you have a plan," he said neutrally.

"Yeah, but it isn't as complicated as Innes's," I said.

"Good. You don't need a goddamn roundup crew to catch a cow in a corral," said Sharp in a disgusted voice.

I began to allow myself the first easy breath I'd had since I'd come over the fence and under the federal guns. As I'd hoped, Sharp was more than a little disenchanted with the FBI's elaborate sting operation. Stings are fine, for a while. And then they go bad. This one had that smell about it, like a skunk in an outhouse.

"OK, Fiddler. Let's hear it."

"Rent 12-12. Cut through the wall to 12-1. Load up that bastard and run for the hills. You're the shooter. I'm the bait. You get the machine and the glory. The Russians get dumped in their shoes. Innes gets his scandal. And I take Fiora and get in the wind."

Sharp's dry laughter curled through the room. It was music to me, though, the sound of a man who enjoyed what he was thinking about. "I like you, Fiddler. Too bad you didn't take after your Uncle Jake. We could have had some fine times out there on the desert east of Calexico, hunting one another."

I waited, knowing as well as Sharp did that that's what we were doing now. Hunting one another.

Sharp smiled at me. "You've got twenty-four hours, Fiddler. After that, Innes will get real restless and wonder why the hell you and me disappeared together. That old boy is dumb like a fox."

I nodded. A day was more time than Volker had given me.

"But, Fiddler—"

I waited, tensed, even though Sharp was too far away for me to jump him before he got the gun out of his holster.

"Don't misunderstand me. I'm not against Innes. I just don't think his fancy plan will work. In fact, I think there's a good chance he'll step on his cock and the Russians will get the damned machine after all."

"I know."

Sharp nodded.

"Anything to be done now?" asked Sharp, smothering a yawn as he turned his back on me.

He wasn't worried about me running out on him. Not now. Not while Volker had Fiora. Sharp knew I needed him. I needed a shooter who wouldn't get buck fever when a man's head showed in the sniper scope.

"I have a few calls to make," I said. "Then Volker has to get in touch."

I picked up the phone and waited for the desk to answer. "Would you check my bill?" I asked. "I made a phone call tonight, long distance, but I've lost the number."

While I waited, Sharp pulled off his boots and loosened the big turquoise buckle on his belt. He shucked off the shoulder holster, put it on the bedside table, then pulled the gun out a few inches and put it back again, making sure the weapon wouldn't hang up on the leather if he made a fast grab.

I picked up a pen and one of the sheets of writing paper the motel had left lying on the plastic dresser. The desk came back on the line and gave me the number Kieu had called earlier. It seemed more like days than hours had passed since then. Adrenaline will do that to you. I wrote down the number Kieu had called, then gave the clerk Benny's number. The Ice Cream King answered on the first ring.

"What do you need?" he asked.

A hell of a way to answer the phone.

"You tell me," I said. "There's one contact alarm, but I'm not worried about it because I'm not going in that way. What worries me is something that looks like a weird furnace filter. The box I want is in a corner, and this gizmo is in front of the box. Nothing connects the gizmo with anything else. No wires, no beams of light, no funny noises."

"Sounds like you're up against an IR or microwave system. Probably IR. Probably cheap, too, if what you saw really was a reflector. A good passive system only costs a couple grand more, for God's—"

"Save it for a magazine article. Just give me a shopping list."

Benny hesitated. I wasn't usually so abrupt.

"Right," he said. "Okay, first you have to locate the transmitter. Get a good, dark red photo filter. Number 24 ought to do it. A camera supply house should have it. If not, try a scientific supply outlet. And while you're about it, get a twenty-foot roll of coated Mylar, like photographers use for bounce lighting."

I was writing fast, way ahead of him now, adding to the list.

"You're also going to need a Husqvarna saw," said Benny.

I grunted and kept writing. After a while, he ran out of items. Our lists matched right down to the big dolly to haul out the machine on.

"No guarantees," finished Benny. "You could have trouble matching that reflector. The Mylar should do it, unless the projector is using the really long IR wavelengths. If you can't spot anything through the Number 24 filter, assume you have a microwave system. No problem. Buy a microwave oven, pull the door, and use it as a reflector. Anything else?"

"I hope not. Thanks, Benny. I owe you."

"Like bloody hell," he snorted. "If the Mylar doesn't work, I'll go your bail."

He hung up before I could. I looked at the dead phone. I wasn't comforted by the fact that the Mylar was more in the nature of an experiment than a sure thing. When I looked up, Sharp was watching me.

"Any more calls to make?" he asked.

"No."

"Now what?"

I shrugged. "We wait for the stores to open or Volker to call, whichever comes first."

"Then it's sack time," said Sharp, yawning.

He sat up and dug in the little leather bag he had carried with him into the room. He came up with a chased silver hip flask. He unscrewed the top, took a belt, then offered the flask to me. Light ran over the flask lovingly, the kind of polish that comes from age and handling. I sniffed at the mouth of the flask. Scotch, single malt.

"Royal Salute," said Sharp.

"Amen," I murmured, rolling thē liquor around on my tongue. Potent, incredible, as smooth as the best Bordeaux.

"A half-century old," added Sharp, enjoying my appreciation of the Scotch.

"Passed down from father to son?" I asked, holding out the flask to him.

"After a fashion," said Sharp, taking the flask and a drink in the same easy motion. "My daddy inherited a truckload of it a long time ago."

I made a sound that was halfway between a hiss and a sigh. I could already feel the Scotch passing through the semipermeable membranes of my body directly into my blood, sliding into the brain like a symphony by Orpheus.

"Daddy was a Customs line rider back in Prohibition Days," said Sharp. He lay back on the pillow and closed his eyes. "Down in the desert. Long time ago, that was. Longer than any lifetime should be." Without looking, Sharp held out the flask to me. "He rode three-week horseback patrols for fifty bucks a month plus two dollars a day for ammunition and oats."

Sounded fair to me, but then I didn't have to do it. I took another swallow, let music wash through every cell of my body.

"Right before Repeal, he stumbled across a truck mired down in a sand wash east of Jacumba," Sharp said, his voice low and easy, an echo of the Scotch spreading through him. "Two men with the truck. One was a bootlegger, and the other was a hijacker. It must have been an even fight, because they both were dead. The truck was full of casks of Royal Salute. Daddy purely loved that stuff. He stashed the load in a nearby cave. It's been there ever since. A little less each year, but enough that my grandson's first legal drink will be the finest Scotch God ever made."

I took another sip. I could feel myself coming apart. Maybe I'd be able to sleep after all. I handed back the flask and sat on the second bed. In the silence I heard the small sounds of Sharp taking a drink and then capping the flask once again. I lay back myself, letting the Scotch kill a few brain cells.

The remaining cells struggled with warring thoughts; the world changes, and the more it changes, the more it stays the same. Sharp's father rode horses and shot it out with bootleggers, yet felt no compunction about drinking their product. Sharp drank the same Scotch and chased another kind of contraband, a machine he hadn't the slightest use for. Not much sense in that, if you want to examine it real close. Or maybe it all makes more sense than anything in the world. Hunters and hunted and a desert as big as the universe.

"Fiddler?"

"I'm here."

"Make no mistake," Sharp said softly. "I'm taking this ride for one reason. That machine. It stays in the U.S. if I have to shoot you and that pretty lady myself."

"I know."

"Yeah, I figured you did. But I had to be sure. I owe Jake that much."

Before I could ask why, I heard Sharp's breathing change and knew that he was asleep. If I called his name he'd wake up all in a piece, ready to go. Cops, like doctors, get used to going from sleep to full alert and back again within the space of a few breaths. I was the same way, usually. But I wasn't a cop or a doctor. I was a man looking for something to kill.

I closed my eyes and willed myself into unconsciousness, hoping I would find Fiora there. I reached out for sleep as though it were an old silver flask waiting to be emptied of dreams. Fiora was there, but she was wrapped in somber music. Other people would have dreamed words, but not me. My perfect pitch heard every note of fear and grief pouring from her mouth. I picked up my violin and played for her, trying to wrap her in beauty, but my fingers were filled with sand and the bow kept dissolving.

I woke up in a cold sweat. The clock on the bedside table said five forty-five. I knew I would not sleep again.

I got up, feeling as though I were still mired in my dream. My reflexes were shot. Not Scotch. Fear and futility. Like a Cobra that had been throttled down too long, I needed to run hard for a time. I swapped jeans and boots for shorts and running shoes. Sharp never stirred as I left the room. Probably he had already factored my restlessness into his subconscious alarm system.

Outside, the dawn mist and coolness were like a benediction. I set out along the road that ran behind the motel, first walking to loosen my muscles and then jogging slowly. After a few minutes I began to feel a little better, more natural, less existential. Directly behind the motel was an open field that was bordered by a dirt farm road. Just beyond was a grove of flat-topped plum trees, their leaves dark green and their fruit a slightly lighter color.

As I approached I heard the sound of running water. It welled up from the short concrete standpipes at the ends of each orderly orchard row. Streams of silver water leaped toward the furrows with a liquid sound. The sun was balanced on the hilltop. Smokelike tendrils of mist rose when sunlight suddenly knifed through the damp air.

Halfway into the grove a Mexican worker in knee-high rubber boots and a straw hat looked up from the collapsed furrow he was digging out. He nodded gravely to me as I went past, my shoes making hollow sounds on the sandy roadway. Then he shrugged and turned back to his work. There is no explaining physical exercise to a man who does manual labor. Further down the road, a pair of gray and white mourning doves flared out of a volunteer pomegranate bush as I passed. They were so close I could hear the rustle and pop of their wings as they fled, a sound like ghostly brushes bounced over kettledrums.

The tension in the muscles of my calves and above my knees was beginning to ease. I could move more freely now,

but I still felt like a man in an iron tube. I was only drawing
on the top half of my lungs and winning a stitch in the side
for my trouble. I concentrated on breathing deeply, evenly,
setting the rhythm until my body moved in concert with
itself and the demands I was making on it. After a few minutes, I was able to draw one deep breath, then another,
oxygen spreading through me, feeding the physical fires.

The dirt ended in a two-lane blacktop road, rough and
potholed in spots. It was one of those roads that had been
abandoned but not officially closed when the area around it
changed as Santa Clara was changing.

Apricot groves replaced the plums, apricots just beginning to reflect the sun on their smooth skins. Once these
trees had been the sole economic raison d'être for the land.
Now they were a holding operation run by tax accountants
and a few stubborn farmers. Someday, too soon, the trees
would go down before a D-9 Cat. Uprooted trees would be
piled into enormous pyres and then burned to ash and bitterness. Their grave markers would be tilt-up slabs with
semiconductor factories inside. Silicon chips in place of orchards. But not yet. For now, orchards still rose gracefully
out of the land.

I had come a mile and a half and was just starting to sweat
freely when I heard the footfalls behind me, somebody
coming on fairly fast, rubber soles slapping the rough asphalt with a hard, unvarying rhythm. I didn't mind being
passed. I moved to the side of the road and kept my pace,
not bothering to look back. I'm a runner, not a racer. Six- to
eight-minute miles are enough for me. Then the footfalls
began to slow a bit, matching my own. I glanced over my
shoulder—and felt that extraordinary silence that comes
just before the symphony begins.

Volker wore a pair of nylon racing shorts and no shirt. He
was indeed a gymnast, broad shoulders and narrow hips and
maybe two ounces of fat on his entire body. His was the kind
of physique that made you realize the antic lunacy of the
belief that all men are created equal. Sunlight blazed in his
pale hair and ice-blue eyes. He moved lightly, like a wolf,
fluidity and power and grace. Sweat shone over his skin. He

was breathing easily, evenly, the way man was meant to breathe.

I glanced further back and saw the dark sedan a few hundred yards behind us. Korchnoi's square form filled the windshield on the driver's side.

"Good morning," said Volker, opening notes of the overture. He was breathing a bit more heavily than if he had been walking, but not much.

"It's morning," I agreed.

Volker's smile was sunlight, warm and undemanding. It scared me like nothing else could have, because I had to fight not to smile back.

"Do not look so unfriendly, Fiddler," Volker said gently. "Things will work out. I have great confidence in you."

"Fiora," I said.

"She is safe," he said. "And not far away. Where is the machine?"

"It's safe. And not far away."

"Then you have it in your possession?"

Volker's question had a sharp edge to it. I knew then that the Vietnamese had already made their move.

"I know where it is," I said, looking sideways at him. "Why?"

Volker's clear eyes memorized me. His pupils were very black, dilated, midnight in the center of all that sunshine.

"A third party called an hour ago and offered to sell us our machine for $100,000," he said. "It is a small price, really."

"They called the consulate?" I asked.

Volker didn't answer, merely watched me as we ran side by side, my longer stride more than compensated for by his superb conditioning. I could feel the stitch in my side return. I was holding my breath again. I concentrated on drawing air deeply into my lungs.

"Are you going to take the offer?" I asked.

"Do you think we should?" he said smoothly. "My guarantee to release Fiora would still stand, once the OxyCon was safely in our possession. If something happened during the trade, of course, something unfortunate . . ."

Volker didn't say anything more. He didn't have to. He

smelled a trap, a pit opening beneath his feet and pungi stakes sliding into his body. He knew how well certain Vietnamese loved Russians. He would rather deal with me, because I valued Fiora's life.

"It's a trap," I confirmed, telling him what he already knew.

"Whose trap?"

"It's not that easy."

"Then it must be your FBI," stated Volker.

"Does that worry you, Volker? The FBI?" I was curious and feeling more than a little cruel. I wanted to see him sweat from something more than a run through the early morning.

"I respect the FBI," said Volker evenly. "They are very professional, very competent."

"But they don't intend to blow your head off the first time you raise it," I said. "You'd survive an FBI trap. But not this one, Volker. Korchnoi should have killed Kim Van Kieu when he had the chance."

Volker smiled coldly and nodded.

"Kieu doesn't like Russians," I continued. "You're a Russian. She'll kill you. The FBI will just parade you through the headlines and deport you. That's assuming you have some kind of diplomatic accreditation and immunity, whether in the name of Volker or Igor Smithovitch."

Volker laughed with real warmth. "Smithovitch! Ah, Fiddler, no wonder Fiora refuses to let go of you."

Volker said nothing about his diplomatic credits. I didn't push, because I didn't care. I wasn't the FBI. Yet I had to fight to keep the fine edge of my anger, for Volker was a cello, vibrating with emotions he himself could not feel. But sweet God how perfectly he turned your ability to feel against you, crippling you and strengthening himself.

"So," said Volker evenly, his words as smooth as the muscles flexing in his legs, "how do you plan to get us out of the trap? For it is your job to free us. It is your field, your game, your choice. You have a freedom in you that I do not, Fiddler. But I will use it, and use it well."

Freedom? I almost laughed. Volker was free because he

could kill and walk away and never be haunted by un-
finished symphonies. I can kill and walk away. That's as far
as my freedom goes. The rest I have to live with.

Starting now.

"Tell Korchnoi to call Kieu," I said. "As of now, I'm your
official negotiator for the OxyCon. Tonight, I'll deliver the
machine to you. Call me at the motel room at seven. I'll tell
you when and where."

Volker ran silently, his eyes like chips of winter narrowed
against the sun. "And the Vietnamese?" he asked softly.

"They'll blow you to hell the first chance they get. I'm the
only one you can trust, Volker. I want Fiora. Period. The
rest isn't worth a bucket of warm spit to me."

"I do not believe that," Volker said after a moment. "Fiora
is not all you want. You also want revenge. I have—inconve-
nienced you. First Fiora, then the machine. You are a
proud man, and I do not discount the effect of pride."

I stopped in the middle of the roadway. Volker ran on a
few steps. Then, surprised by my action, he also stopped. I
could hear the sedan a few hundred feet behind us stop, as
well.

"Volker, listen to me," I said slowly, as though by speaking each word clearly, carefully, I would guarantee his perfect understanding. "If killing you right now would free
Fiora, I would kill you and feed you to the crows. But killing
you won't get me what I want. Fiora. So I plan to take the
machine from the Vietnamese and deliver it to you. You
plan to take the machine from me and get it out of the country.

"Our plans are pretty simple, each in its own way. Two
simple melodies making a simple harmony. Let's not com-
plicate it with revenge or pride or anything else. I would
crawl on my knees from here to Moscow if I thought that
would do any good. I'm a pragmatist, Volker."

He stood and watched me with the look of a man whose
mirror has just showed him another face. I turned and
started running again, because despite my words I didn't
trust myself not to kill Volker and then try to cut a deal with
Korchnoi, who was also a pragmatist. This was the best shot

I was likely to get at Volker. My hindbrain was howling for the feel of his jugular beneath my thumbs. The forebrain knew better, though. So I ran. Hard.

Volker caught up. For once, he was the one who was showing discomfort. I had gotten to him, somehow. His breathing became audible, ragged, and finally he raised his hand in a signal to cut the pace. I had burned off the worst of my rage, so I dropped back to an easier speed.

"I am sorry that we were born on the opposite sides of too many things," Volker said finally. "We are so much alike, mirrors facing each other, reflecting endlessly. But mirrors are not an exact reflection of reality. Mirrors reverse images. You can see yourself, but not really. And you cannot touch yourself at all." He turned and looked at me, his blue eyes like crystal in the slanting early morning light. "Seven o'clock, Fiddler."

Then Volker smiled at me and began to run, legs flashing, hair burning gold in the sun. I stayed with him for a few strides, stretching out, but it wasn't enough. He ran perfectly, everything in harmony, racing through dawn like a god.

There is a reason that men sometimes call Lucifer the Lord of Light.

13

I jogged back to the motel at half speed, but my mind was going flat out. The Vietnamese could be a lethal complication. They had more freedom of action than Innes and the FBI and were less rational than Volker and Korchnoi. God, how volatile zealots can be. I'd sooner try to set fractured emeralds in a bench vise than to predict the reactions of political hardcases from a culture as alien as one which considers it polite to belch in public but extraordinarily offensive to use a toothpick.

Yet I had just nominated myself as go-between in an impossible deal. The Vietnamese wanted the Russians dead, and I wanted Fiora alive. So long as the Vietnamese had the machine, there was no meeting ground. So long as the Vietnamese had the machine, Fiora's life could be measured in very short hours. Somehow I had to convince Kieu that her best hope of revenge on the Russians was me. And if I couldn't do that, I had to steal the machine while both the Vietnamese and the FBI watched.

I'm good, but I'm not that good.

I was nearly cool and moving easily by the time I got back to the room. Sharp was awake.

"You look like hell," he said, squinting through the smoke at me. He laughed, then started coughing. That's the problem with getting up in the morning when you smoke. You need a push start from a D-9 Cat in order to get it all heading down the road in the same direction.

"I've just been run into the ground by the opposition, as Innes so manfully calls it," I said, heading for the shower.

"Korchnoi?" asked Sharp, coming to a point.

I closed the shower door and let the hot needles of water slam into me. "No," I said loudly, "Volker. Korchnoi sat on his butt behind the wheel."

"I knew that old boy had to be brighter than he looked."

Sharp's voice was clear. He had followed me into the bathroom. When I got out of the shower, he was leaning against the wall, using Royal Salute to cut the taste of late nights, early mornings, and filtered cigarettes. He held the flask out. I took a modest sip and let that incomparable Scotch shiver through me. "Beats mouthwash all to hell, don't it?" said Sharp, smiling. "Did you learn anything from Volker?"

"He wants the machine."

"No shit," Sharp said sarcastically.

"The Vietnamese have opened negotiations."

Sharp repeated himself, this time with a question mark at the end.

"Volker didn't admit it," I continued, "but it's a good bet he has diplomatic immunity."

"Not here," said Sharp. "I've been thinking about that. Probably he's something like third economic attaché at the Russian embassy in Mexico City. The Russians have over six hundred people accredited there. Bet he's one of them."

"No wonder Volker hired a Mexican pilot," I said.

"Most of the contraband just went from that Omnitronix plane right to the KLM or Alitalia air freight offices across the apron at Mexico City. The Mexicans don't give a shit about things like that," said Sharp. He capped the flask and put it in his back pocket. "Then the stuff was all shipped to dummy corporations in Zurich or Helsinki. Somebody over there just slapped a different label on it and shipped it to Zelenograd. Nothing fancy. The Russians aren't fancy folks."

I said nothing, because I was chasing a sour note. I lathered up and shaved quickly, still chasing the off-key sound. As I rinsed, it came to me. "Would Volker use that name in Mexico?"

"Yeah."

"Wonder what they call him at the San Francisco consulate?" I muttered. "He's too smart to leave himself open to an espionage charge in the U.S. He's probably a gardener."

Sharp flipped his cigarette butt into the toilet. "It do purely piss me off to catch diplomats," he said roughly. "Like kissing your sister. No punch at all."

"Bullets don't know about diplomatic immunity."

Sharp looked at me quickly, then gave me a shooter's smile.

"There's a phone number in the hip pocket of my jeans," I said, toweling my hair dry. "Can you run that through somebody at the telephone company? I need the address."

"I already ran it. Belongs to one Tran Van Nguyen in Palo Alto," said Sharp, stretching and wandering over to the toilet. "I wrote the address under the phone number."

I gave Sharp a hard look. "I suppose you went through my wallet, too," I said, walking out to the bedroom.

"Your driver's license expires this year," called Sharp from the bathroom. "So does the concealed gun permit."

I pulled on fresh underwear and old jeans. A clean rugby shirt finished the job. I glanced in the mirror, decided I looked as harmless as someone my size could, and pulled on my boots.

The toilet flushed. Sharp came out into the room, stuffing his shirt back into his pants, zipping up and settling his turquoise belt buckle back into place.

"I understood most of the list, but what's a Red Number 24?" asked Sharp.

"I'll explain it after breakfast."

The coffee shop wasn't crowded. The waitress took our orders, poured our coffee, demanded that we have a nice day, and left. A smart waitress. Sharp and I attacked the coffee in silence. The waitress brought refills and eggs in the same trip. When we were both finished, Sharp shoved back his plate, lighted up a cigarette, and waited for me to talk.

"The Vietnamese are offering to sell the OxyCon to the Russians for $100,000," I said.

Sharp exhaled a dirty stream of smoke over the egg yolk

hardening in the middle of his plate. "Sounds like a fair price."

"Plus all the bullets they can carry."

He threw me a fast glance. "Set up?"

"I'm betting on it. After I talk to Kieu, I'll know for sure."

"Why should she talk to you?"

"I'm Volker's designated hitter. She pitches to me, or there's no game."

"Volker know about the FBI?"

"Not from me. He doesn't know about you, either," I added. "He's shrewd, though. He smells a trap."

With his thumb, Sharp flicked ashes into his plate. "He's got his choice of traps. The Feebees, the tonks, or you."

"Yeah. With all of us scrambling over the bait, the tiger might just get away. So I'm trying to subtract the FBI and the Vietnamese."

"How?"

"I'm going to let them chase one another all over the Bay Area while you and I walk out with the machine."

"Nice trick, if it works."

I shrugged. "Never know until you try."

Sharp took a quick, double drag on the cigarette and killed the glowing ash in the viscous egg yolk. "Which comes first, Kieu or the Red Number 24?"

"Kieu. While I talk to her," I said, pulling the list out of my hip pocket, "I want you to find the local building supply outlet and buy the stuff that I put your initials after."

"If Kieu has the keys, wouldn't it be simpler just to unlock the door? Unless you get a kick out of sawing through walls," he added.

"Kieu may not be feeling cooperative."

Sharp took the list, scanned the items that were marked with his initials, and looked up. "No Number 24?"

"I'll get it myself."

"Don't trust me, huh?"

"They don't speak Good Ol' Boy in high tech specialty shops."

Sharp smiled slightly and rubbed the gray stubble along

his chin with his knuckles. "All I have with me is my standard issue sidearm."

"What do you need?"

"What's the range?"

"Anything from fifteen to fifty yards. Downhill. You'll be up on a bank near a bridge."

"Night?"

I nodded.

"Will my target be holding the hostage?"

"Probably."

Sharp let out a long breath.

"One chance," I said quietly, "and if it isn't a bull's-eye, Fiora is dead. That's why I wanted someone who won't flinch. A shooter."

Pale blue eyes weighed me, then Sharp nodded. "You got one. I'll need an M-16 with a zero-aim laser sight."

I unhooked my belt, unzipped the compartment that was all but invisible between the seam marks, and pulled out ten one thousand dollar bills and gave him six of them. This wasn't the first time the banks hadn't been open when I needed cash. As I gave the folded bills to Sharp, I said, "Don't buy the rifle with big bills. I don't want anyone remembering your face."

"Kiss my ass," said Sharp, his voice rich with disgust.

I laughed. I'd had that one coming. Sharp was hardly an amateur.

"What about Volker?" asked Sharp, tucking the bills into a worn leather wallet.

"By the time you dump Korchnoi, Volker will be a moving target. Or he'll be dead."

Something in my voice caught Sharp's attention. "You think he'll let you close with a gun?"

"Men killed each other for a long time before guns were invented," I said.

"He'll toss you for weapons, Fiddler, just as sure as God made little green apples. Don't count on keeping a boot knife."

I looked at my hands. Large, long-fingered, calloused, able to open a bottle of wine or a man's head with equal ease. "I'll manage, Sharp. If I don't, feel free to spend a bullet or two. And if Volker has hurt Fiora, spend them all."

Sharp's pale eyes narrowed, but all he said was, "Anything else?"

"Are the Vietnamese using radio communications?"

"Nope. They switch guards every eight hours, regular as a factory."

"You know the FBI frequencies?"

"That's a problem. Oh, I know the numbers, but the Bearcat you've got on the list won't get it done."

"Why not?" I asked. "A Bearcat can pick up any frequency you want. Just punch in the numbers and listen."

"Innes uses a scrambler. All you'll hear is garbage. Can we fit the OxyCon in the Plymouth? Its radio has a scrambler."

The idea of driving metropolitan streets with an OxyCon hanging out the trunk of a government car made me want to laugh and swear at the same time. My expression must have said it all, for Sharp didn't mention using the Plymouth again.

"We'll have to pull the scrambler and wire it into the Bearcat," I said.

"That's your department. You need a car hot-wired, though, let me know."

"I think I'll just rent a van, not steal one."

"Whose name you gonna use?" asked Sharp blandly.

Which told me that he had found the concealed compartment in my wallet where I carried spare driver's licenses and other miscellaneous ID. None in my name, of course. Names for all seasons and reasons. "I'll think of something," I said. "Trust me."

He snorted and pushed away from the table.

"Be back by two," I said. "And, Sharp—"

"Yeah?" he said, standing up, looking over his shoulder at me.

"Even if this goes well, Innes is going to be pissed."

Sharp laughed unpleasantly. "In Russia they send the hard cases to Siberia. In America, they assign them to work the Mexican border. So what's Innes going to do—give me life plus ninety-nine years in Calexico? You watch your own ass, Fiddler. I'll take care of mine."

Sharp dropped me off at my Mustang. Nobody was watching it. Nobody even had bothered to steal the hubcaps or run a beer opener down the side. Nobody followed me as I ducked and turned and finally headed for the freeway.

I found the address in Palo Alto without much trouble. The numbers belonged to a tiny bakery in a small Asian shopping center. Nothing unusual. There were dozens of shops and shopping centers like it in Little Saigons all over California. This one was more profitable than many. Some of the storefronts had been redone with Oriental facades and enigmatic signs in Chinese ideographs: oriental grocery, pharmacy, newspaper and travel agency with Air France posters. The businesses were all open, and the parking lot was half-full.

I spotted the watchers, but didn't take it personally. Yet. The Vietnamese have survived for thousands of years by keeping an eye on one another as well as the other guys. And then there's the fact that their culture tolerates certain human activities that Americans consider vices. When you're an immigrant in a Puritan land, you put lookouts in the parking lots and try like hell to learn the local palm-greasing etiquette.

The watchers here were teenage boys who sat on their heels on the sidewalk in front of the bakery Kieu had called. The boys were eating pastries and casually keeping an eye on cars and people. I pulled into a parking spot. Before I had the Mustang shut off, one of the kids was up and striding nonchalantly toward an unmarked door next to the travel agency.

I let him go. At the moment, I was interested in the bakery, where the Nguyen phone was registered. A brass bell tinkled happily as I entered.

The display cases were filled with fresh goods. Half were Vietnamese and half would have sold well along the Champs Élysées. A Vietnamese man of middle age emerged from the back room. He greeted me with a polite smile and a heavily accented "Good morning."

I ordered a half-dozen of the croissants with glistening butter crusts. "Were you trained in France?" I asked as he bagged the croissants.

"It is my wife, she who bakes," he said with an ambivalent smile. "At the Cordon Bleu was her education. I was diplomat to embassy of Republic of Vietnam in Paris. Now . . ." He smiled again weakly.

"The fortunes of war," I said.

He politely agreed.

"Tell Kim Van Kieu that I wish to see her," I said in the same cordial tone.

At first the request didn't seem to register. Then, so quickly that I almost missed it, the man's glance flicked past the bakery window toward the unmarked door where the teenager had disappeared. The look was entirely reflexive, the gesture of a man taken off guard. He had been a merchant too long.

He turned and watched me with blank, dark eyes. Buttery croissants soaked through the brown paper bag in his hand. "Thousand pardons," he murmured, tipping his head in a slight bow as he handed me the bag. "No good English."

For an instant I was tempted to try him in French. Then I shrugged. The look out the window had told me all I needed to know. There was no point in further embarrassing the former diplomat. I took the bag and dropped a couple of bills on the glass countertop.

I tossed the bag into the Mustang and crossed the parking lot, moving quickly without seeming to. The unmarked door was my target, but I looked at the Air France travel agency instead. The second teenager had been monitoring my progress from outside the bakery. When he saw how close I would come to the unmarked door, he tried to stay cool and at the same time beat me there. It was close, but I had the stride on him. I collared him with one hand and boosted him through the door. He said something in Vietnamese that I ignored.

There was an office consisting of a paint-splattered desk covered with papers and a table piled with ragged stacks of pamphlets. On the wall were a couple of posters in Vietnamese script, broadsides in red and black. One of them had a large photo of a Vietnamese man. He wore the stern, statesmanlike look that politicians affect when confronted by cameras. I recognized him as a former cabinet minister who had fled Vietnam in early 1975 with several planeloads of gold. He was said to be living in Paris and leading the resistance to the new government in Saigon—Ho Chi Minh City, that is.

The boy's yelp had brought a man from the back office. He was in his late twenties and looked like one hard son of a bitch. I was immediately reminded of Fiora's description of the surprised cat burglar: Oriental, very strong, very silent, with a wispy mustache. He was no more than five feet six inches tall but he moved as though he had steel springs in his feet.

I headed toward the doorway he had just come through.

"What you want?" he demanded in broken English as he moved to block my path.

"Hi," I said, smiling ingenuously and moving fast. "My name is—"

That was all I got out. He arched his hand and pointed it at my sternum. The movement is common to many of the fighting styles of Asia. I parried it, turning his hand upward, then catching his wrist and turning with it. He was strong and well schooled, but his mistake had already been made: He had underestimated the smiling, clumsy-looking round-eye. I had him spun around with his arm barred and his palm shoved up between his shoulder blades before he had time to curse his error.

I kept the pressure on. He felt like a handful of steel braids beneath his shirt. I had no desire to find out what fancy moves he might know that I didn't. I crowded him right up against the wall and leaned hard, giving him no room to do anything but bunch his muscles.

"My name is Fiddler. The woman who calls herself Kim Van Kieu knows me."

I felt his body change at the mention of Kieu's name. I took advantage of the instant of surprise to pull my Detonics and lay its cold muzzle just behind the man's ear.

"Now I'm sure you have enough black belts to stock a men's shop," I continued, "but no matter how good you are, a bullet in the ear is better. Send your boy to get her. English only, please."

The man said only two words. "Bring Kieu."

The teenager hesitated, then ran through the back door. He returned almost instantly with Kim. Her amber eyes took in the scene. She dismissed the teenager with a single look. Then she said a few Vietnamese words to the man I was holding. I could literally feel the change in him. Muscles relaxed, his breathing changed, even his spine seemed to loosen. He nodded and said a single word.

"You may release him, Fiddler," said Kieu, her voice uninflected.

I lifted the gun. His muscles remained relaxed. I holstered the gun and stepped back beyond the reach of his feet. He turned around, looked at Kim, and then left the room.

"Come," she said to me, turning away.

I followed her into another, much larger, office. Kieu sat behind a clean-lined teakwood desk. A dozen straight-backed chairs faced her desk. Behind her was the flag of the Republic of Vietnam. A side wall was covered with a twenty-year-old map of Indochina, the demilitarized zone between North and South Vietnam still darkly marked.

Kieu was dressed in the uniform associated with our former enemies in Vietnam, the black loose-fitting blouse and trousers that looked like pajamas. Actually, it was the costume of the common man on both sides in Vietnam, like the business suit in the United States or the *guayabera* in Mexico. Kieu filled out her uniform rather uncommonly, though. She was arrestingly beautiful, and well aware of her effect. Her makeup was understated but as careful as a television anchor woman's. Her posture was both elegant and at ease, like a queen. This woman knew how to use the trappings of office instinctively. I felt a distant regret that I

hadn't met her in different circumstances, for she had
strength.

"What do you want?" asked Kieu. Her voice was cold and
correct. If she had any regrets, she wasn't sharing them.

"Did Korchnoi call?"

"Yes."

"Then you know what I want."

"No. I have not agreed."

"You don't have any choice," I said, my voice as cold as
hers.

"I don't trust you."

"Well, lady, we finally have something in common. I
don't trust you."

Amber eyes watched me with the unblinking attention of
a cat.

"But that's OK," I continued. "We don't have to trust each
other. All we have to do is cooperate. That shouldn't be too
hard. You've had a lot of practice at crawling into bed with
unlikely allies."

"We don't need you."

"The hell you don't. The FBI has a snitch in your organi-
zation. If you go to the bathroom, they know how many
times you flush."

Black pupils dilated, then went back down to tiny points
glittering out of narrowed eyes. She didn't bother to protest
or deny or ask futile questions. Betrayal was something the
Vietnamese understood very well indeed.

"Why are you telling me this?"

"Because I want you to know that I'm your best hope of
revenge on the Russians," I said bluntly. There was no sense
in a fancy lie when the truth would serve just as well.

Kieu watched me for a long moment. Then she said
quietly, "You Americans have no stomach for politics. It is
the reason you lost our war. You could not bring yourselves
to do what had to be done for victory."

"We lost because we could never figure out what would
have constituted winning," I said. "I don't have that problem myself. I know exactly what my idea of winning is, and
I'll personally destroy any Vietnamese who gets in my way.

Nothing racial, Kieu. I'm planning on doing the same to the Russians and the FBI."

There was another long silence, another long scrutiny from amber eyes. Then Kieu smiled faintly, enigmatically. "I believe you will." For the first time, she looked at me the way a woman looks at a man who interests her. When she spoke, her voice was faintly lilting, husky with half-remembered French accents. "What is winning for you?"

"The Russians dead," I said, half the truth and the less important half at that, means rather than end. The end was Fiora alive, but Kieu wouldn't understand that anymore than I understood the devils that haunted her.

"Why?" asked Kieu.

"It doesn't matter. What matters is that we want the same thing."

Kieu narrowed her eyes, then accepted it. Pragmatism was not a foreign concept to her.

"What do you want from me?" she asked.

"I want you to take the FBI on an extended tour of the Bay Area. While you're gone, I'll bring in Volker and Korchnoi. And then I'll kill them."

"I will stay to see them die."

"No. If you don't leave, the FBI won't believe that the sale is going down."

"I will see the Russians die."

Never argue religion with a fanatic. So I tried a minor variation. "Volker demanded to see the machine before he paid for it. But if he comes here while the FBI is hanging around, they might get impatient and jump in before the killing starts."

Kieu waited.

"You and I will agree on a place to hand over the Oxy-Con," I said. "Volker will come to see the machine in the storage yard. Once Volker is convinced that you actually have the machine, we'll go to the meeting place. By that time you'll have dumped your FBI tails and be waiting in ambush. Then you can see the Russians die."

Kieu's long black eyelashes moved down slowly, concealing her eyes. She looked up at me suddenly. She nodded, once. "I will choose the meeting place."

I shrugged. It didn't matter to me. I wasn't going to be there. "Fine." I held out my hand. "Keys."

"No."

"Then how is Volker going to see the machine without setting off every alarm in the place?" I asked reasonably.

"There is a tiny window. Ventilation. He can look through it."

Yeah, just like I had, only he'd have to stand on tiptoe. But I kept my mouth shut. "That won't be good enough."

"It will have to be."

"Kieu—"

"No," she interrupted, her voice hard. "We will do it my way. It is the only way *I* can be sure of winning." She wrote an address on a telephone message pad. She tore off the sheet and handed it to me. "We will meet here. You may name the time."

I swallowed a sarcastic comment about generosity and the brotherhood of man. On the other hand, I hadn't expected anything else.

"Volker will call me between three and five," I said, lying this time because the truth wouldn't serve at all. "That means you'll have to take those feds on a long tour so they don't come back and find Volker peeping through the ventilation hole. If you get tired of driving, go someplace and look like you're waiting or the Russians. That way the FBI will stick with you no matter what. They want the Russians as bad as you do." I turned to leave, then paused at the door long enough to say, "Just be sure you dump the FBI in time to meet me here"—I waved the address—"at seven-thirty. Otherwise, you won't be in at the kill."

I left before she could answer. I crossed the parking lot quickly. Just as I put my hand on the Mustang's door handle, I heard the click of high heels behind me, then a woman's laugh, light and lilting and sassy and alive. For an instant I thought it was Fiora, her hand brushing my arm, her voice whispering my name. I spun around.

Sanity returned, bringing an echoing silence. There was nothing but an expanse of cracked asphalt and worn cars, hope and adrenaline hammering uselessly in my veins.

14

I was asleep when Sharp came back. I woke up fast. Sleep hadn't been that kind to me. I kept hearing Fiora's voice.

"Get everything?" I asked, kicking out of bed and into my running shoes.

"Yeah. You?"

"All of it, including a unit called 12-12." I stood, feeling used up by dreams. "What time is it?"

"Nearly two."

An hour until Kieu's charade began.

I shook my head, hoping to dispel the ghosts. It didn't work. Nothing would get that done but a first-class job of exorcism.

"Help me jerk the Plymouth's scrambler," I said, heading for the door.

"Don't you want your change?" asked Sharp, digging into his pants pocket.

I shook my head. He looked surprised, then shrugged. He started to say something, looked closely at me and decided to wait until later. When I glanced in the mirror, I didn't blame him for walking lightly. My face would have fit nicely beneath the half-mask of an executioner. I grimaced and looked away. Some people wake up looking like Pollyanna. Even under the best of circumstances, I'm not one of them.

These weren't the best of circumstances. I kept hearing Fiora's voice like a broken melody. I knew I should be calm and smooth, a still pond waiting for sunrise. Don't think about what will happen, what could go wrong. Just remember what the Zen master told you. You don't aim the arrow at the target; the arrow is *already* there. Nothing to be nervous about. A dead sure thing.

And a lousy choice of words.

I walked out into blinding afternoon sun. As I'd hoped, the scrambler was an afterthought rather than a built-in factory job. It was a cigar-box-sized rectangle wired into the radio between the antenna and the transceiver. No reason it shouldn't fit into the Bearcat. Two skinned knuckles, some hot words, a few connections, and a short walk to the Bearcat, which had been put in the rented van's front seat. Repeat on the knuckles, add new words, make connections.

While I worked, Sharp loaded his purchases into the back of the brown Dodge van I'd rented. Then he cleaned out the room and threw that stuff in back, too. By that time I'd finished fiddling with wires, paid for the room, turned in the Mustang, and mentioned to the clerk that an airport limousine would pick me up. If anybody asked for me, I was gone.

"Ready?" I asked as Sharp rolled the van's side door shut with a harsh sound.

He nodded curtly.

"You drive," I said. "I'll play with the Bearcat."

Sharp backed the Dodge van out of the parking lot with a skill that suggested vans were familiar to him. I concentrated on the Bearcat, feeding in the frequencies that Sharp had given to me earlier. When I was finished, Sharp looked over at me. Shrewd, pale eyes and a humorless smile.

"You wake up meaner than I do," he said.

It sounded like a compliment. Probably it was. Fiora had always complained about my morning temper. I shied away from that thought. I'd promised myself I wouldn't think about her for a while, because it wouldn't do any good and might just blow the whole thing to hell.

"White bag in back," said Sharp.

I looked over my shoulder, climbed into the back of the van, and retrieved the bag. Back in my seat, I prowled through the paper sack. Inside were such items as two baseball caps and two pairs of sunglasses, tennis shoes, a truly awful plaid shirt, and a thick gray mustache. I was relieved

that only the cap and sunglasses would fit me, and I already
had a mustache. Sharp tossed the straw cowboy hat he usually wore into the back. His government issue, paramilitary
sunglasses followed. I gave him an orange and black Giants
cap, reserving the Coors cap for myself. He put his cap on
backward. A pair of dark, plastic-rimmed sunglasses followed. He smoothed on the mustache as he drove.

"Take the wheel," Sharp said, unbuttoning his shirt and
pulling it out of his pants.

For the first time I realized that his blue slacks had been
traded for prewashed jeans. His distinctive turquoise belt
was gone, too. I normally don't miss that kind of thing but
I'm not normally haunted, either. I held the wheel with one
hand. Steering wasn't a problem on the highway. Besides,
with a van you aim rather than drive, anyway. While I kept
us in the lane, Sharp traded his wilted white shirt for the
awful plaid. He didn't bother to tuck it in. With quick motions, he pulled off his boots, chucked them in back, and
put on the tennis shoes.

"I'll be the front man," said Sharp, taking the wheel
again. "It's easier to change my profile than yours."

I didn't argue. When you're big, the only way to change
your profile is to put on high-heeled, high-soled boots and
go for gigantic. No way to look small. Sharp, on the other
hand, was average height, lean and as versatile as a good
model. Put him in a three-piece suit and you have a banker.
Put him in beard and jeans and you have a doper. Put him in
jeans and a plaid shirt and you have John Doe renting a
storage unit for all the stuff his wife picks up at garage sales.

Particularly from one to three hundred feet, which was as
close as any surveillance was likely to be. As for my profile,
I'd try to stay out of sight. When that wasn't possible, there
was the baseball cap, sunglasses, rugby shirt, and running
shoes.

Sharp wheeled the van into the parking lot of the coffee
shop at two forty-four. I turned on the Bearcat and started
scanning frequencies. The reception was marginal. I could
hear a few conversations from other FBI sectors in the Bay
Area, but nothing nearby. Either Innes wasn't talking or we

weren't drawing him in. I looked at Sharp. He shrugged. All we could do was hope that we were in the same meter band as Innes.

In silence, Sharp and I waited and listened to the Bearcat. For a time, all we got was a running commentary from a couple of Oakland G-men, who had been dispatched to investigate a $900 stickup at a branch bank in the Piedmont hills. I looked at my watch. Three minutes after three. I wondered if Kieu had scented betrayal and gone to ground.

Suddenly the radio blared with such clarity that Sharp and I both scrambled to lower the volume. The voice was very soft, and had the flat, professionally neutral tones of a cop on surveillance.

"They're moving. Stand by."

Sharp turned toward me. His oversized sunglasses were like two patches of night. "That's the point man. He was going to try to move up close in a motor home today. He's got the eyeball on the storage bay and on the Vietnamese, too. Hope he's pulled off with the rest, or we're going to be in deep shit."

Another FBI voice came back on the radio: *"What's happening, Twenty-two?"* It sounded like Innes.

Twenty-two was silent for a minute. Then: *"Can't see, for sure. A car just pulled up to the Chevrolet that's been sitting on the machine. Three male subjects in it. They're out now, talking to the guy in the Chevy."* The agent's voice was low, even, unexcited.

I remembered the Chevrolet from last night. If the Vietnamese sentry was still parked in the lot where I had seen him, the FBI motor home probably could have gotten close enough to take voice prints of the conversation.

A third agent's voice came in, describing the scene from another angle. They had the storage area blanketed. I looked at Sharp. He nodded.

"There are two more units that haven't reported in," said Sharp, lighting a cigarette. "Might be more. The Feebees have men and money to burn."

There was more than a little envy in Sharp's voice. At budget time, Customs always sucked hind tit. The only federal enforcement agency that was lower on the totem was the Border Patrol.

"*All units on the surveillance, there are weapons in the second car,*" said Twenty-two. "*I can see two AR-15s or M-16s and a handgun. This looks hot.*" His voice was more animated now, but still soft. "*The new car is a 1979 or 1980 black Camaro. Three men. All male Orientals, mid-twenties.*"

Twenty-two continued with descriptions of all three. One sounded like the man who had followed Kieu and me last night.

"*Here comes another car. A black Z-28,*" reported Twenty-two. "*It's the Dragon Lady.*"

I allowed myself a small feeling of relief. Kieu was holding up her end. It was her presence, rather than the firearms, that would convince the FBI that something was going down.

"*More guns,*" reported Twenty-two. "*They're moving a shotgun case from the Dragon Lady's car to the Chevy. A U-Rent truck just pulled into the storage yard. It's backing up to 12-1.*"

Sharp threw a look at me. I shook my head. Was Kieu going to take the machine, leaving me to Korchnoi's tender care when Volker stood on tiptoe and peered into an empty storage bay? I swore very softly and began to think of all the things I would do to Kieu when I caught her.

"*They're opening the bay door. I can't see a damn thing. Truck is blocking the opening.*"

Innes broke in, his voice hard and sure. "*All units get ready to take up rolling surveillance. We have five units on the Viets. How many are hanging back in reserve?*"

Static and a disembodied voice coming from a distance. "*Three at the freeway.*"

Through the smoked glass blister windows on the van, I looked around the parking lot. Nobody was in any of the nearby cars.

"The fence," said Sharp, watching the driving mirror.

I looked out the tiny rear door windows and spotted three vehicles parked against the chain link fence at the rear of the storage lot—a van, a sedan, and a Pacific Telephone service truck. Each vehicle was manned by one driver and one passenger, all appropriately dressed. The telephone truck was driven by a woman in a phone company uniform. There was a very convincing tool belt around her waist. All six members of the surveillance team had been gathered around the van, probably listening to radio transmissions the way Sharp and I were. Now, though, the agents were walking quickly toward their vehicles, ready to take up their assigned slots for a moving surveillance.

"*Are they loading the machine?*" demanded Innes.

Twenty-two didn't reply. There was a triple pop, as though someone had punched the mike button three times.

Sharp laughed softly. "Poor bastard. They're so close he can't talk."

Nearly a minute later, Twenty-two's voice came back softly, "*They were standing right beside me. The truck is still blocking the bay. I can't see what's being loaded.*"

"*Any unit. Can you see into the bay?*"

No response.

Innes muttered a word that it was a misdemeanor to use on the public air waves. But then the average citizen wouldn't be using a scrambler to eavesdrop on federal obscenities.

"*They're saddling up now, everyone including the sentry. Bay doors are closing. Stand by.*"

Three seconds. Seven. Ten.

"*They're away,*" said Twenty-two. "*All three vehicles are headed for 101, even the sentry. They're moving quickly, in convoy. You call it, Innes.*"

There was a short pause. You could almost hear Innes's mind whirring and clicking like a slot machine as the calculations were made.

"That's one heavy machine to move so fast," muttered Sharp, frowning.

"How much?" I asked quickly.

"Over two hundred kilos, including the crate."

"*Okay, we're going to have to assume they have the machine,*" said Innes.

And I was going to have to assume they didn't.

I waited while Innes assigned primary responsibility for each of the Vietnamese vehicles to a pair of his surveillance cars. Keeping a moving surveillance on three separate vehicles should clean out even Innes's reserves.

From where we were sitting, we could see the road. We watched as two cars and the rental truck rolled by in the moderate traffic. During the next few minutes, we saw several other cars that were probably FBI surveillance units, although it was hard to tell. I did see Innes in one of the cars, looking like an Ivy League plumber in artfully stained work clothes. The surveillance team blended skillfully into the surroundings. Even the motor home that brought up the rear didn't look out of place in the traffic.

"I do like to see competent work," said Sharp, half irony and half truth.

The three vehicles that had been in the lot with us were preparing to roll out as the mobile reserve when the roof fell in.

"*One to seven*," came Innes's voice on the radio.

I saw the woman driving the telephone truck reach for a microphone.

"*Seven, go ahead*," came a female voice on the Bearcat.

"*Circle back and set up as the eyeball on the storage bay*," said Innes. "*I'd hate to be following a truckload of smoke.*"

I hoped he was following a truckload of smoke, too, but I'd just as soon he hadn't thought of the possibility.

Sharp smiled grimly. "Innes left his best shooter."

"The woman?"

"Yeah. I fell in love with Sally the first time I saw her at the range. She put a rapid-fire clip in the black from twenty meters."

"Does she love you?"

"Doubt it. She's never seen me shoot." Sharp smiled and resettled the baseball cap on his weathered forehead. "Looks like you'll get to use that fancy saw I bought you."

Sharp flipped his cigarette out the window and started the van. We pulled into the storage yard, stopping in front

of the office. Sharp went inside to finish off the paperwork
and get the keys.

*"One, this is seven. We're in place. I'm going up to watch
the roof."*

I looked in the driver's mirror and spotted the FBI telephone truck. It was parked on the street at the front of the
storage yard. The truck's door opened, and the woman
came out. She went up a nearby telephone pole like she'd
been born to it. A bearded, barrel-chested man in a white
hard hat got out of the truck, stretched, and leaned against
the fender.

Sharp sauntered out, his eyes invisible behind the dark
glasses. As he got in, I said, "Their shooter is at the top of
the telephone pole."

"Helluva woman" was all Sharp said.

We weren't the only ones moving about the yard. There
was an old man and his wife cautiously unloading household
goods, a man making pottery to the accompaniment of a
very loud ghetto blaster, and a low-rent cabinetmaker cutting pine into shelving on a table saw in front of his bay. The
sound of that saw was sweeter than any music I'd ever
heard. I hoped he had thousands of boards to rip before the
day was over.

Sharp drove the van past 12-1. From where I sat, the lock
looked solid. Maybe Kieu had left something in there to
protect. I tried not to think about it too much. One thing at
a time. The first thing was to get into 12-12, punch a hole in
the wall, and see if there was anything in the bay but concrete and shadows.

It seemed as though Sharp was moving in slow motion,
dragging seconds into minutes into eternity. I started to tell
him so, then realized that it was me, not Sharp. Since I'd
seen that U-Rent truck pull up to 12-1, time had entered a
new, unspeakably slow dimension. It would stay that way
until I found out what was—or wasn't—in 12-1.

We turned right and disappeared around the back of the
building, where 12-12 was. Sharp hopped out and opened
up the bay. I backed the van in, shut it down, and began
passing equipment out to him. No one, not even the woman

at the top of the pole, could see what we were doing. By the time we were finished, we were sweating heavily in the early afternoon sun.

Sharp drove the van forward, came back inside the bay, and pulled the door shut behind him. I turned on the work lights as the door came down with a metallic rattle. I moved the lights until they shone on the wall separating 12-12 from 12-1.

"Thank God for greed," I said as I inspected the wall. "I was afraid the interior would be cement block curtain walls. This is just a sandwich of plasterboard and wall braces."

Sharp picked up the block saw with a small grunt. The blade was unshielded, shining brightly in the harsh light. The chain glistened with oil. "Don't know why they call it portable. Bastard must weigh forty pounds."

"Closer to fifty," I said absently, my mind on the wall. I pulled on canvas work gloves and a dust mask and impact goggles. The air was going to get very dirty, very soon.

Sharp touched the curving carborundum teeth with a respectful fingertip. "Best that money can buy. You could cut through a battleship with this." He hefted the chain-driven saw over to me and stepped back out of the way, pulling his own mask into place.

I started up the gas-powered engine. In the closed room, the sound ripped through my head like a knife. I looked at the wall, but I wasn't seeing it. Not as a wall, a barrier. If you look at it that way, you'll only think of finding ways through it that already exist. Like doors or windows, which are always wired for sound. Instead, I was seeing how the wall had been built, framework of steel or wood, wires and plaster, paint.

What had been assembled could be disassembled. It was as simple as that.

I rested the whirling blade lightly against the first layer of ⅝" plasterboard. White dust exploded as a surgically clean cut appeared behind the blade. I ran the saw blade down the wall to the floor, then stood up.

"I think the box is nearly four feet wide," I said loudly, trying to be heard over the saw's harsh snarl.

"Make the hole five," said Sharp. "We have to maneuver the bastard."

I moved over five feet and ran another parallel cut down the wall. Five feet above the floor, I joined the two parallel cuts with a perpendicular one. Then I shut off the saw, wiped plaster powder off my face, and began ripping out wallboard. Sharp joined me. Within minutes we had revealed the metal studs that separated the two layers of wallboard. There was a lot of dust in the air, and the saw had made a lot of noise. Thank God for ghetto blasters and cabinetmakers out front. Even if the sounds in here got out, they wouldn't attract much attention.

It took five minutes to rip out the first layer of chalky plasterboard. I revved up the saw again and started cutting out the metal studs. Sharp played surgical assistant, ready to pull out the steel braces as I sliced them free. Between times, he huddled over the Bearcat, listening to the chase.

The studs were slower work, but they were what the saw had been made for. I didn't think about time. I didn't think about anything at all. The arrow was already in the target, so why worry?

Sharp gave me a running commentary on the game of Vietnamese tag. For a while Kieu's vehicles stayed together, heading into San Francisco. Once they got downtown, though, the game plan changed. I shut down the saw and stretched my arms. Holding that damn saw at arm's length and cutting through steel will do until real work comes along.

"This is six. Our target turned off onto surface streets. Green Street."

"Five, back him," said Innes.

Sharp grinned. "The second car just split off. Innes will be stuck with his men chasing all over hell, freeway and surface streets both. He'll go nuts trying to keep tabs on everybody, especially the car that turned down Green Street."

"That's where the Soviet consulate is," I said.

Sharp's grin hardened into a predatory line.

I nodded. "A nice touch," I said. "You'd like Kieu. She's the Vietnamese version of a shooter."

I wiped my forehead and started up the saw again. The saw blade spat a straight, bright line of sparks as it worked. The dust mask was soaked with sweat by the time I cut through the last stud. I shut off the saw, set it aside, and picked up a tiny keyhole saw. Sharp was chuckling and listening to the radio. I ignored that. Despite my best attempts to make my mind like a smooth, untroubled pond, a hard sense of urgency was riding me.

"Do they still have Kieu's car under surveillance?" I asked as I gnawed at the second layer of wallboard, the backwall of 12-1, with the keyhole saw. I tried not to cough. The air inside the storage bay made a third-stage smog alert look like 100 proof oxygen.

"Yeah, but it's a struggle. He's having to call up reserves. Seems Kieu's driver likes to make U-turns on one-way streets. Helluva way to burn tails."

I smiled. Apparently the Vietnamese learn fast. "Hope they hang onto her. I don't want her showing up here until we're nothing but a memory."

"Why would she do a thing like that?" asked Sharp blandly. "Doesn't she trust you?"

"About as much as I trust her."

"Think she took the machine with her?"

My only answer was a sideways look that shut him up.

The point of the keyhole saw penetrated the wallboard of 12-1, making it easier for me to work. I rotated the punch quickly until I had a peephole. I looked through. I couldn't see anything, of course. No windows, no light. The ventilation shaft was so small as to be useless. I grabbed the tiny saw, put the blade in the hole, and went to work carving an opening that was about four inches by four inches. As soon as I was done, I yanked out the ragged square of plaster.

"Flashlight," I said curtly.

Sharp handed it to me. Automatically, I muffled the beam with my palm, even though I wasn't worried about setting off alarms with the light. I shone the flashlight into the opening. Bare wall. Cement floor. Darkness. Then light glanced off rough pine.

The machine was there, not in a rental truck leading feds on a tour of San Francisco.

Or at least something that looked like the machine was here. Big pine crate sitting in a corner, odd metal mesh object set in front. It looked like nothing had moved. Perhaps Kieu had simply decided that the only sure way to pull off the FBI was to appear to take the machine with her.

"Well?" demanded Sharp.

"Looks like the machine is still here," I said.

"Good, because Innes just lost the Dragon Lady."

"*Shit.*"

"That's about what Innes said."

So much for finesse. Time was more important now. I revved up the big saw and cut out a two-foot by two-foot window. No wires surprised me. I played the light over the far wall, where the bay door was. There was a contact alarm system rigged on the front door, as I'd suspected. It was nothing special, simply a hard wire system, magnetic touch-switches tied together by copper wire, and an alarm box. Open the door, the contact breaks, and the alarm goes off, unless you've keyed into it already. In all, about a hundred bucks at any hardware store. If their other alarm system wasn't any better, that box was all but in the van right now.

I stepped back. "Looks good so long as we stay away from the front door. I want to check something first, though."

I went over to a pile of equipment. Off to one side was a small, rectangular box full of carefully machined photo filters. I selected the Number 24, a ruby-colored circle of glass, and walked over to the small window I'd cut. I leaned in slightly, holding the filter to my eye. I spotted the IR source instantly. Through the filter, the source looked like a huge red eye. Swearing none too silently, I withdrew.

"Have the Feds found Kieu yet?" I asked, replacing the filter in its box.

"No." Sharp looked closely at my face. "Trouble?"

"They've got an infrared alarm system."

"How do you know?" Sharp asked.

"I can see the light source through the Number 24 filter."

"Now what?"

"We try to convince it nobody's home."

Even knowing where to look, it took a few passes with the flashlight beam before I spotted the IR source. It was a dull black box tucked catercorner from the big shipping crate. There was no way to approach, much less move, the Oxy-Con without tripping the IR alarm.

"How does it work?" said Sharp, peering over my shoulder.

"Like an invisible electric eye," I said, reaching for the big saw again. "The source sends a steady beam of IR radiation toward a reflector, which bounces the IR back to the source. So long as nothing interrupts the round trip, everything is quiet. Break the beam, and you're up shit creek."

"So?"

"So you're going to grab the plasterboard chunks as I saw them free. If one drops through to the other side, school is most definitely out."

The saw snarled to life. I went to cutting. Sharp worked in close, showing a remarkable trust in my skill with the heavy saw and its naked, lethal blade. We didn't stop until we had an opening big enough to dolly the crate through. My watch told me that we had made the door very quickly. My mind told me it had taken just under a month.

Sharp dragged over the work light so that it illuminated the bay of 12-1. We could take one or two steps before we risked infringing on the invisible IR beam. One or two steps wasn't enough. That understanding was clear on Sharp's plaster-dusted face. He transferred his attention to what I was holding, another purchase from the well-stocked camera store. The reflector looked like a large white Frisbee. I grabbed the frame and twisted my wrists, releasing the coiled reflector, which had been folded in upon itself. It popped open to make a circle the size of a four-foot, metallic-finished trampoline, large enough to do the job and handier than the flimsy Mylar sheets Benny had suggested.

"What in hell is that?" asked Sharp.

"It's a photo-flash reflector for professional photographers. Great for bouncing light around. It should reflect in the shorter IR wavelengths, too."

Sharp didn't ask if I was sure. The sweat on my face told him more than he wanted to know. He went and unlocked the bay door, ready to throw it open and make a run for it if things went sour. I didn't tell him that I wasn't sweating over the reflector. I was sweating because I didn't know if the IR alarm was sophisticated enough to measure the elapsed time between source and reflector and return. If it was, there was no way to bugger the system. Given the cheap bay-door alarm the Vietnamese had installed, I hoped that they had settled for a cheap IR system, too.

There was only one way to find out. I took my reflector and moved into 12-1, being very careful not to stray away from the wall. I eased along the wall until I was as close as I dared come to the IR source on the opposite corner. Nothing on the box told me whether or not the IR beam was timed for the round trip. I backed up to the wall again and kept my back there as I inched toward the shipping crate that was shoved into the corner. I played the flashlight beam over the reflector. It looked like a weird mix of bicycle reflector and furnace filter.

I inspected the crate more closely. Either it was the right one or a very cleverly made dummy. A stylized "OxyCon" logo was stenciled onto the pine with black spray paint. A shipping label bore the name "Omnitronix" and the storage yard's address. Something about the label was odd. I looked more closely and saw that there was another beneath. Probably one to Irvn, not Brlngme. I wondered whether Kieu had posed as Danny's secretary in order to switch the shipping address. Then I shrugged. It didn't matter now. Danny was dead, and Kieu was on her way here.

I eased the photographer's reflector up over my head. Then I hesitated, wishing that the King's advice came with a money-back guarantee. I lowered the reflector, cutting off the plastic mesh from the IR beam.

Silence. Wonderful and deafening, broken only by my long sigh of relief. Just a few more feet to go. I stood behind the circular reflector and inched toward the IR source. Everything stayed quiet. I inched some more and felt sweat dripping down my ribs. More quiet. More inches. More sweat. By the time I was within five feet of the emitter, I had enough adrenaline in me to jump over the moon.

"Okay, Sharp," I said. "Move in behind me. Don't get between me and the source."

I waited until I heard Sharp breathing behind me, close enough to smell his sweat the same way he was smelling mine. Neither one of us said anything, though. It wasn't the first time either one of us had sweated with fear.

"Take the reflector," I said. "Hold it steady. I'll get the box on the dolly and into the next bay. Then you back up, prop the reflector in the corner where the machine was, and slide back down the wall. Got it?"

"You're gonna need help with that machine. It's a heavy bastard."

"Take the reflector."

Sharp took it. I went and got the big dolly, wheeled it into the bay, and addressed the problem of getting two hundred kilos of machine onto the dolly. In the end, I simply wedged the dolly's steel lip under the crate's edge, leaned and heaved and swore and heaved until I'd walked the crate onto the dolly. I strapped everything in place, gave a last heave to tip the dolly onto its wheels, and aimed the works toward the hole in the wall. I made it on the first try. Then I waited in 12-12, taking in great whoops of dusty air while Sharp inched backward with the photo-flash reflector until he could prop it against the wall where the OxyCon had been. With an audible sign of relief, Sharp retreated along the wall to the doorway I had sawed.

Sharp trotted across 12-12's bay, unlocked the door, and disappeared into the van. He backed up until the van was practically parked inside the bay. The rear doors popped open and a ramp came down. With him pulling and me pushing, we finally horsed the OxyCon into the van. I grabbed the Bearcat, closed up the bay door, jumped into the back of the van, and slammed the doors behind me.

Forty-six minutes gone.

If Kieu was coming straight back from ditching her tails, she'd run right over us in the driveway.

When we passed the front of the storage area, the woman was still on top of the telephone pole. She was calling down to her partner. Seconds later, the Bearcat started talking.

"Seven to one. My partner just spotted what looks like Kieu's Z-28 approaching the storage yard along the back road."

"Get us out of here," I snapped.

Sharp didn't need the advice. He had floored the accelerator before the radio transmission was finished. We slid out the front gate and turned right, moving away from the direction Kieu was coming in.

As we gained speed on the freeway, we heard Innes give orders to close in on the Vietnamese U-Rent.

15

Sharp pulled into one of those roadside rests that the federal government provides for travelers whose bladders aren't built to go the distance. He shut down the engine, stretched, and fished around in a greasy paper bag he had dragged out from under the seat. He came out holding a cold, bulging burrito.

"This is yours," he said, offering it to me.

"I've had enough."

"You haven't had any part of it," he protested, looking at the burrito's white, oozing body. Thick green salsa dripped between his fingers onto the sack.

"I've looked at it. That's enough."

Sharp laughed and tossed the burrito in my direction. "First rule of surveillance: Close your eyes when you eat."

"And hold your nose," I said in disgust.

I dropped the burrito back into the bag. Then I remembered the croissants from the Vietnamese bakery. I rummaged under the seat until I found the bakery bag. The croissants were a little bag-worn but still flaky and light. I ate them while Sharp delivered the coup de grace to the suffering burrito.

I looked at my watch. Six-thirty. Too soon. Time running backward.

Sharp finished the burrito, balled up the bag, and threw it in the back. He followed shortly, a cigarette hanging out the corner of his mouth. I closed my eyes and thought about arrows and targets, but arrows kept turning into guns and the targets all had green eyes and round mouths calling my name. After a time, I gave up and looked over the seat into the back of the van, puzzled by the energetic, metallic sounds that had been nagging at my concentration.

No wonder guns had intruded into my thoughts. Sharp had several weapons spread out across the long OxyCon crate. The light wasn't very good inside the van. Sharp didn't care. He was working by Braille and long, long experience. A field-stripped semiautomatic pistol lay next to a .22 derringer. Sharp was running an oily patch through the barrel of the automatic pistol with the same practiced motions that an accountant would use to sharpen a pencil. At the end of the crate was a gun case that had been customized to accommodate a special sight mounted on the barrel.

"Looks like you bought out a gun store," I said.

"All government issue, one way or another," he said. "This was the Philippines insurrection in 1911," he said, indicating the larger handgun. "The marines wanted a sidearm that would knock down a guerrilla with one shot. For that, no handgun can beat a .45."

"What's the little one for?"

"Infighting. Backup. I carried one like it all the way through Korea. Made it to Pyongyang before the Chinese pushed us back. Little guns like this have done a hell of a lot more real damage to world communism than all our fancy nuclear bombs."

I got up and sat on my heels in the back of the van. It was crowded, but so was my mind. I motioned toward the closed black case. "Which war was that?"

"Vietnam," said Sharp, peering down the barrel of the big pistol. "Take a look."

The case was lined with thick, resilient foam rubber. It cradled a black M-16 with what looked like a handgun mounted on top of the barrel just above the trigger. It wasn't a handgun, though. It was a sighting device that used coherent light the color of blood. Both the zero-aim laser and the M-16 itself were black. The power pack and bipod were black. The little light that warned when the laser was on had been covered with black tape. Even the on-off toggle had been blacked. There were no shiny surfaces anywhere on the piece to catch stray light and betray the shooter's presence or position. It was a pragmatic weapon, an ambush weapon, just the right weapon to use on a man who hid behind a woman. Fuck chivalry.

Sharp reassembled the big pistol and turned to the M-16. "You ever use one of these?" he asked.

"Not with a laser."

"It's pretty," said Sharp, running his hand over the rifle and laser. "Real pretty. Not many can use it worth a damn, though. They either turn on the laser too soon and are spotted downrange, or they can't get the hang of the sight and miss by a foot or more."

"Thanks for telling me," I said harshly. "Why the hell didn't you get a star scope and be done with it?"

"Tonight will be short range, fixed position shooting," said Sharp. "I know how to use lasers. I spent two hours on a range adjusting this one and the rifle before I came back to the motel. So back up, Fiddler. My laser will give you an edge. And you're gonna need it." He looked up at me, his eyes pale and intent in the dim interior light of the van. "When you see a red circle on the forehead of the man holding Fiora, you move and you move fast, because two bullets are coming down that red beam *now*. That's all the warning you'll get. With a star scope, you wouldn't get any warning at all."

I wanted to argue, but didn't. Sharp was the shooter, not me. "You're the man with the balcony seat. I'm going to be in the orchestra."

Sharp smiled. It was a hard, ironic expression that wrinkled the skin around his eyes as though he were squinting down a rifle barrel. "You want to be the hero, you get the good seat," he agreed. "Me? I'm just the hired gun."

I put the black rifle and its odd laser aiming device back in the case and dropped the lid. My watch glowed up at me. Six-fifty. I moved to the front of the van and out the door. As I approached the pay phone, a car turned off the freeway. I stood and talked to a dead phone while a man got out, went to the rest room, came back, and drove away. Then I started feeding in coins.

The man who answered the phone at the Soviet consulate was surprised to hear from me. In fact, he did one hell of an impression of a guy who hadn't the faintest idea what the crazy American was talking about. After about thirty seconds of that routine, I got impatient.

"Listen up," I said, cutting across the man's polite protestations of ignorance. "I'm going to give you a phone number. You're going to pass it on up the ranks to a man called Volker, who you never heard of. I'll wait ten minutes here, then I'll be gone, and this whole deal will be in the toilet, and your career as a diplomat will be right there with it."

"But—"

"Got a pencil?"

"Yes, but—"

I gave him the number and hung up.

Volker's call came precisely five minutes later.

"I trust you have the machine," said Volker.

"Yes."

"Is it intact and operational?"

"Is Fiora?"

"Of course."

Volker's voice told me he hadn't liked the question. He liked what I said next even less. "Put her on the line."

"No."

"Good-bye, Volker."

I hung up and stood sweating in the thick, cool afternoon light. He would call back if Fiora was alive. He had to call back. I repeated that like a litany for the two minutes and twenty-six seconds until the phone rang.

"Fiora," I said, afraid to make it a question, afraid to doubt.

"Fiddler . . ."

I ignored the relief that went through me like a shock wave, just as I ignored the emotion underlying the surface of Fiora's voice. We didn't have time to feel now. Just to survive.

"Are we alone on the line?" I asked.

"Yes, I'm fine," she said.

Scared but thinking at top speed. The best damn woman I've ever known.

"The first time I say your name tonight, hit the ground and roll like hell. Got it?"

"I've always loved the way you say my name," Fiora said, her voice husky.

"Don't look back no matter what happens. Run and don't stop until you're safe. And, Fiora, I lo—"

The phone was wrenched away from her grasp before I could finish. I heard her excoriate Korchnoi in a few razor phrases, venting her feelings and telling me at the same time that the second Russian was present.

"All right, Fiddler," said Volker. "You've talked to Fiora. She has assured you that she is all right. I would like similar assurances about the machine. Bring the OxyCon to me within one hour at the following address."

"Wrong, Volker. I'm tired of playing your tune. You're going to play mine. Don't bother to argue. I'll just hang up and leave you with a woman you might have loved and will have to kill for no better reason than you were afraid to trust your own reflection in the mirror."

There was a long, long silence.

I waited, hoping I'd read Volker's weakness correctly. We were alike, yes. We were also different. I was capable of love. Volker wasn't. His weakness was that he didn't know that. He believed that he could predict my ultimate reactions on the basis of his own. Pride and pragmatism. Volker. I was betting that the pragmatism, the need for the Oxy-Con, would overcome the pride that made Volker want to control every aspect of this situation, and me.

"I see that we are both gamblers," said Volker finally.

I spoke quickly, before he could change his mind. "Tonight. Nine o'clock. Page Mill Road in the Santa Cruz Mountains. There's a small creek about a mile west of Skyline Drive, and a small concrete bridge with a steel railing. You take the east side, I'll take the west. Just like Berlin, Volker." I heard his laughter, brief and warm, genuinely amused. "Yeah, I thought you'd enjoy that. We'll switch vehicles, but before we do, I want to see Fiora."

"And I want to see the OxyCon."

"Then bring a crowbar. The machine is still in its shipping crate. So you'll look and I'll look, and then we'll stare at each other and try to figure a way to play winner-take-all without dying."

"Like looking in a mirror," murmured Volker.

I didn't disagree. "One other thing."

"Yes?" he asked.

"Come alone. Just you, me, and Fiora."

"Of course," he said smoothly. "Just as you will be alone. No guns, Fiddler. Come unarmed, as I will."

I said nothing. I had the oddest feeling that Volker was telling the truth about the guns. He wasn't going to be armed—which meant that Korchnoi would carry enough for a raiding party.

"Pray that no helicopter flies over that bridge, my friend," continued Volker. "I would dislike for Fiora to die through sheer bad luck."

I fought the rage rising in my throat. I'd deliberately chosen a lonely place, but I wasn't God or the FAA. Flight patterns were beyond me.

"Listen to me, Volker," I said, hardly recognizing my own voice. He said nothing but I knew he was there. I could hear his breathing, slow and even. "If Fiora doesn't live, no one does."

I heard the faintest intake of breath just before the line went dead.

I hung up and turned around. While I had talked, the sun had died. Crimson light bathed the rest area and pooled on walkways where sprinklers had just run. I looked away and walked quickly toward the van. At the moment, blood red wasn't my favorite color.

"Is it on?" asked Sharp.

"It's on."

Sharp smiled. I wondered if Korchnoi ever smiled like that.

Sharp had changed shirts. He wore a black, long-sleeved turtleneck. No belt for the blue jeans, no buckle to gleam or catch on brush. A dark navy watch cap was pulled over his grey-streaked hair and receding hairline.

"I'd have been glad to buy you real camouflage gear," I said.

He snorted. "You crawl on your belly in the dirt long enough, you fade right into the landscape."

My preparations didn't take long. I peeled off the rugby shirt, put on a bullet-proof vest, and pulled the rugby shirt down over it.

"Ready?" I asked.

"No gun?" asked Sharp, looking at the naked rugby shirt and equally naked running shoes.

"Volker asked so nicely that I couldn't refuse."

Sharp's mouth twisted down. "Yeah, I'll bet." He leaned over and produced a belt from his personal bag. He held it out to me, worn brass buckle and leather gleaming in the thick light. "You need a belt."

I looked at him. Usually I don't bother with belts, which I mentioned to him.

He put two fingers through the nondescript brass buckle and yanked. Suddenly he was holding a wicked knife with a triangular two-inch steel blade. It reminded me of a large shark's tooth. He pulled his fingers out of the buckle and handed the weapon to me. It nestled in my palm with the sharp tooth extended between my index and second finger. When I made a fist, the blade became a deadly extension of my hand. Even in the waning light, the edges of the blade gleamed. Both sides had been honed recently by an expert. Respectfully, I drew the blade along the back of my hand. Black hair curled over steel and then drifted to the floor. I whistled softly. The blade was sharper than the razor I had used this morning.

"This government issue, too?" I asked, turning the knife over, watching red light run down the blade like insubstantial blood.

"Nope. Range is too short for balcony jobs. Just right for you, though."

Sharp lighted a cigarette, dragged hard, and exhaled, letting the smoke mix with the last red light seeping into the van. He watched as I reassembled belt and buckle and strapped everything in place on my jeans. I moved to the driver's seat and fired up the van. Next to me, Sharp looked over the USGS map of the area we were going to.

"The moon will be above the hills," he said, looking at his watch and then back to the map as I accelerated down the highway. "I'll set up on the east side of the bridge with the light behind me. I don't figure to be any more than seventy-five feet from the target. I might get off four shots, two each, before it all goes from sugar to shit."

"I've seen Volker move," I said. "If he's your second target, you'll be lucky to find him, much less shoot him."

"Then we'll just have to hope that he's the one holding the lady," said Sharp. "Otherwise you're betting that you'll be close enough to Volker to cut his throat before he can react to the first shots." Sharp paused. "If he's as fast as you say, I wouldn't bet those odds unless I was using somebody else's money."

"Can you think of a better way?"

Sharp dragged on the cigarette again and shook his head. "You could get yourself killed, Fiddler," he said calmly. "You know that?"

"It's occurred to me about once every five minutes."

Sharp shrugged. "So long as you know."

He reached around to check the leather pouch at the back of his jeans. A distributor cap for the van was inside. Satisfied that everything was in place, Sharp lighted another cigarette and added, "Volker's gonna be pissed when he finds out you threw the van's distributor cap into the drink."

"He'd better be dead before he finds out. Besides," I shrugged, "it's the only way to be sure that no matter what happens, the machine stays here."

"A closet patriot," Sharp said mockingly. "Never would have suspected it."

I turned, a nasty remark poised on my tongue. I swallowed the words. Sharp was looking at me with something uncomfortably close to compassion on his weathered features. "Call it pragmatism," I said, turning my attention back to the road. "Volker and Korchnoi can't afford to let either Fiora or me out of there alive. They have too much ground to cover with that machine."

"Yeah, that's the way I had it figured," said Sharp, nodding. "So it's them or us. Makes the choice easy. Real easy."

The moon slipped up over the horizon as we passed beneath the 280 freeway and climbed into the Palo Alto foothills. Sprawling hilltop houses loomed in the silver-blue light. Fences threw dense, geometric shadows beneath the rising moon. A shooter's moon, radiant and calm, deadly transparent light. I wondered whether Volker was looking at the moon and thinking the same thing. Probably. That was the risk of dueling with a mirror image.

We left the gentrified foothills behind and moved into the first of the oaks and madrones. Leaves were black against the lighter grasslands. The open windows brought a mixture of smells. The most potent was the last of the warmth curling out of the asphalt, rich and tarry. Grass cured to the color of sunshine, the smell of silence and summer heat. And in the arroyos, the first coolness was sliding down from the Santa Cruz Mountains, bringing intimations of deep night and fog.

The road curved and dropped into a hidden valley, breathtaking beneath the moon. Grapevines in neat rows wound over the gently rumpled land. Rainbirds poured out water rhythmically, silver curtains of mist sweeping over the thirsty vines. Against a grove of massive oaks gleamed the lights of a home already closed up for the night. The home was unearthly in its beauty, more dream than substance, a symphony in light and shadow. I yearned toward it, wanting it as I had rarely wanted anything. Someday I would own a home wrapped in light. Maybe Fiora would live there with me. Someday.

When we both had burned most of the craziness out of ourselves. If we lived that long.

Someday.

I looked over at Sharp. He wasn't watching the house or the vineyard or the valley. He cared only for the ridgelines black beneath the flat white eye of the moon. He was watching the countryside like a hawk watches the fields below as he soars on transparent currents of wind and need.

"You live for this, don't you," I said quietly.

Sharp didn't answer for a minute. Then: "Tell me you don't."

I couldn't. Short of love, this was as real as life got.

I drove in silence while night condensed around us. We passed only one vehicle, a battered pickup heading the other way. Just before we reached the last turnoff, Sharp moved into the back of the van. Unless the Russians used a helicopter, I didn't think Volker could beat us to the bridge no matter how fast he drove. Even so, there was no point in taking a chance on Sharp being spotted. He wouldn't be comfortable in the back of the van, but he'd be invisible.

The road wound around, rising as gradually as the moon. Ragged stands of redwoods blackened distant ridgelines. Head-high brush grew up to the edges of the road. I rounded the shoulder of a steep hill. There was a long road cut and then a hard turn onto a small concrete and steel bridge. I couldn't see any vehicles. Slowing to five miles an hour, I approached the bridge from the east side. I heard the back door open.

"Good hunting," I said softly.

All that came back was a quiet chuckle.

Sharp timed his move perfectly, stepping off the rear bumper and into the shadows so deftly that I almost missed his exit. The brush at the edge of the bridge approach quivered very slightly. It could have been the breeze.

Between one second and the next, Sharp was gone.

I pulled across the short bridge and scouted the west side for a few miles. The country was virtually uninhabited. The nearest dwelling was more than a mile away. The only car I saw was at the bottom of a ravine, a wreck rusting in the damp air. I turned around on the narrow road and went back to the bridge. On my side, the west side, the land was flatter, an ancient river bench that grew boulders and oaks in equal numbers. There was a turnout at the bridge abutment. I backed the van off the road until I was beneath the

black-lace moon shadow of a huge oak. Then I turned off the
engine and waited.

At first I heard only the pinging sounds of metal con-
tracting as it cooled. Then came the light breeze playing
through the leaves of the oaks. Beneath that was the small
murmur of the creek. Gradually, my eyes grew accustomed
to the vague light. I discovered that I could pick out surprising detail, even in the shadows. Twice I caught flickers of
movement. The first time I froze, expecting to see a man,
but it was only the blurred gray shadow of a hunting owl.
Coyotes called to each other from the ridgelines, singing in
primitive harmonics older than man. I could have been the
first person on Earth. Or the last.

I got out, pulled off the distributor cap, and hurled it into
the darkness and water below the bridge. As I closed the
engine compartment, I heard a vehicle topping the ridge
two miles to the east. At first the sound was diffuse. Gradually it settled into the smooth outpourings of a six-cylinder
engine. Korchnoi's Volvo. I listened hard for a second engine underneath the first but heard none. I was neither surprised nor pleased. Whatever trap Volker had prepared
wouldn't be as easy or as obvious as a carload of shooters.

The sound of the approaching car diminished as it
dropped down into the valley to the east, then increased as
it topped the closest ridge, a half mile away. The moonlight
shone silver on the little bridge. The Volvo stopped, as
though reluctant to enter the narrow road gouged out of the
side of a hill. I closed my eyes to save my night vision and
pulled the headlight switch to call the Volvo in.

When I opened my eyes, I thought for a moment that the
Volvo had backed out. I couldn't see its headlights. Then I
realized that the headlights were off. Using only moonlight,
the Volvo crept down the narrow road to the bridge. I got
out and stood in the shadow of the bridge.

The Volvo stopped short of the bridge. I heard the sound
of a door opening. Two figures emerged. Korchnoi's brick
shape and Fiora's hair gleaming in the moonlight. She was
moving awkwardly, her hands pinned behind her. Korchnoi

turned sideways so that I could see the gleam of a sawed-off shotgun jammed against the nape of Fiora's neck.

I didn't see Volker. He must have been driving. There was a soundless explosion of white as Volker tripped the Volvo's high beams. I swore and shut my eyes, knowing it was too late. My night vision was gone. Volker's wasn't, though. He'd planned it that way.

"Can you see her, Fiddler?" Volker called out.

Fiora's voice came to me out of blinding light and darkness, calling my name, fear and hope, a nightmare come true. I stepped out of the shadows because there was nothing else to do.

"I'm here."

Immediately, Korchnoi grabbed Fiora with his free hand and pulled her back into the Volvo, using her like a shield. I swore bleakly, silently, knowing that the car would protect Korchnoi from Sharp's gun.

The headlights went out. Volker appeared in the shadows beside the car.

"I'm coming over," said Volker, his voice conversational, carrying easily in the increasingly damp air.

He wore Levi's, a white shirt, and running shoes. He walked across the bridge with the confidence of a superb athlete, as though he had not the least worry for his own safety. And why should he? He knew I wouldn't move so long as Fiora was under the gun.

Volker was halfway across the bridge before I noticed that he carried a dark, slender crowbar at his side. If he had a gun as well, it didn't show.

"Step into the moonlight, Fiddler."

Volker's voice was clear and cold, a perfect match for the moonlight. I stepped into the moonlight.

"Stand between me and the Volvo."

As soon as I was in place, Volker switched on a small flashlight. "If this light moves quickly, Fiora dies. Hold very still, my mirror."

I barely breathed while Volker searched me for weapons. He didn't give the belt a second look. When he stepped back, he was smiling. His free hand moved to his collar,

jerked sharply, and then fell to his side. Beneath his white
shirt he was wearing a bulletproof vest. Like me.

"Mirror," murmured Volker. He shook his head sadly.
"You should have taken my offer, Fiddler. Fiora and a few
months of time together. Then we wouldn't have been here,
now, like this. Enemies. Hating each other, hating ourselves."

I said nothing. Hate is like that sometimes. You hate so
much you are all but paralyzed. I would have given everything but Fiora's life to feel Volker's throat beneath my
hands. It showed on my face, for he nodded.

"I know," said Volker softly.

And the worst of it was that he did know.

He clicked the flashlight on and off three times, telling
Korchnoi that all was well, the fish was in the net and the
gaff raised, ready to sink its lethal curve through living
flesh.

"Walk before me to the van," said Volker.

I hesitated, half expecting to hear the shotgun blast that
would kill the only woman I'd ever loved. When it didn't
come, I turned and walked to the van. Another gamble
won. Volker wouldn't kill me or Fiora until he was very sure
of the machine.

And perhaps, just perhaps, he was in no hurry to see
Fiora die.

I walked to the van, hearing a symphony of despair in my
mind. I refused to add my violin to it. I was a soloist, iso-
lated, a long chord quivering with hatred and hope.

At Volker's command, I went first into the van. He swept
the flashlight beam around and found nothing but the crate
and a plaid shirt and the paper remains from a fast-food
dinner. The shipping crate filled half the space, leaving no
room to hide a man.

Volker shone the light on the shipping sticker that had
routed the machine from Irvine to Burlingame, and in
doing so had killed Danny Flynn. With a harsh Russian
phrase, Volker jerked the sticker off. The Irvine address
showed through. He nodded abruptly and turned his attention to the crate itself. He went over the fastenings mi-

nutely, ensuring that the crate hadn't been opened since it left the factory.

At least, I assume that was what Volker was doing. It's what I'd have done if I were in his shoes.

Volker kept an eye on me all the time. Habit, not real worry that I would do something foolish. Jumping Volker now would be the death of Fiora. If Volker had carried a gun with him into the van, I would have tried for him. If I were armed, I could hunt Korchnoi myself. Which was why Volker wasn't carrying a gun. He knew what would tempt me, what would hold me, how to control me with the hope of Fiora's life.

Mirror.

He pried up the crate's top with a great shrieking and squalling of nails against green wood. One side of the crate was hinged. He left that alone. When he was finished, the top stood ajar, nails like steel teeth protruding down. With one hand, Volker lifted the top. With the other, he played the flashlight beam over the OxyCon. The machine looked like a small iron lung, cylindrical and festooned with stainless steel lugs and clear glass inspection ports. It didn't look like $20 million, much less a woman's life.

"Satisfied?" I asked.

"With the machine? Yes. With the rest of it?" He looked at me suddenly. Lighted from below, his eyes looked as clear as glacier ice and as inhuman. "No, I'm not satisfied."

I felt my skin tighten and adrenaline pour through me. Whatever was coming wasn't going to satisfy me, either.

"I have been instructed to offer you employment," said Volker.

I laughed. I couldn't help it.

Volker smiled ironically. "Yes, I told them as much. Like me, you are not a man to bend. Even if death is the alternative."

He fell silent, watching me with transparent eyes, waiting for the moment when the knowledge of death would change me. He'd wait a long time. I'd already heard my own death written into the score, sung with Fiora's voice.

"It is as I feared," he said softly. "Even if you agreed, I

could never turn my back on you. We are too much alike. Put your hands on the edge of the crate, Fiddler."

I didn't move. I knew as surely as I knew my own name that when my hands touched the crate the lid would slam down, impaling my hands, pinning me, destroying me.

"It will not hurt much more than landing on a broken foot," said Volker.

"I wouldn't have guessed you were a sadist," I said honestly.

Volker's smile was sad. "No more than you. But I am a pragmatist. Like you. You are too big," he said calmly. "Too fast. Too hard. I will take you to Fiora so that you may die with her, giving her what comfort you can. But first you must put your hands on the edge of the crate. Or," Volker added quietly, "Korchnoi will make Fiora's death . . . difficult. She will die screaming your name, and you will be alive, watching her, hearing her."

That was the instant I learned what hate really is. Black and cold, burning to the bone. I was going to kill Volker. But not yet. Fiora.

Slowly, I put my hands on the edge of the crate.

Volker nodded. He hesitated an instant, then moved with incredible quickness, slamming the lid down. I barely had time to flex my right hand, taking the brunt of the blow on it, sparing my left. There was an instant of overwhelming pain as nails rammed through my flesh and the edge of the crate slammed against bone, bruising, breaking. Nausea kicked through me. I swayed against the crate, trying not to black out. Sweat ran from my face onto the rough pine, mixing with the scarlet flow of blood.

I took a breath that sounded more like a groan and threw my head back. Volker jerked up on the lid, freeing me.

"Fiora will never know that she is going to die. I promise you," said Volker, stepping back quickly, beyond my reach.

I clenched my teeth against the rage consuming me. I wanted only to get through the moments between now and the instant I killed Volker. All that kept me sane was the agony. My right hand was broken. Bone flashed whitely in the instant before blood welled. My left hand was a question mark written in pulsing waves of agony. It had two holes in it where nails had gone through, but no broken bones showed. I tried to move the fingers of my left hand. A mistake. Nausea and darkness closed in.

I felt Volker's hand on my arm, pulling me out of the van. My breath made an odd, hissing sound through my teeth as my right hand bumped against the back door. I kept trying to move the fingers of my left hand, ignoring the nausea and blackness that followed each effort. Pain came through like lightning, illuminating everything. I hurt, therefore I am.

The night air revived me somewhat. That, and the body pouring endorphins into the gap between agony and unconsciousness. I walked slightly bent over, cradling my hands against my belt, fumbling with weak fingers at the buckle. Volker, walking behind me, could see nothing. I hoped it would be the same for Korchnoi.

The brass felt cold against my thumb. I hooked, twisted, and staggered against the bridge railing on the east side. Sweat ran down my ribs and made my hands sticky. Or maybe it was blood. I shook my head, trying to clear away dizziness. Below me was nothing but blackness and water flowing. Above, only night and a shooter's moon.

"That's it, Volker," I gasped. "Bring Fiora to me before I pass out."

I sensed Volker looking at me, measuring my pale skin and the sweat gleaming, quick breaths and hands bleeding blackly in the moonlight. If I looked as bad as I felt, he should be comforted.

Volker called out in Russian. The Volvo's door opened, but Korchnoi didn't get out. Fiora came out first, closely followed by Korchnoi. Her hands were still bound. A shotgun muzzle still rested against the nape of her neck. No chance for Sharp. Korchnoi was bent over behind Fiora as though he sensed cross hairs resting on his skull.

Sharp, where the hell are you?

"God damn you Volker, untie her," I said harshly. "She's too good a woman to die like that."

I heard Volker's quick intake of breath, felt the sudden rage in him as he turned on me. I knew then that he loved

Fiora as much as he could love anything. It wasn't enough, though. With men like him it never is. I tugged weakly on the buckle and felt it slide free of leather.

Volker spun around and hurled a torrent of Russian at Korchnoi. Korchnoi argued, then subsided when Volker flayed him with guttural phrases. In a moment Fiora's hands were free. Korchnoi's hand was buried in her long blond hair, holding her. The gun was still at her neck, though. No pleading on my part would change that. As they came closer, Fiora saw my hands.

"Oh, Fiddler—" Fiora said, her voice breaking.

She tried to run to me, only to be yanked back by Korchnoi. The motion pivoted him slightly, presenting his shoulder to me. And his profile to Sharp, I hoped.

"It's okay, love," I said. "A little blood. Nothing to worry about."

She bit her lip and shook her head. Tears gleamed in the moonlight. I wanted to touch her but my right hand was useless and my left was curled around a deadly little blade.

Come on, Sharp. For Chrissake, what are you waiting for?

I slowly began to straighten up, holding my hands close to my body. I had as good a grip on the knife as I ever would with two holes through my hand and the whole mess slick with blood. Pain hadn't done much for my reflexes. I told myself it didn't matter. The arrow was in the target. Better yet, the knife was in the throat.

And then Volker started to speak.

Sharp, it better be now. Volker is going to—

I saw the scarlet circle of light bloom suddenly on Korchnoi's cheek.

"Fiora!"

I started to move even before I spoke her name, but she was already falling, anticipating me, knowing me better than Volker did, better than I knew myself. She kicked out her feet and went down as though she had been clubbed. Before Korchnoi could adjust, two bullets exploded in his head. He was dead before his knees got the message to collapse, dead before twin reports shattered the night.

I spun, using the heel of my hand as a brace while I tried to ram that knife all the way through Volker's throat. He was incredibly fast. He ducked and tried to grab my hand in the same motion. His fingers slipped over bloody skin and the blade slashed. Instantly he changed directions, diving toward Fiora. I brought the knife back and slashed along the underside of his arm, where the vest would offer no protection. Volker gasped as the blade slid in, then ground against bone in the instant before his momentum took him beyond my reach.

Volker regained his balance instantly. With a single fluid motion, he leaped for the concealment of the brush and boulders that lined the road.

And he vanished.

I waited, holding my breath. I heard the sound of a man retreating through brush. Steady sounds, rhythmic. I had wounded Volker, but not badly enough.

"Sharp!" I yelled.

"Yo." The answer came from the roadcut on the east side of the bridge.

"Volker's going west. Can you see him?"

There was a long silence. Red light lanced through the bushes.

"Can't spot him."

"Cover us."

"Yo."

"Fiora?" I called softly.

My only answer was a broken sound from dense shadow inside the bridge. She had rolled as far as she could. I staggered over to Korchnoi, kicked the shotgun away from his lifeless hands, and went to Fiora.

"Fiora? Are you hurt?" I asked, and my voice echoed hoarsely.

"N-no."

With a groan I knelt beside her. I wanted to touch her but my hands just wouldn't cooperate. She sat up slowly, then knelt and put her arms around me. For a long time we simply held each other.

I heard Sharp walk slowly onto the bridge.

"Volker's gone. We won't find him until morning. Maybe not even then." Sharp paused and I knew he was looking at my bloody hands. "Ready to go home?" he asked softly.

Fiora and I looked at each other. Neither of us had a home. Not really. And we knew it.

Tears streamed down her cheeks. She put her hands on either side of my face and kissed my lips very gently. "I love you, Fiddler. For what it's worth."

I smiled but it only made her cry harder. "I love you, too."

For what it's worth.

Epilogue

Sharp never found Volker. After a few days, Innes called off the search. He said that some hiker would probably come across Volker's bones, but then Innes had never seen Volker move. Volker was the most gifted man I'd ever met. Intelligent, witty, strong, a radiant fallen angel. And, like Lucifer, Volker wasn't quite human. Empathy and compassion were only words to him, and lives were nothing at all.

I knew that Volker had survived as certainly as Fiora knew that Danny had not.

Sharp agreed with me. He kept the rifle and laser I gave him, but only after I promised to call him the next time Volker surfaced. Or the next time I needed a shooter, whichever came first. All I had to do was pass the word on down to Calexico, where Sharp was doing life plus ninety-nine years patrolling a piece of desert nobody else gave a damn about.

I hope that I won't make the kind of mistake again that requires a shooter to bail me out. It could happen, though. To remind me of that, I put Danny's diamonds in a small Mason jar and set it on the windowsill in my bedroom. Every day when I wake up the stones are there, morning sunshine pouring through them like a silent symphony composed out of glittering shards of light. Every color. Every possibility.

And the diamonds themselves, dead as only stones can be.

I was alive. Pain told me so for the weeks it took my hands to heal. Long weeks. I won't say my hands are as good as new, but I could play the violin again if I were fool enough to try. Fiora stayed with me, cooking for me, but—

toning my shirts, bathing my hands, touching me as only she can. I did what I could for her, holding her, giving her the silence she seemed to need. She took longer to heal than my hands. Crying comes hard for a woman like her, but she spent a lot of dark hours grieving for the twin I hadn't been good enough to save. Not that she blamed me. She didn't.

I did, though.

Somehow, I should have figured it out. I should have been able to put the notes together sooner or better or at least differently. Surely there must have been a way that Danny wouldn't have died and I wouldn't have lain in bed cursing silently while Fiora wept in my arms until neither one of us could speak, only hold on to each other.

Then one day I woke up, and Fiora was gone. I'd been expecting it for two weeks, wondering whether she would wait until we fought or if she would do what I had done years ago, simply leave. No anger, just a visceral understanding that it wasn't going to work this time, either. Not the way we wanted it to. Not this time.

Maybe next time . . .

ABOUT THE AUTHOR

A. E. MAXWELL is an award-winning writer, a journalist, and the author of two previous novels, *Steal the Sun* and *Golden Empire*, as well as a nonfiction book, *The Year-Long Day*. A. E. Maxwell lives in Southern California.

MAX BYRD PROMO: CALIFORNIA THRILLER, FLY AWAY JILL AND FINDERS WEEPERS

By Max Byrd

☐ **A CALIFORNIA THRILLER** (26179-7 • $2.95)
Mike Haller is hired to hunt down George Webber, a journalist for the San Francisco Constitution. Carlton Hand, Webber's robust editor, is sure that his reporter's suffering from a mid-life crisis and is off on a fling with a woman. So does Webber's wife—he's done it before. But Haller's search reveals a truth more sordid than an extramarital fling. A truth that turns the peaceful Sacramento Valley into a death trap for Mike Haller.

☐ **FLY AWAY JILL** (26178-9 • $2.95)
Mike Haller's second mystery sends Haller on a mission to England and France to find Caroline Collin, the missing daughter-in-law of a very rich California businessman, Carlo Angeletti. But Angeletti wants to find more than Caroline. She has disappeared deliberately, it turns out, taking with her the plans of her father-in-law's international drug smuggling operation. Haller tracks Caroline through Europe, tangling with hoods and hired killers as he untangles the secrets of the drug network's chain of command.

☐ **FINDERS WEEPERS** (26177-0 • $2.95)
Private eye Mike Haller gets deeply embroiled in a case with a lot at stake. There's money—nearly a million dollars—and a strange beneficiary, prostitute Muriel Contreras. There's self-respect, as Haller is deprived of his license by a cop who's itching for revenge. With little more to go on than a photograph of a woman in a black bikini, Haller embarks on a journey that takes him through the kinky underside of San Francisco, into the boardroom of a superlawyer, and forces him to make the worst choice a man has to make—between the woman who can clear his name and the woman he loves.

Buy these novels wherever Bantam books are sold, or use this handy coupon for ordering:

Bantam Books, Inc., Dept. BD20, 414 East Golf Road, Des Plaines, Ill. 60016

Please send me ____ copies of the books I have checked above. I am enclosing $_____. (Please add $1.50 to cover postage and handling.) Send check or money order—no cash or C.O.D.'s please.

Mr/Ms _____

Address_____

City/State _____ Zip _____

BD20-7/86

Please allow four to six weeks for delivery. This offer expires January 1987. Price and availability subject to change without notice.